ASSAULT
ON THE
PRESIDENCY

ASSAULT
ON THE
PRESIDENCY

Acacia Imprints

Omaha, Nebraska

Email the author: john@johnachor.com

Author's Links:

BLOG:	http://www.johnachor.wordpress.com/
FACEBOOK:	http://www.facebook.com/jachor1
TWITTER:	twitter.com/caseyfremont
WEB SITE:	www.johnachor.com

1st Edition, 2020

10 9 8 7 6 5 4 3 2 1

ACACIA IMPRINTS

Acacia Imprints

TO MY WIFE PAT FOR HER UNDERSTANDING,
PATIENCE AND ENCOURAGEMENT.

ACKNOWLEDGMENTS

My profound thanks to: Kathleen Nicely, Karen Edmisten and Mark Achor for editorial assistance, suggestions, and who always give me inspiration and encouragement. Rich Schooler, M.D. did his best to educate me regarding the medical aspects. Larry Malanish of Bloomfield Press directed me to several sources of information. Mr. Alan Korwin and his book Gun Laws of America set me straight on the aspects of carrying a weapon. John Wood, Director of Law Enforcement Services for Shooter's World (Phoenix), gave me a comprehensive education on weapons.

Any number of coffeehouse and bookstore managers who didn't run me out, but allowed me to linger over a cup of coffee as I wrote. The Flamingo Hilton, Laughlin graciously provides numerous places for an author to sit and write while his wife beats up their slot machines. Last but not least, thanks to the critique group I met with, Cindy Goyette, Wanda McLaughlin Val Neiman, Judy Pearson, and Gary Ponzo.

My reference sources shared their time, knowledge and expertise providing me with more help than an author could expect. If there are any errors in this work, they are mine. If I strayed from the straight and narrow, I hope it was because of writer's license and fictionalization and not pure error.

MAIN CHARACTERS AND CODE NAMES/NICKNAMES

Greek Name (Symbol) Assigned to, "Nickname"

Alpha (A) [unknown]

Beta (ß) Lieutenant Colonel Alexander Chase Hilliard, Air Force, "Alex"

Gamma (Γ) Master Chief Petty Officer Charles J. Eaton, Navy, "Duke"

Delta (Δ) Master Sergeant Rayford T. Pickens, Army, "Hillbilly"

Delta Two Staff Sergeant Rebecca Nathan, Army, automatic weapon

Delta Three Master Sergeant Marion Dwayne Newcomb, Marine Corps, shotgun, "Bull"

Delta Four Master Sergeant Lewis Roundtree, Army, sniper, "Dozens"

Delta Five Sergeant First-Class Phillip James Lexington, Army, additional team member, "PJ" or "Lex"

Theta (Θ) Master Sergeant Nathan K. Tucker, Marine Corps, "Tuck"

Lambda (Λ) Sarah Crawford, GS-9, civilian employee

Sigma (Σ) Staff Sergeant William G. Tufts, Army, "Scrounger"

Reserved: Xi (Ξ), Pi (Π), Upsilon (Y), Phi (Φ), Psi (Ψ) and Omega (Ω)

Not used: Epsilon, Zeta, Eta, Iota, Kappa, Mu, Nu, Omicron, Rho, Tau and Chi

OTHER CODE NAMES/NICKNAMES

Code Name	Assigned to
TopHat	President-elect Ahern
White Tie	Vice President-elect Ryder
Batman or Mister Two	Corbett Chapman (rogue agent)
Robin or Mister One	Dickie Brocklin (rogue agent)

Table of Distribution and Allowances (T D & A)

Description	Quantity (Assigned to... Team Member #)	Ammunition per Weapon
Auto Pistol, Glock 19, 9mm, 15 round magazine, 2 spare magazines	1 per team member + Beta	45 rounds
Auto Pistol, Walther TPH, .22 caliber Long Rifle, 6 round magazine, 2 spare magazines, with AWC sound suppresser	1 per team + Beta (Team Lead)	18 rounds
Auto Pistol, Calico M950, 9mm, 50 round magazine, with spare magazine and Shurfire 2581 laser aiming device	1 per team (Number 2)	100 rounds
Shotgun, Mossburg Persuader 500, 12-gauge, pistol grip, 6 round magazine	1 per team (Number 3)	18 rounds
Holster, Shoulder, Galco "Miami Classic" for 9mm Glock or 9mm Beretta	1 per weapon	
Holster, Waist, Guardian "Belly Band" for .22 caliber Walther	1 per weapon	
Rifle, Sniper, McMillian M89, .308 caliber, 5 shot magazine with scope, Leupold Vari III, 3.5-10, STD Police	1 per team (Number 4)	15 rounds
Flashlight, Penlight, Halogen	1 per team member + Beta	
Rope, Nylon, 1/4", 50 feet	1 per team	
Name Badge, Bright Yellow (Team ID)	1 per team member + Beta	
Widgets	1 per Beta, Gamma, Delta	
Voice Modifier	1 per team Leader	
Radio Communication, headset/mike for hands-free communications	1 per team member + Beta	
Radio, Miniature, 4 frequency	1 per team + Beta	
Cell phone	1 per team + Beta	
Tape, Duct, 3" by 100'	1 per team	
Lantern, Battery Powered	1 per team	
Kit, First Aid, Combat	1 per team	
Grenade, Smoke - Precision Ordinance M359	2 per team	
Distraction Device - Def-Tec AA1, "Big Bang"	2 per team	

GENERAL ORIENTATION
OF THE PENTAGON

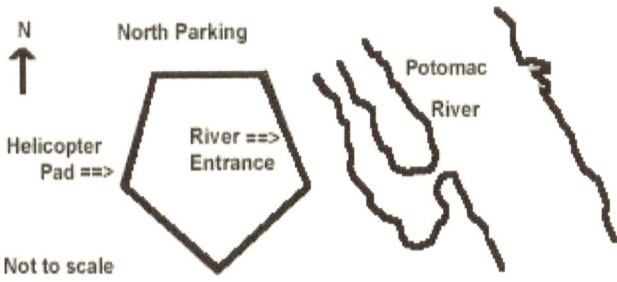

N

North Parking

Potomac

River

Helicopter
Pad ==>

River ==>
Entrance

Not to scale

Though most people refer to the building as being in Washington D.C., the structure is actually located on the Virginia side of the Potomac River

The Pentagon has been in use since January of 1943. It is the equivalent of five buildings, each in the shape of a pentagon. Each "building" is inside the next larger one and all are five stories tall. On each floor and running through the center of each building there is a corridor following the pentagon shape with access to offices on both sides of the hall.

The outermost or the largest of the five buildings is designated "E" Ring. Its corridor is referred to as the "E" Ring corridor or just E Ring. There are perpendicular, numbered corridors connecting the buildings. The smallest or inside building is the "A" Ring. The open courtyard in the center is large enough to hold three football fields.

Escalators and stairs provide access from floor to floor. The building design was selected to provide maximum office space while reducing the time it takes to walk from one area to another, even if widely separated.

SKETCH ALEX USES TO BRIEF
MASTER CHIEF EATON ON NMCC ACCESS

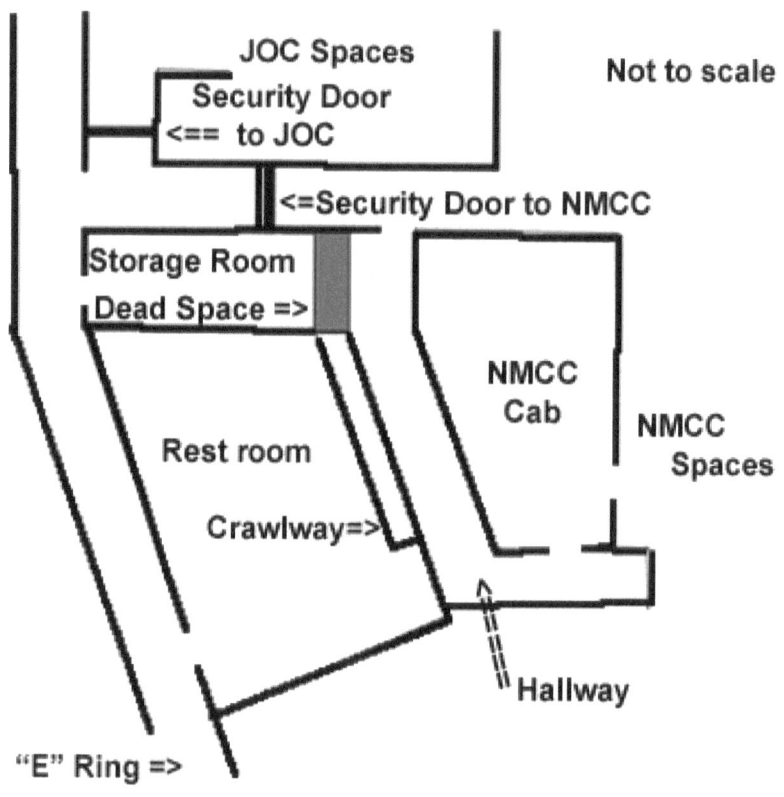

THE MYSTIQUE OF THE SCROUNGER
A JEEP IN THE CRATE

Staff Sergeant William G. Tufts (Scrounger) was not an illusionist in the typical sense of the word. He didn't perform on stage, but he used their tricks of the trade to accomplish this particular feat. He made the jeep appear "out of nowhere" in the desolate Georgia woods while they were looking the other way.

Scrounger planned this illusion long before they went on maneuvers. He arranged with several of his friends to disassemble the jeep, place it in three crates, and transport all three crates to a spot near where they would be camped. This occurred several days before the departure for the maneuvers deep in the piney woods.

The night before the jeep's "magical" appearance, Scrounger manipulated his conversation with Master Sergeant Pearson toward the subject of transportation indicating, it would be convenient if they had something to ride around in, like a jeep. Pearson took the bait more quickly than even Scrounger anticipated. Pearson said, "I'd give a hundred bucks for a jeep right now."

With this opening, Scrounger led Master Sergeant Pearson into the bet and said he could produce one by the next morning. When the master sergeant went to sleep, all Scrounger did was pull the brush back from the previously concealed crates and—Presto!—the jeep was there when Master Sergeant Pearson arose the next morning.

Just another in the long line of feats that were part of the mystique of the Scrounger.

ASSAULT
ON THE
PRESIDENCY

PROLOGUE

NOVEMBER 11th, THE PENTAGON

Only minutes ago, Lieutenant Colonel Alex Hilliard folded his lanky frame into the Mustang. Now he eased his car to a stop before he left the North parking lot. As he checked traffic, he could see the building over his shoulder. The massive, gray outline of the Pentagon loomed behind him. An icy, prickly sensation crawled up his spine.

He realized this would, in all likelihood, be the most important briefing he would ever give. *It's going to be a damn long night and day...twenty-four hours...drive two hundred and fifty miles one way—tell The Man a story that even I have trouble believing. The drive will be the easiest part. Telling him won't be that hard. Convincing him...that may take more time than I have. After that, all I have to do is retrace my steps and be back to work.*

* * *

As this phase of Alex's life—moving into the last decade of the 1900s, he hoped for more and more promising events. At times, the USAF didn't like to cooperate, but he decided life without hope wasn't a path he would choose.

Even studying for his doctoral dissertation, Alex found there was ample time for boredom in this job. He managed to complete a Master's Degree during a previous assignment. He was fortunate there was an excellent program at the university located just eight miles from his base.

Now it was time to push his education further. He enjoyed the challenge of learning and something in the back of his mind was telling him to go for it. It could be another punch on his ticket to future promotions. Alex was beginning to suspect he had a sponsor who helped him attain his current rank.

There was havoc in the promotion process. Making lieutenant colonel usually wasn't the world's toughest feat, but reduced threats abroad and the resulting military drawdowns made it difficult. The year Alex was eligible for lieutenant colonel, there were a half dozen people qualified for every open slot on the promotion list. If I do have a sponsor, I may as well give him more ammunition for the next go around, Alex thought. So as soon as he settled into his Pentagon assignment, he looked for a good school where the Ph. D. program could fit his work schedule.

Boredom paved the road to the trip—he wandered the halls and poked his nose into cubicles here and corners there. He looked, probed, and learned the myriad details that made the big building tick in the dark, quiet hours of the night.

* * *

It started innocently enough, routine duties and looking for ways to pass the long hours on a dull shift. Alex's workspace was just off the National Military Command Center. The NMCC was on the second floor of the Pentagon, a structure that after nearly five decades remained the world's largest office building. Inside the River Entrance to the big building, teams assigned to the NMCC staff faced eight-hour shifts, rather than the twelve he worked. Alex was upset at first, but it did give him an overlap with them and the opportunity to know more of the NMCC team members. Representatives from the services and the various civilian agencies having an interest in intelligence gathering around the world formed the teams.

Alex's normal work area was smaller and more cramped than the NMCC, but he did have the satisfaction of knowing that most of the folks next door were not allowed in these spaces. Part of his duties required him to deliver message traffic to the Cab in the NMCC, a glass enclosure where the senior duty officer, a general or an admiral, sat with his aide.

He also knew when he delivered message traffic to the Cab there were only a handful of people over there who had the necessary clearances to read it.

At times, he even felt a bit smug when he made these trips. He could move past dozens of people who outranked him, and walk into the Cab. He would usually just gaze out over the panorama of the people staffing the duty desks, and the large screens representing the current state of affairs throughout the world.

Occasionally someone he knew would catch his eye and their body language told him that they wanted to know what was up. Alex would shrug his shoulders as if to say, "beats me" and turn back while the duty general finished reading the messages. The general would indicate whether he wanted a copy of the message for his "read-file" or whether he would simply enter the subject on his log. More times than not, they asked for a copy, so the daylight "wheels" could read it also.

* * *

There was something Alex couldn't put his finger on, but it continued to gnaw at him. Like waking in the morning and knowing that during the night you dreamed. Try as you might, those snatches of the dream fighting their way to the conscious mind would drift away and leave that empty, frustrated feeling.

He felt the frustration. As if he knew something, but didn't even know what it was that he knew? It wasn't there all the time, but was an occasional feeling Alex sensed. It seemed so vague that he nearly dismissed it from his mind, but in the wee hours of a dull night shift, it surged back into his mind. The feeling was akin to being part of a wall of water rushing down a dry riverbed. "There is something going on." Alex didn't intend to verbalize his thoughts and the flood continued to fill his mind.

* * *

He drifted back over the years of flying. The times the bird didn't feel quite right—the strange noises an airplane can make, as if she's talking to you...telling you what is happening or about to happen. Telling you that it's time to pay attention or you'll be so far behind her mentally when the trouble starts, you'll never catch up.

It's seldom one horrendous emergency gets you...it's not a catastrophic failure. More often, it's the cumulative effect of a dozen little kinks you ignored. In one blinding instant they'll come together and if you haven't prepared yourself they will reach out, grab you by the throat, and choke the life out of you. The myriad details which happen, right or wrong—that put you and your airplane together at that particular instant in time, in that particular piece of the sky.

Sometimes it's the silence that sounds a warning. The humming and rumbling that should be there and isn't. Or the times you think that your mind has wandered and that you haven't been scanning the gauges. They were all in-the-green and the subconscious recorded that fact, so why clutter the consciousness with such trivia.

Then there was the opposite reaction. Glance up to scan the dials and let just one of the needles, on all those gauges, point the wrong direction and a mental alarm bell sounds. The conscious mind is jerked to the reality of something out of place, and the adrenaline begins to pump.

* * *

An automobile horn behind him jerked Alex back to the task at hand—the trip. He cut the Mustang's steering wheel hard right and accelerated. *It's hard to believe that it's only been three weeks.* He wheeled his little coupe onto the freeway and headed south wondering what the next three weeks would bring.

BOOK 1

DISCOVERY
(THE PREVIOUS MONTH)

OCTOBER 19th, THE PENTAGON

That's it. Something that looks so ordinary I didn't pay much attention to it. I've seen something out of place and the "something" is trying to tell me what's wrong.

"There is something going on."

"What's that Colonel?" The question came from Master Chief Petty Officer Eaton, Alex's watch NCO for this night shift.

"Nothing Duke, just thinking out loud," Alex said in an attempt to cover his mental lapse. "Everything quiet on the machines?"

"Aye, sir. Everyone is on time and where they should be."

"Then I think I'll wander the halls for a while. If you need me, give a beep on the pager and I'll be back in a flash...or something simulating a flash. Need anything from the snack bar?"

Duke shook his head and reached for his handset as one of the hundred phone line buttons flashed on his console. He answered the incoming line, "Joint Operations Center, Master Chief Eaton speaking." He listened for a moment and then asked the caller to "stand by" and punched the Hold button. "Routine traffic, sir."

Since his watch NCO put the person on Hold, Alex already knew it was a routine call. Duke was a pro and Alex respected him for a no-nonsense approach to his duties even when those duties were tedious. "Don't let World War III start while I'm gone," Alex said. The smile and the wink let Duke know Alex trusted him to handle the console in his absence.

"No sweat sir. The world can sleep safe tonight—I've got the con." Duke was also grinning as he punched the button and took the line off Hold.

Alex made his way through the heavy security door that separated his workspaces from the rest of the people in the Pentagon. In all the time he knew Chief Eaton, he still wondered about the nickname. He reminded himself for the hundredth time to ask Duke where his nickname came from.

He headed for the escalator that would take him to one of his favorite corridors. Now that he felt certain there was something to his gut feeling, he was more relaxed. *Now at least there are options—a plan to develop, and theories to test. Whether it proved to be something large or small, it was real, not the vague anxiety of the unknown.*

The escalator took Alex down one flight and he strolled along the corridor devoted to Armed Forces history. There, among the models of fighting weapons, portraits of military figures and battle flags of distinguished units, it seemed as if he could draw on the ideas and intellect of those who came before him.

Alex found he could do his best thinking while talking aloud. He often wondered what a casual observer would think seeing him there, for at times it appeared that he was talking to the portraits. "I guess I'll only be in trouble if I tell anyone you folks on the wall are answering my questions."

* * *

In an effort to appear environmentally aware and reduce the reams of paper going through the copiers, bean counters dictated there would not be a duplicate read-file of the NMCC message traffic. Each morning, the Joint Operations Center Watch Officer picked up the read-file, briefed the contents to the J.O.C. Ops Chief and then returned the file to the NMCC Cab. Following the brief, the J.O.C. Watch Officer could call his night shift done.

Alex felt that wall of water rushing down the dry riverbed again. He stared at a portrait of General "Hap" Arnold. *What was unusual about the message traffic? Why did something in the stack of communications stand out?* He racked his brain for an answer. *Why should a message seem unusual if it is just routine traffic?*

* * *

Only moments before, Alex and Duke had been watching CNN on the television located ten feet in front of their watch console. The correspondent was reviewing the candidates for the upcoming presidential election. Next they ran film clips of the candidates and their speeches from earlier in the campaign. It was the sitting president's turn to deliver a speech supporting his handpicked successor. The camera had zoomed in on Lamar A. Bancroft and picked up a speech in progress. "...We must watch over the land from our tower—not an ivory tower where we are isolated and nothing happens, but a high place from where we can watch our country, where we can watch our economy, and where we can watch our people. Not only watch, but also identify the problems that plague our country, our economy and our people. And when we identify those problems, roll up our sleeves and solve them, so we..." Alex noted that this cliché, along with other shopworn platitudes, were often woven into Bancroft's speeches.

I know I saw something out of place. About a week ago...I delivered a message to the NMCC Cab. As General Watkins read it, I scanned his message log and read-file. I remember one message, about the middle of the log. It had an unusual title and I leafed through the message traffic and skimmed it. Tower Watch. That was it. Tower Watch, the subject line of the message. Now he realized what had been gnawing at him was not what he had seen, but what was missing.

That following morning Alex briefed his boss, Captain Bedford, "That's Navy Captain, Hilliard," the man used as his introduction the first time they met. During that first meeting, his boss also said that this office would never be pronounced using initials since it would sound like a JOCK and we don't want to be an athletic supporter; hence, it would be referred to as the Jay-Oh-Cee.

Alex mentioned the NMCC traffic anomaly. Just before the briefing, he picked up the file in the NMCC and reviewed it again to be able to cover any items of concern to the J.O.C. Ops Chief. There was little in the file of direct interest to the J.O.C., and Captain Bedford in his usual Navy style wanted to get the "decks squared away" before the old man arrived for the day. Alex flipped through the messages on the clipboard looking for the one which caught his eye, but the actual message was not on the clipboard he handed to Captain Bedford that morning. He remembered thinking it was odd the message was missing. He scanned the message log for the subject title, and realized it wasn't there either. There was however, one entry redacted with a heavy black marker. He mentioned the discrepancy between the log, the read-file and what he showed to Captain Bedford when the interruption came.

The PA speaker crackled, and the security guard announced, "The Admiral's on deck." Captain Bedford knew he had three minutes before Admiral Eastland picked up his morning coffee and made his appearance in the Watch Area for his briefing. Captain Bedford muttered, "Must be some EYES ONLY traffic or something like that, forget it." The discussion ended.

The admiral appeared in the Watch Area and Alex began his morning briefing to the J.O.C. Director. About five minutes into the briefing, Admiral Eastland waved his hand in front of Alex and announced that he needed to depart for an important meeting. Alex did not have an opportunity to mention the missing document again.

* * *

Alex looked up again at the portrait of General Arnold and said, "Thanks General, you helped me put it all together."

He was more at ease following his walk through the Pentagon halls. The gnawing in his stomach was relieved. He knew what he was looking for and now he could begin to dig for more information and fill in the gaps.

OCTOBER 19th (Later the same day)

Duke briefed his day shift replacement and now Master Sergeant Rayford Pickens, sitting at the watch console, reviewed message traffic. With a name like Pickens, most folks expected him to answer to "Slim." He would respond to such a nickname if required, but he preferred his friends call him "Hillbilly." Being a rather private individual, not many people were offered the opportunity to address him in that manner. If you've been invited, Pickens would smile broadly and do nearly anything for you. If not invited, his glare could shrivel a person of any rank and they seldom tried it a second time. Rayford Pickens grew up the only child of a hardworking blue-collar family in Wheeling, West "by God" Virginia. The "by God" reference was to make sure you understood he was from West Virginia and not from the western part of that other state.

As an only child in a neighborhood of large families, Hillbilly felt a bit out of place. Those who knew him well decided that early solitude led him to be selective in his choice of friends in later life. Though his circle of friends might be small, there was genuine loyalty in both directions. Pickens graduated from high school in the top five percent of his class. Following high school, he decided he spent enough time inside of schoolhouses and the military was the best way to see what the rest of the world looked like. He joined the Army and during his first hitch he completed Ranger school, gained the rank of staff sergeant, and went into training with the elite Green Berets.

The Green Beret training qualified him as a weapons and demolition expert and his first in-country tour to Vietnam gave him another two promotions. He didn't talk much about the incident that busted him back to sergeant first-class, but those who were aware of the details knew someone handed Hillbilly the shitty end of a stick he didn't deserve. He never held the incident against the Army, but there was one officer still on active duty who always looked over his shoulder whenever he heard a voice with anything like a West Virginia twang.

* * *

"Hillbilly, I'll be over in the NMCC for a few minutes," Alex said. "I should be back in plenty of time to brief Colonel Sanchez." Today, Ray Sanchez would be taking over the day watch in the J.O.C. and it was Alex's responsibility to bring him up to speed.

Just inside the entry point to the NMCC, Alex paused and scanned the entire room. *I wonder who would be my best bet for more background on Tower Watch.* His eyes stopped on the CIA Watch Desk and he saw Mike Reilly. During this tour, he and Mike shared a study group, years before they shared much more. Both were doing some catch-up work on graduate level courses and found themselves in the same class. He stopped to chat with a couple of other Watch Officers he knew as he made his way to the CIA desk.

"Mike, I've got a favor to ask."

Mike looked up from the papers on his desk. He didn't bother shuffling any of the documents on his desk into the classified folder. "Sure, Alex, what can I do for you?"

Alex spent about five minutes covering the events that put the questions in his mind. He finished by saying, "Mike, it may be none of my business, but it sure looks strange on the face of it. If it's something that falls into the 'I don't have a need to know category,' you tell me and I'll back off."

"Sounds fair enough to me, buddy. I'll check it out with my folks at Langley and get back to you. I won't be back on duty for three days. When's your next shift day, Alex?"

Alex checked his calendar. "I'm going on break this morning and won't be back on duty for four days."

"Let's meet for lunch on the twenty-first, which should give me enough time. Alex, I'm sure there's nothing to this Tower Watch business…but just in case, let's avoid the phone till we can get back together."

OCTOBER 21st, OFF DUTY ⬠

Alex arrived at the little restaurant near Seven Corners at 11:30 a.m. Since traffic had been light, he made good time, and was a half hour early for his lunch meeting with Mike Reilly. With some time to kill, Alex ordered a draft beer and assumed he could nurse it till Mike arrived. The first beer was warm by the time Alex decided it wasn't going to last. He ordered a second draft thinking *Mike'll be along soon. He's not the type to stand me up without a phone call.* The third draft was flat, warm and nearly gone. The waiter was looking at him with one eyebrow raised as if to say, "Are you ever going to order, or are you one of those who wastes my time and leaves a small tip."

Alex asked the waiter where he could find a public phone. Old "one eyebrow raised" nodded over his right shoulder without uttering a word. The quarter Alex dropped into the slot gave him the usual gong and he dialed Mike's home number. How many times had they called each other with questions about the study group? The voice that muttered "ullo" gave Alex a start. He knew Mike well enough to know even from this short grunt that this was not Mike's voice. "Who is this?" Alex said.

"This is Mike's friend," the strange voice on the other end replied and asked, "Who is this?"

Military habit formed the reply in Alex's mind and the first word "This" was already out of his mouth before he stopped. "Mike's friend" was not much in the way of identification. Instead of replying, Alex repeated his original question.

The voice on the other end said, "Knock it off fella', *who* is this?"

The emphasis in the terse question implied an "or else" situation. Alex repeated his question for the third time and received an "official" threat from the voice. The uneasiness increased. Alex knew if something was wrong, his time on the phone was long enough for the Company types to trace the source. It was time to terminate the call and get out of the restaurant. As his hand moved the receiver toward its cradle, he could hear the repeated threats coming from the earpiece. He brought the handset close enough to his mouth, so "the voice" would be sure to hear the "put it where the sun don't shine buddy" and hung up.

OCTOBER 22nd, OFF DUTY ⬠

It was a day off for Alex, but he couldn't wait three more days to find out why Mike missed their lunch meeting. So Alex found himself in uniform heading for the Pentagon. As he turned into the North parking lot entrance, he felt the hair on the back of his neck rising. He pulled to the curb and braked quickly, keeping his eyes on the rearview mirror. Several cars passed the entrance. A dark sedan slowed, but continued without turning into the lot. *Wonder if I'm just jumpy or is someone keeping an eye on me? Well, no one there now.*

He parked, walked to the building and went in through the River Entrance. The guard noticed Alex's empty hands and asked, "Where you hidin' your lunch if you ain't got that briefcase, Colonel Hilliard?" He knew from previous inspections, the briefcase usually carried not only Alex's study material but also a meal or a snack. During the two years of Alex's assignment to the Pentagon, he came to know most of the civilian security guards. He knew them well enough to use their first names and to chat with them as he passed their posts.

"Earl, you don't miss much do you? It's one of my off days, but I'm missing some papers. If I don't find 'em, my faculty adviser will eat me alive," Alex said hoping the lie didn't show on his face. He didn't want to make an overt attempt to learn Mike's whereabouts. If something were wrong, this would be a reasonable cover. It was plausible his notes could be at the officer's Watch position in the J.O.C. or even in the NMCC. He hoped that thin veil would hold and not arouse suspicions.

* * *

He made a cursory search in the J.O.C. after casually telling several people about the misplaced school notes. Next he made his way past the security door into the NMCC and retraced his steps of two days ago. His first stop was the NMCC Cab, again explaining his reason. Then he passed the watch desks he visited before and only then did he let his eyes go to the CIA Watch Desk. Someone new, someone Alex never met was taking the CIA Watch. "Hi, I'm Alex Hilliard, J.O.C. Watch, don't think we've met," he said. He felt a tingling on the back of his neck as the man responded to the introduction.

Alex covered his alibi with the CIA rep and asked if he noticed any unclassified handwritten notes on the current situation in Argentina. At least this part of the world tied into his current studies. Jim McKee, as the CIA rep introduced himself, looked around the desk and indicated nothing about Argentina caught his eye. Alex turned, as if to leave, making his next comment sound like an afterthought. "Son-of-a-gun, Mike was on your desk two nights ago when I was lugging those notes around. We were in the same study group at one time, and I'll bet he saw them and recognized my lousy handwriting. If he did, I'll bet he probably stowed them somewhere for me."

The comment produced the desired results. McKee said, "Don't know. He might have, but I don't think he'll be covering the desk for a while. You might try him at home. Do you have his home number?"

"No, I don't," Alex lied again. "Do you have it?" Nice try, Voice, Alex thought as he realized why the back of his neck tingled since he reached out to shake this man's hand. It was McKee's voice he heard on the phone when he called Mike's house from the restaurant. "I hope Mike's not sick or something."

McKee looked at him through narrowed eyes and said, "Nah, on special assignment I think. No, I don't have a home phone for him. If it's that important, I can get back to you."

"No thanks. With luck I can remember most of the information," Alex tossed over his shoulder.

* * *

Once outside the NMCC, he turned right and reentered the J.O.C. Alex saw that Sergeant Pickens was alone at the console and asked the sergeant to meet him for lunch. "Just come alone, Hillbilly."

Sergeant Pickens squinted one eye and raised the other eyebrow but maintained his silence. He nodded and went back to his duties.

Sanchez returned to the Watch console. Ramon Sanchez was a lieutenant colonel in the Air Force. He came up through the reconnaissance ranks in the Strategic Air Command and through the Strategic Reconnaissance Center at SAC Headquarters near Omaha, Nebraska. Alex knew of Ray and the birds he flew—the ones that were big, black and faster than a speeding bullet. On more than one occasion, Ray kept listeners spellbound with tales of flying the SR-71. They shared similar backgrounds, reconnaissance—and similar assignments like SAC Headquarters, but their paths didn't cross until Ray arrived in the J.O.C. three months ago. For a moment Alex considered discussing Tower Watch with Sanchez. *No. I really don't know Ray well enough. I'll stick with people I've known long enough to trust.*

* * *

Alex spotted Hillbilly as soon as the NCO entered the cafeteria. Alex watched Pickens as he moved through the line, stacked the tray high with food and ambled toward the table. Alex marveled at the quantity of fuel it took to stoke this man's furnace. He was also aware that Pickens' physical regimen would never let that fuel accumulate around his waist. They sat several tables away from everyone else, so their conversation would not be overheard. Alex covered the events of the last couple of weeks, the message, the code name Tower Watch, the aborted meeting with Mike Reilly and the new guy on the CIA desk.

"Hillbilly, I could sure use your help finding out what this is all about. I can't put my finger on anything specific yet—it's just a feeling. If there is something to this mess, Lord knows what it could mean…and if it turns out to be nothing, we may be sticking our necks out to get them chopped off…at least career wise."

"Colonel H…" Sergeant Pickens said. "I'd work for you anytime, but then I guess you know that or we wouldn't be a talkin' like this. I'll see what I can dig out for you, Colonel."

"I appreciate the compliment, Sergeant."

"Damn, now, Colonel. If you're gonna go all formal on me, I may have ta take that back."

Alex grinned as Hillbilly slid in and out of his West Virginia accent. "Hillbilly, it's probably best we stay off the phones. The shift change-over when I come back on duty will be a good time for an update." They also agreed on some recognition signals.

As Alex started to leave the table, Sergeant Pickens looked up quickly and said, "Colonel H, I darn near forgot. Ms. Crawford said she's got a message for you. I told her I'd probably run into you before you left the building. She didn't say what it was about, only that if I saw you I should tell you to stop by and see her before you leave."

"Thanks, Hillbilly. I'll do that. I don't want to disappoint the light of my life."

It was Hillbilly's turn to grin. He also winked.

Sarah Crawford was a civilian secretary, a GS-9. In less than two years since her arrival in the J.O.C. as Captain Bedford's secretary, Sarah's talents earned a promotion. Three months ago, she moved to the front office where she became Admiral Eastland's secretary. When Alex arrived, Sarah told him she received an anonymous call. The caller told her to give Alex an envelope she would find on her desk addressed "To A." Sure enough, she found it buried in her IN basket. "Alex, what's going on?" she said. "It sounded like Mike Reilly...but why the mystery?" She felt a right to ask the questions. First it was unusual for a mysterious envelope to appear on her desk. Beyond that, she believed the nature of their personal relationship outside work afforded her that privilege.

* * *

"Sarah, I really don't know what might be in the letter." That part was true, but then Alex skirted the truth. "I'm not sure it was Mike. I do know something strange is going on around here and that even knowledge of this note may be dangerous."

"What do you mean dangerous?" she said.

"You are going to have to trust me on this Sarah. Just trust me for a few days until I figure it out. As soon as I know, I'll tell you. In the meantime, please don't mention this to anyone. No one...please."

"You know I trust you, Alex. Tell me when you can."

Alex left the J.O.C. *Better get somewhere to read what Mike has to say before I leave.* He entered the restroom nearest the J.O.C., went into one of the stalls, lowered his trousers and sat down. He opened the business size envelope, unfolded the single sheet of paper and began to read the small cramped handwriting that he recognized as Mike's.

A

Sorry I missed our lunch meeting. You must be right. Something is going on but I'm not sure what. I mentioned TW over at Langley when I got off duty and all I got was vacant stares. I also heard whispered comments as I left a couple of offices. Couldn't hear the words, but figured I was the topic of conversation. Before I could get out of the building, my boss sent me to a "conference." Turned out to be a batch of bull that wasted the entire morning. I tried to beg off, but he wouldn't relent. By the time I left, about one-thirty p.m., I figured you gave up on me, so I headed home. When I got there, I found someone tossed my place. Damn good thing Cindy and the kids were visiting Cindy's mom. The whole house was a mess—no stopping point like they found what they were looking for—just a mess from top to bottom. That told me why there was a "mandatory conference" for me to attend. I'll nose around a bit more tomorrow morning and see you later. Kept a low profile and talked with some folks I knew I could trust. I still don't know what is going on, but I've seen some TW traffic. Weird stuff—talk about "polls show the wrong guy ahead," "need to get the troops alerted," and a lot more that doesn't look like typical military or Company traffic. By the time you read this, I'll have some copies of the traffic. Meet me for lunch (10/23). The place we went to on your birthday and the same time. Also check inside the plumbing panel in the restroom just outside your spaces. I think you'll find some interesting widgets there. Take the case, you'll find it interesting too.

Hang tough buddy, and WATCH YOUR SIX

M

Alex smiled at Mike's reference about "watching your six." Alex did his best to instill into an ex ground-pounder and now a Company man a pilot's mentality. He felt he succeeded to some extent. The phrase indicated he needed to watch his backside if he wanted to stay alive.

Before leaving the restroom, he checked the area Mike's note mentioned. He opened a metal door, about two feet by three feet, which provided access to the plumbing. Inside he found a brown leather briefcase. The case contained some nondescript paperwork, two packages each about one-fourth of an inch thick filled with some writing paper, a copy of *The Washington Post* and a couple of pencils. He closed it, left the restroom and headed back to the River Entrance. Alex approached the guard post and noticed that Earl was wolfing down an appetizer before leaving for his regular lunch break. Briefcases are not considered a threat on the way out of the building and are ignored. Alex was counting on that fact. It worked; Earl didn't seem to notice Alex leaving with more than he carried in.

* * *

Back at home, he examined the case more closely. It was brown, good quality leather and about five to six inches deep. He opened it again. This time, a more detailed examination revealed the interior was a little less than four inches deep. He slipped a knife blade along the edge of the bottom and found that it would pop up. Below the first bottom was a space the size of the briefcase and nearly two and one-half inches deep. In that compartment, Alex found another note from Mike and three items. There were two small black boxes each with two wires coming out of them. Each wire ended at a flat object that looked like it might be a two-inch diameter speaker with an elastic band attached to it. To Alex's amazement, he also found a 9mm automatic pistol and what looked like a sound suppressor. The note read:

A

By now you have no doubt discovered the items (oops, forgot, "widgets") in this compartment. I included two of them. I know you are good for them, so I'm letting you borrow some of the Company's latest technology. I think you'll be needing them. They're sophisticated encryption devices (scramblers) for phones—battery powered (a type that's easy to replace), just put the disk with the embossed "ear" on the speaker part of the phone receiver, with that "ear" facing out (may need the elastic band to hold it) and the other disk goes over the mouthpiece in a similar manner with the embossed word "out" facing away from the handset. Keep use sparse—the built-in microchips containing the security coding will only last four or five weeks depending on the amount of use and the traffic intercepted by the other side.

Still not sure what is happening, but it is big. I've gotten several raised eyebrows when I even mention TW. Pay attention to my previous warning about covering your tail. Be careful who you share this with—I think it could get hairy real fast. I'll bring the copies of message traffic with me when we meet for lunch. Again, the place we met on your birthday. Until then - - -

1041 - 5, 290 - 24, 206 - 1/ 1194 - 15, 888 - 6,
297 - 17, 457 - 7,

412 - 30, 921 - 32, 747 - 8, 842 – 1

M

At first the cryptic numbers at the end of Mike's note didn't register. Then he remembered that while they were in the study group, Mike showed him a simple code involving a book. Both parties needed access to the same edition of the same book. The references were to page numbers and then to the number of words until you arrive at the one you want to use. Since they chose a paperback encyclopedia, it contained too many words to try to count. They settled on only those words or initials that were in bold type. For numbers, they circled numbers zero through nine on various pages—always making sure that both copies reflected the same references. They marked several references to each number to avoid repetition. One other rule they observed—they would use commas as delimiters. *If only I kept the damn book. What was it? What was it?* Alex ran his finger along the bookshelves in what he laughingly referred to as his study. *Here it is.* "The New American Desk Encyclopedia."

In a matter of minutes Alex tracked the coded references in Mike's note to the encyclopedia. The decoded numbers read:

Samuel Cooke Canary Trust 5 5 5 1 2 7 2 Home

The third word didn't make much sense until he remembered their rules. Slashes used to separate words would also mean to chop the word—don't use the entire word. The numbers must be a phone number for Sam. So, the message read:

Samuel (or Sam) Cooke, can trust, home phone 555-1272

Of course we can trust Sam—we met him years ago during the fiasco at the Modesto airport. He also helped bring down the crooks after my wife was killed. *Has it really been more than a decade ago?* Alex nodded to himself.

OCTOBER 23rd, OFF DUTY

Twelve-thirty. Time to meet Mike and see what this is all about. Better wander around for a while and keep an eye on the rear view. I should be able to spot anyone following me.

Alex swung onto the interstate that headed south toward Springfield, Virginia. He brought the car up to the speed limit and then tacked on an extra ten miles per hour. That was pushing the speed which attracted the attention of the state police who patrolled this stretch of the Shirley Highway. But, it would give a better picture of anyone interested in his destination. He passed two exits and was approaching a third one still in the middle lane. He planned to swing onto the exit ramp at the last minute like many of the cars traveling the interstate tend to do. With several car lengths between himself and the one behind and to the right, he cut the wheel hard and barely made the exit ramp. He slowed quickly with an eye on the rearview mirror. Only one car followed him off the interstate. A blue Chevrolet sedan moved up the ramp and Alex could see three people in the car.

The traffic signal on top of the exit overpass turned red, and Alex stopped. He was in the center lane, and the painted arrows on the concrete indicated he could turn either right or left. The Chevrolet was on his back bumper when the light turned green. Alex drove straight ahead. The blue Chevy turned left and Alex could see that no one in the car was looking his direction. He pressed his right foot to the floorboard and he was soon back on the interstate and up to cruising speed. Halfway to Springfield, he left the interstate again. Reaching the stop sign at the top of the exit ramp, he turned left onto the overpass. Once across the overpass, he again turned left and put himself on the entrance ramp to the interstate heading the opposite direction. Alex repeated the same maneuver at the next exit. Now he was headed south again, his original direction and during the two U-turns he didn't identify any cars following him.

The maneuvers cost Alex an extra thirty to forty minutes getting to the restaurant; but he was still a few minutes early. Mike was usually prompt, so he might be there already. He remembered the last time he visited this bar. Mike tried hard to get tickets to the Washington Redskins football game scheduled at RFK Stadium on Alex's birthday. He was not successful. The next best alternative Mike could think of was to find a bar with the biggest television screen imaginable and take Alex to see the game. They both enjoyed the game and one another's company. Now Alex was on his second draft and once more he felt uneasy. *Damn, not again. Where the hell are you, Mike? This is not like you.*

An hour and three draft beers later, Alex left the bar. Mike missed another appointment, leaving Alex with nothing to do but head back home. He couldn't shake the uneasy feeling. Mike would have been there unless…Alex couldn't fill in the blank. He barely caught the traffic report on the all-talk-all-news station on his car radio, "Big tie-up on the GW Parkway, southbound near state Route 120—one-car accident, but plenty of lookie-loo's slowing everything up. Stay clear if you can." Alex dismissed the traffic problem. *Opposite direction from me. I won't be going so far north anyway.*

* * *

Mike allowed plenty of time to drive from CIA Headquarters at Langley, Virginia to meet Alex in Springfield. He also built in extra time for a couple of detours while he watched for a tail. Rather than using the Beltway, he decided to take the slower route down to Springfield. It was only a short way to the George Washington Parkway. Then he could head southeast until he hit the Shirley Highway and finally southwest into Springfield. In less than a minute on the GW

Parkway, he saw them. Looked like two, and at this distance he could only tell the driver was a Caucasian and the other was Black. The black Ford carrying the pair accelerated and came up on Mike's right rear. The man leaning out the back left window of the Ford was holding what appeared to be a .410 gauge shotgun. Mike even recognized the weapon—the Company kept a number in the armory available to check out—modified Snake Charmer II's with the barrel under eighteen inches—making it illegal. Mike hit the accelerator hard, but it was already too late.

The failure of a rear tire, in a rear wheel drive car like Mike's, caused him to lose power to one of the wheels providing traction. Mike's action aggravated the problem by shoving the accelerator to the floor and adding maximum power to the rear wheels just as the shotgun roared. The blast hit his right rear tire, the car swerved violently out of control and off the highway. It crossed the right-hand shoulder and careened down the embankment. His last conscious thought was: they planned it just right to put me into the trees.

* * *

Mike's car plowed through a grassy area and smashed head on into an elm tree that must have been growing there for nearly a hundred years. The black Ford came sliding to a stop on the shoulder of the road opposite the crash site. The two men jumped out and ran to the wrecked car. The tall thin Caucasian hunched over the driver's door to block any view from the highway while the shorter Black man ripped open the left rear door of Mike's car and jumped into the backseat.

"Is he dead?" said the tall man outside.

"Not yet." said the man in the backseat as he reached toward Mike's head. Then he stretched over into the front seat and grabbed a large envelope. He stuffed the envelope under his shirt and then stepped out of Mike's car. Both men were standing there as the first casual observers arrived on the scene.

"Looks like he died when he hit the tree," the tall man said to no one in particular.

* * *

Corporal Wheeler of the Virginia State Police was cruising the northbound side of the GW Parkway. He received the accident call shortly before he saw the cars parked on the shoulder of the southbound lanes. He hit his lights and siren, made a U-turn across an open space in the median, and was on the scene within minutes of the reported accident.

"Looks bad. Better roll the paramedics," Corporal Wheeler shouted into the microphone of his police radio as his patrol car skidded to a stop. His purposeful stride brought him to the scene in minimum time as well as giving him an opportunity to survey the area. He saw four people near the car, three men and a woman. He cataloged them into his memory to help him with the report he would have to write later.

The man nearest the woman said, "Doesn't look like there's much anyone can do for him. These two fellas were the first to get here."

"Anyone checked for vital signs?" said Corporal Wheeler. Responding to the head shakes from all four witnesses, he reached through the open driver's window and placed two fingers on Mike's neck feeling for a pulse. He knew before he tried he wouldn't find one. The ambulance was pulling off the highway and attempting to get as close as possible to the accident scene. "I'll need formal statements from all of you. Please stay here for a few more minutes," he said to the witnesses as he started toward the ambulance. He waved it to a stop and warned the driver not to risk coming any closer. The EMTs would have plenty of time to take care of the details now.

The officer retrieved a clipboard with the appropriate report forms from his cruiser and returned to the wrecked car. The man and woman, a couple from Bethesda, Maryland, were still there. The other two men were nowhere in sight. Corporal Wheeler wrote down the few details the couple provided about the accident, He wished his glance at the parked cars when he arrived was a more detailed one. There were two. The couple confirmed the car the other two men were driving was black, that it might have been a Ford or Chevrolet. They also stated that they didn't have the slightest idea of the license plate number or the state of registration. Wheeler was reasonably sure it was a Ford, but like the couple, remembered little else. "I hope the appointment those two needed to keep was real important. I sure would like to know what they saw," he said.

OCTOBER 25th, ON DUTY, THE PENTAGON

Fortunately, this was the beginning of another shift where it appeared there would be little for Alex to do. *The more time I'll have to dig for details about Tower Watch. Let's see what's going on over in the NMCC. Mike should be on duty by now. I hope. At least I can find out why he stood me up for two free lunches.*

The man on the CIA desk looked familiar. Between routine chores, Alex talked with the people on several of the other desks. Finally he approached the CIA desk and stuck out his hand, "Hi, I'm Alex Hilliard, J.O.C. Watch."

With a face devoid of expression, the man said, "I'm Sam Cooke, good to know you." Then dropping his voice to less than a whisper, he added, "Restroom, thirty minutes."

Alex barely contained his surprise. "Yeah, me too. I guess I'd better get back to my desk," he said to cover his departure. Alex entered the restroom twenty-eight minutes after meeting Sam. Four minutes later, Cooke arrived. He held an index finger up to his lips and said nothing until he finished checking the entire room. "Alex, good to see you after all these years."

"Same here. Where's Mike?" Alex said.

"Damn, I thought you must have heard by now. He died—was killed—the day before yesterday. Reports suggested an auto accident, but I have my doubts," Sam said.

The words slammed Alex like a sledgehammer. He clenched his teeth, fought back the anger and felt tears sting his eyes. Mike was more than a friend in the early days. Way back, Mike was there for support when he lost his wife, Ellie. Later, during the time they were in the same study group, Mike invited him to their home so often that his two kids adopted him as "Uncle Alex." Cindy and Mike were only children like Alex. His status as a parent was too painful to discuss, so he reveled in being an uncle to Robert Matthew and Elizabeth Mary. Bobby was five and Liz was a precocious eight.

"How, when, what happened…and most of all, why Mike?" The words spilled out in a torrent.

Sam put his hand on Alex's shoulder. "Mike briefed me on your suspicions about Tower Watch. I believe both of you were on to something big. I did some digging and got my hands on most of the same message traffic Mike carried with him when he went to meet you. Mike briefed me on the docs before he left. Did I mention the Tower Watch messages were missing from Mike's car after the accident?…I also got copies of the original, handwritten highway patrol and autopsy reports. Damn quick to complete a full autopsy report—looks like the Company put pressure on the state. Tuck these papers away and be careful who you let see them."

Before leaving, Sam and Alex coordinated two subsequent meeting places. With the locations preset, they would need only to set a time and date to confirm a meeting. They also prearranged a code to disguise the actual timing should they have to communicate by phone.

* * *

Now he knew how much he needed Hillbilly's help.

"Anything interesting going on over in the NMCC, Colonel?" Hillbilly said as Alex returned to the J.O.C.

"There sure is. Do you remember our discussion the other day about Mike Reilly?" The sergeant nodded and Alex said, "I just learned that Mike died two days ago."

"Damn, Colonel. I'm sure sorry to hear that. Is there anything I can do?"

"Damn straight there is. The talk we had the other day...I told you about some of my suspicions. Well, we may have some of the answers right here. I got these papers from a contact Mike recommended. Hillbilly, take a look at these messages while I go over these reports about Mike."

Alex chose the accident report first. The description of Mike's body and position and of the two unidentified witnesses stood out as he read it.

* * *

COMMONWEALTH OF VIRGINIA
State Highway Patrol
Accident Report

Section I - General

Date: October 23

Reporting Officer: Cpl. Jeffery D. Wheeler

Arrived, On Scene: 11:20 a.m.

...

Section III (D) Description of Vehicle (Interior)

...body in driver's seat, slumped forward on steering wheel, seat belt/shoulder harness around body but attaching buckle was not locked into stationary part of the restraint system...

Section IV Witnesses (use additional sheet if more space required):

Alvin and Whitney Webb, married, 12664 North Holmes, Bethesda, MD interviewed—did not witness actual crash. Identified 2 other possible witnesses who were on the scene when these two witnesses arrived.

The potential witnesses left scene prior to interview & AFTER being warned by investigating officer to remain on scene—they were driving a late model four door, black Ford with Virginia registration. Witness descriptions follow:

#1 - White, male, 6 feet 1 inch—180 lbs., hair-light brown, eyes-blue, mustache.

#2 - Black, male, 5 feet 8 inches, 160 lbs., hair-black, eyes-brown.

No other distinguishing marks or features noted.

Alex turned to the autopsy report. Again, only parts of the report leaped from the pages.

COMMONWEALTH OF VIRGINIA
ARLINGTON COUNTY
Autopsy Protocol

Cover

1. Name of Deceased: Michael John Reilly

2. (A) Date of Death: October 21st

(B) Time of Death: 11:25 a.m. - estimate, established from report by on scene police officer who investigated auto crash

3. Date of Autopsy: October 22nd

...

42. Conclusions: ...Gross examination of the neck shows 1st cervical vertebrae (C1) rotated relative to C2—supporting facets dislocated and extensive damage in the supporting ligaments of C1/C2. Compatible with sudden rotational injury while head turned to right. Injury is somewhat suspicious, however since body apparently not restrained by the seat belt, it is not totally inconsistent with vehicular accident type trauma ...

...

56. Cause of Death: Accidental, dislocation trauma to C1/C2 (see item 42) sustained in automobile crash.

Signed: Willis J. Cafferty, MD

Alex and Sergeant Pickens traded documents. It took several minutes for Alex to compose himself after reading the impersonal details of Mike's death, like the "bruising, bleeding and swelling" of the neck. He reminded himself the authors of the reports were following protocols and didn't know Mike. To them, he was another body in a long string of bodies they viewed day after day. The words in the messages Hillbilly handed back to him began to take his mind off Mike.

Continued references to presidential polls taken by various organizations all pointed the same direction—"the wrong man is leading the field." Further references suggested the "wrong men" were those running for the office of president from both parties. There were signs "those in office" believed it would not be in the best interest of the country if the "incompetents" were to gain the day. Innuendo, euphemisms and deceptive descriptions disguised the authors and the parties in question. Alex reached his own conclusions, but he needed to put names and deeds to the words.

At the next to the last message, Alex paused. He looked up and noticed Hillbilly's completed stack of documents, and that Hillbilly was staring at him. "Do you believe what you just read, Colonel?"

They discussed the details. Neither could believe what they faced. This particular message carried a classification that was far above Top Secret. Even the name assigned to the classification was classified. The name was therefore never mentioned or printed outside fully secure areas. According to that message which quoted a Top Secret Executive Order, the president's decision was:

...If any person incapable of providing strong leadership for the country were to win the coming election, the future of the economy and the country would be in grave danger.

Should such a condition come to pass, it would be the duty of the incumbent president to ensure the nation is preserved.

Any and all means would be used to secure the future of the country.

Tower Watch would henceforth carry the classification of this document—it would not be discussed with anyone not on the TW Access List—and would also be marked SPECIAL CATEGORY (SPECAT) EYES ONLY...

OCTOBER 26th, ON DUTY, THE PENTAGON

Master Chief Petty Officer Eaton relieved Sergeant Pickens on the day watch. Alex took the Chief aside and discussed his suspicions and the message traffic with him. Since it was a weekday, they would have trouble keeping the rest of the normal staff from interrupting and seeing the documents. "Duke, use a call of nature to get a little privacy and time to read these. I'll cover the Watch Desk till you get back," Alex said.

When Duke returned, he seemed incredulous. "Colonel, I'm not sure I can believe what I just read..." he said, echoing the words Alex and Sergeant Pickens used, "Does it really mean what I think it means?"

"Give me your take on it, Master Chief."

His thoughts again mirrored those Pickens and Alex used to interpret the meanings in the messages.

"Well, it seems spooky, but reading between the lines, it sure sounds like that message is quoting the president as saying he'd do anything to stay in office, if the wrong person is elected."

"That's pretty close to my thoughts on it. Who do you think would make the determination about who is a 'wrong' person?"

"From the tone of the Exec Order, I'd say the person who wrote it would."

"That would incriminate the president. Is that what you're saying?"

"Yes sir, and I think your suspicions are right on target. Whatever it takes, Colonel, you can count me in."

"Hillbilly told me he would lend a hand," Alex said. "Now we need to really start organizing and do some serious recruiting."

"How many people do you think we might need?"

"I'm not sure at this point, but I'm going to need several like you and Hillbilly to be extra eyes and ears."

"I think we could count on Tufts and Tucker," Duke said.

"I think you're right. I have their names on my list of potentials. Also, considering the sensitivity of what we may be getting into, I think we should have some method of protecting ourselves. We'll all use code names when communicating or referring to one another."

He told Duke that when discussing TW, Hillbilly will be Delta—and if written the symbol "Δ" could be used. For Duke, Alex decided on Gamma which is written like this "Γ"…like an upside down "L."

Alex discussed the rationale of his decisions with Chief Eaton. They needed a way to conceal who or how large the group was. He wondered whether this cloak-and-dagger aspect was really needed—he decided that it was better to feel foolish and stay healthy than the opposite. Since they would be recruiting shift workers, he decided a large number of people would be required. He would, of necessity, need to know everyone. Team leaders would know one another, but not team members of teams other than their own. In that manner, the integrity of teams could be maintained with the least danger to the group as a whole. He decided to use the Greek alphabet, but only those letters that would not be confused with English letters when written. He discarded ones like Mu and Zeta. The only letter that came close to violating the rule was the name he assigned to himself, Beta.

Alex developed a list of people he believed he could trust. He handed the list to Duke for input. "Duke, I want you and Hillbilly to be part of my first level coordinators—Delta will be in charge of weapons and munitions—I want you to head up intelligence. I'm going to ask Sarah to give you a hand on that side. If she says okay, I'll use Lambda to identify her." He formed an upside down vee with his index and middle fingers.

Eaton nodded. "Delta's experience in the Special Forces should be just what we need for the weapons side."

"Since I want people I know and can trust, I'm not going outside the J.O.C. for warm bodies. For logistics, I was thinking of Sergeant Tufts—he seems to be able to put his hands on anything he wants." Getting another affirmative nod from Duke, Alex continued. "Tufts will be Sigma." As he spoke, he drew the symbol "Σ" on a piece of paper. "We are also going to need something in the way of communications. I've got some widgets, that'll help, but I think Tuck would fit the bill." Duke nodded again as Alex referred to Master Sergeant Nate Tucker. He was a tough Marine with an extensive background in communications. His sphere was wide and included a circle of friends in services beyond the Corps. "I've kept it to the NCOs since I don't know the officers on the watch staff that well. There is one I am considering, Ray Sanchez. I know his background even if I have only known him personally for a few months."

Duke agreed with Alex's assessments and choices. Duke would see Tucker on the shift change-over and recruit him. Alex would contact Tufts during his time between duty periods. They felt they could trust these two even if their decision was not to participate. At the same time, there was no doubt these two NCOs would be excited by the invitation.

* * *

Alex managed to have lunch with Sarah and found a place to sit where they could share some privacy. Sarah was shaken at the news of Mike's death. She accompanied Alex to Mike and Cindy's home on several occasions. Alex reminded her of their conversation when she found Mike's letter to Alex. He warned her again it could be dangerous to get involved. By now even with her emotions in check, she was still getting angry. "You're damn right I'm scared, Alex, but I want to be part of putting them away, whoever they are. Mike deserves that. What can I do to help?"

"For now, just sit tight and keep your ears open," Alex said. "I've got some information I want you to see. Maybe tomorrow. I need to check out some details first. I'll stop by before I leave today." Sarah and Alex took the escalator back to the second floor and returned to the J.O.C.

* * *

Alex saw the obituary about Mike in the Sunday edition of *The Washington Post*. It was short, terse and contained little detail. Mike's occupation was listed as "government employee." It said memorial services would be private and burial would be at National Memorial Park at 11 a.m. on October 27th. The interment location surprised Alex. He put a call through to Cindy Reilly. He was not looking forward to this second call to Cindy. He talked to her shortly after he learned about Mike's death, and that call was tough enough. He knew this one would be even more heartrending. "Hi, Cindy this is Alex. How are you doing?"

"Thanks for calling, Alex. I'm doing okay, I guess." They carried on a casual conversation for a few minutes, and then there was a long pause on Cindy's end of the phone. Alex was sure he could hear a sob and tears choked back.

"It's all right Cindy, just take your time, I can hang on here as long as you need. Let it out if you need to…it's okay to let the tears out," he said and held the phone in silence waiting for Cindy to gain enough composure to speak again. He felt the tears forming in his own eyes.

"Thanks again, Alex," she said. "Sometimes I can talk about Mike and it's no problem, and then in the next breath it hits me and I come all unglued. The kids are doing pretty well too. Bobby is too young to really understand that his Daddy won't be coming back. Liz is something else. She doesn't understand everything, but she knows enough to realize that Mike will never come home. Oh God, I miss him, Alex." Again there was silence on her end of the phone.

"I know you do, Cindy. I miss him too. Hang on as long as you need to, I'll be here." When Cindy was able to speak again, Alex asked about the cemetery mentioned in the paper. "I thought Mike wanted to be buried at Arlington, and the paper said services were to be private. I would like to come if you don't mind."

"Alex, you know you are always welcome. I want you to come, and Sarah too if she can get away. I guess the Company put Mike's obituary together—I didn't talk with anyone about it. I've seen the National Memorial Park and it's nice. Mike did prefer Arlington, but they told me that Arlington is running out of space. I guess Mike didn't have enough rank to allow him to be buried there."

"I'll see you tomorrow Cindy. Take care of yourself and the kids. Remember I'm here if you need me," Alex said as they finished their conversation. I've made a promise to Cindy—now I have to find a way to keep it, he thought.

* * *

Alex knocked on Captain Bedford's open door. The captain nodded him in and finished his phone call.

"Boss, I lost a good friend over the weekend. I'd like to attend his funeral tomorrow. I'll need someone to cover my shift in order to make it. Can you give me a hand on a replacement?" Alex said.

Captain Bedford was far more understanding than Alex expected. "Good friends are hard to come by. If you need the time off, I'll cover the desk for you tomorrow. What time do you need to leave?"

"The funeral isn't till eleven-hundred, so I can cover tomorrow's shift up till about ten-hundred. Burial is out at National Memorial, about six or seven miles west of here—so I should be able to be back by thirteen-hundred or so," Alex said.

"Don't bother coming back here after the funeral, Alex. I'll see that your shift is covered till the night team arrives," Captain Bedford said.

Alex thanked him and headed to Sarah's office. "Can you get off tomorrow morning for Mike's funeral? I just talked to Cindy and she'd like us both to be there."

"If I was Cindy, I know I'd appreciate all the moral support I could get. What time do we need to leave?"

OCTOBER 27th, ON DUTY, THE PENTAGON

This was the last of Alex's current stint of day shifts. There was one task remaining before leaving to attend Mike's funeral. He dialed a number in the J3 Directorate of the JCS and heard, "General Watson's office, Miss Harper speaking."

"Miss Harper, this is Lieutenant Colonel Hilliard. I've known the general for a number of years. I'd like to visit with him if he has some time available in the next few days.

Could you help me out?"

"Why yes, I believe I've heard General Watson mention your name. He is in his office, so I could check with him if you'd like."

"Yes ma'am, I'd be happy to hold." Miss Harper was back on the line in under a minute.

"The general would be pleased to see you. He left it up to me to put you on his calendar. When would you be available?"

Alex was pleased to find General Watson's schedule allowed time two days from now. Alex would be off duty on the 29th, and coming in on an off day was an advantage. He could use the Visitors' parking lot, which was much closer than the area he used on normal workdays.

* * *

Alex and Sarah walked to the North parking lot and found Alex's car. Since Alex's afternoon was free, he decided to drive, so he could drop Sarah back at work following the funeral and then head home. He started west on the Arlington Boulevard part of Route 50, planning to take it into Falls Church where he could cut northwest through town and pick up the Lee Highway. From there, it would only be about a mile and a half more to the cemetery. With plenty of time, he was not pressing the speed limit. He glanced in his rearview mirror and winced when he noticed a black Ford two cars behind them. "Sarah, don't turn around, but I want you to use the courtesy mirror on your sun visor to check behind us. Two cars back, black Ford sedan. Can you make out what they look like?"

Sarah took a comb from her purse and lowered the visor. She pulled the comb through her hair even though she couldn't see herself in the mirror. "There are two men in the front seat. The one driving is Black and medium to short height. The other one is fairly tall, I can't see the top of his head—he's white. Do you know who they are, Alex?"

"Not for sure...not even sure they're following us, but we'll soon find out." On the outskirts of Falls Church, instead of going on through town, he continued west on Route 50. He passed under I-495 and a quarter-mile later, turned north on a state road. The black Ford was still there, three cars back. Another half mile and he turned east, back onto the Lee Highway. Only someone going out of their way would have taken this route to the cemetery. The black Ford was now only two cars back. As Alex exited the Lee Highway and turned into the cemetery entrance, the Ford disappeared.

* * *

Alex spotted the canopy and he parked on the shoulder of the road. As they approached, Alex and Sarah could see Cindy and the children seated to the side of the elevated, flag draped casket. They were under a green canopy that matched the lawn surrounding the grave site. Even though artificial turf hid most of it from sight—the brown, overturned earth created a stark contrast. The ceremony was short and moving. The minister conducting the service had known Cindy and Mike for several years. He spoke as a friend who was experiencing a great loss. Since Mike served four years in the Air Force, he was entitled to a full military funeral and burial in a national cemetery. Three riflemen fired a three volley salute—Cindy winced at each of the volleys. Six officers wearing their Army dress uniforms, flanked the coffin. They would remove the flag from Mike's casket, then fold it into the familiar triangle and present it to Cindy "on behalf of a grateful nation."

Mike, old buddy, you deserve better. You wanted to be buried at Arlington National Cemetery and I swear I'll do whatever it takes to see that happens. And don't worry about Cindy and your kids. There are people here who care and will make sure that they will never be forgotten.

The ceremony was over, so Sarah and Alex made their way to Cindy's side. They each kissed her and told her how much they cared for Mike and how much he would be missed. They promised they would be there if she needed anything.

* * *

Cindy appreciated their concern and offers. In the back of her mind she felt the offers were well meant but would be forgotten in time. Later, she would find out just how wrong her assumption was.

* * *

Swinging his car up to the River Entrance at the Pentagon, Alex intended to drop Sarah off so she could return to work. She leaned over, kissed him and pulled the door release. As Sarah began to slide out of the car, Alex reached across and took her hand. "I really don't feel like being alone, Sarah. Do you have to go back to work today?"

"Admiral Eastland said I could take the rest of the day off if I wanted to. I don't feel like sitting at my desk all afternoon either. Let's get out of here."

* * *

Midday traffic was light. Alex covered the distance to his house in Alexandria in twenty minutes. This was only the second home Alex ever owned. Years ago he sold the first one in Alaska, and it took a long time for him to buy another. The first one held memories that took years to conquer.

As a single officer, Alex's budgeting problems were small. Over the years, he managed to save and invest a substantial amount. When he arrived in Virginia, he found real estate high, but decided his budget could handle the prices. His job and finishing the doctoral thesis did not allow him time to maintain a house. If that wasn't a good excuse, he rationalized; *I just don't enjoy spending time mowing lawns and painting houses.* He looked for a townhouse where he was responsible for the interior and others, for a monthly fee, took care of the outside. He found just what he was looking for in Alexandria, Virginia. It was a well-kept three-story townhouse about four and a half miles south of the Pentagon. His commute was an easy drive or a short Metro subway ride. His home was about halfway between the Metro Blue Line route on the west and the Potomac River on the east.

His walking distance, whether he drove to the Pentagon or took the Metro, was the same. The only difference was which end of the trip required the walk. He could walk to the Duke Street station, catch the subway, and get off at the stop virtually inside the Pentagon. If he drove, the distance to walk was the same after parking his car in the North lot. A third and more remote alternative would be to walk to the Pentagon from the boat dock on the Potomac River. He considered buying a boat. He could run the boat up the Potomac River to the basin on the east side of the Pentagon, tie up at the dock leaving only three hundred yards to the Pentagon's River Entrance. While owning a boat was an intriguing idea, he decided not to take on that third mode of transportation.

* * *

During the drive to his home, Alex told Sarah about the documents he got from Cooke. He omitted the source of the information. "I want you to read them, Sarah. Then I hope you can tell me it's just my imagination running wild."

Sarah settled into the overstuffed armchair in Alex's study on the third floor and began reading. As Alex watched her, a large Maine Coon cat padded into the room. Sarah caught the movement in her peripheral vision and looked up. "I'll never get over the size of him. How much does Caesar weigh now?" she said.

"He's up to about sixteen pounds or better. I can still feel his ribs, so he really isn't overweight," Alex said. Caesar curled up on the floor near Sarah's chair. "I think he's sayin' he's comfortable with you."

Sarah could hear the loud purring, smiled and reached over the arm of the chair, so she could rub the big cat's neck. The purr grew louder. She turned her attention back to the documents and went over them spending several minutes on each document. On several occasions a frown wrinkled her brow. She would refer back to previous pages cross-checking her memory. She finished the final document and was quiet. After a few minutes, she looked at Alex and said "I'm having trouble believing this...and I certainly don't believe it's your imagination. Alex, does Mike's death figure in this?"

"I couldn't prove it in a court of law," he said. "But I think it does. So does the person who got these to me. These are copies of at least some of the documents Mike was going to show me the day he died. Died, hell. My source suspects he was murdered. I've also read the accident and autopsy reports on Mike."

"Let me see them," Sarah said. Alex pulled the two reports from a desk drawer and handed them to her. This time when she looked up there was a flush of anger burning through the tears. "Damn. I agree with your source. At least there are enough questions here to warrant an investigation. And the description of the two witnesses who left the accident scene. Alex, do you realize how close their descriptions match the two in the car who followed us today? Even the car matches."

"Exactly. That's what I came up with too. I thought of the descriptions being a coincidence, but I don't much believe in coincidences. Anything else you picked up on that we haven't discussed?"

"No, not really. I am wondering if you're going to trust me enough to let me in on everything you know. Referring to your 'source.' Alex, why are you holding back?"

"It's not that I don't trust you, darling. I'd trust you with my life. I'm afraid to involve you any deeper. I'm afraid of the danger I might bring to you. From the day I walked into the J.O.C. and met you, I knew you would be something special in my life. I'm afraid I'll lose you." Alex's voice trailed off. "I seem to lose everyone who is dear to me."

"Alex, you know as well as I do that fear and pain are a part of life. What was that saying you shared with me? The one about being too careful in life."

"You mean the one...if I am careful enough, nothing good or bad will ever happen to me?"

"That's the one. I don't want either of us to end up with such an empty feeling about our lives. I know you've felt terrible pain, but we both know in our heads, that you could not have altered the events. Are Ellie and Robbie really gone? Aren't they both still a part of your life?"

* * *

Alex didn't answer. He felt emotion well up in his throat. He felt the tears sting his eyes. Sarah must have sensed the pain and reached out to him. She moved from the chair and sat beside Alex on the threadbare old couch he kept there.

"Sweetheart," she said, "I know they're still here. I see Robbie's picture moved from time to time. My guess is that as he slides to the back of your mind the picture moves back on the table behind some of the other photos. When you're afraid you're forgetting him, his picture comes out to the front where you can see it. You haven't lost him. He's still here—he'll always be with you, Alex. I'm not part of that life—I want to be a part of your life now—today."

Overwhelmed by the emotions, Alex couldn't say anything. He could only take Sarah in his arms and hold her. She reached up and pulled his mouth to hers. It was a long and passionate embrace. Then without a word, Sarah rose, took his hand and led him from the study and down one floor to his bedroom. As they entered, Alex pushed the door closed and took Sarah in his arms. The door stayed closed for a long time.

* * *

By late afternoon, Caesar was standing guard at the bedroom door. Guard duty being a rather relaxed position for him. Catching short naps while curled into a large furry ball was a more apt description. Normally Caesar only kept this mealtime vigil in the morning. Alex either fed him on time or the automatic feeder clicked open for him. Alex kept the door to the bedroom closed when he slept. If he didn't, he could expect to find Caesar standing on his chest and purring into his face to remind him it was time to get up. Caesar decided this quiet vigil lasted long enough and more drastic measures were called for.

* * *

Sarah rolled over and kissed Alex on the cheek. She playfully put her tongue in his ear just to make sure he was aware of her. "Your buddy outside the door thinks it's supper time," she said. By now the purring and chirping meows were loud enough to be heard through the door, and a playful paw could be seen reaching under the door and into the room.

Alex wrapped his arms around Sarah and pulled her over on top of him. Their mouths and tongues sought each other. This embrace was as long and passionate as the one that led them to the bedroom. Alex said, "That cat knows he owns the place. If I don't get up and feed him, there won't be any living with him. How 'bout you? Stay for supper?"

"Since you ask, of course. What's for dinner?" Before Alex could respond Sarah added, "If you have any more of that white wine we drank last time, I'll put a salad together for us. Just give me a couple of minutes to shower."

"Only a couple of minutes… won't give you much time to get dressed before we eat," Alex said.

"I wasn't planning on overdressing. I figured that if you were to have some more lascivious thoughts later this evening, too many clothes would just slow you down. I was assuming you might ask me to spend the night…or do you have other plans?"

"Sounds like a great game plan to me," he said. "I'll feed ol' Caesar and be back to help you shower."

"Oh no you don't. If we shower together, we'll never get around to eating and I'm starving. You can take yours when I'm finished and I'll get supper while you're in there."

Sarah was innovative when preparing meals in Alex's kitchen—a requirement since Alex devoted minimal attention to meal planning. He enjoyed the variety being a good cook provided, but he hated spending time at the market. It was about the only area where he did not plan ahead. She found some ham and chicken in his refrigerator to add to the greens and other vegetables. Alex's robe was large on her, and Sarah rolled up the long sleeves several times to keep them out of the food. She topped the salad with a honey-mustard dressing the two of them developed on their own. During dinner, the robe she wore slid open down the front. Alex wasn't able to concentrate on his food. He was certain Sarah wasn't wearing anything under the robe.

They finished their meal, put the dishes in the dishwasher and took the rest of the bottle of wine into the family room. "I want to go over those papers again. Grab a CD and put it on," he said. "I'll pour some more wine."

* * *

They read and reread the copies of papers and messages hoping that some new revelation would leap from the pages. Nothing did. They discussed what they knew and what they suspected, but they were no further along than before. At last, Sarah reached over and touched Alex's cheek. She spoke softly and at the same time with quiet strength, "Alex, I know you care for me and want to protect me. I appreciate that and I love you for it, but I'm a big girl now and I'll accept the responsibility." Alex started to speak, but Sarah placed her index finger to his lips and continued. "You're going to need more information. You're going to need files you can't get to. What you need is someone inside the secretarial grapevine. And I'm that someone. Besides, I want to do this. I want to be part of it. I want to take down the bastards who did that to Mike. I think of Cindy and their kids, and I get so damned mad I could shoot them myself." Her voice was rising—her anger reflected in clenched fists and her rigid posture.

It was Alex's turn to put a finger to Sarah's lips. "Okay, okay. I'd hoped to keep you out of this, but deep down I figured that wasn't really a possibility. I guess we go with Plan B—you'll be my person on the inside."

Sarah moved closer to Alex. She smiled, curled her feet up under her on the couch as Alex continued. He told her about his recruits. He went over the Greek names and symbols and told her the code name he selected for her.

"Lambda, it's written like an upside down Vee, isn't it?" she said. Sarah was leaning forward toward him, the oversized robe slipping open revealing the fullness of her breasts, and at the bottom, most of her shapely legs.

"That's right," Alex said. "Sarah, I'm having a tough time… ah, concentrating on the subject matter," was all Alex managed to whisper.

"I think we've exhausted the subject anyway. It's about time to switch to more interesting activities," she said. Alex nodded and she uncurled and rose from the couch. She stood in front of him. There was a sparkle in her hazel eyes and a devilish smile on her lips. She bent over and kissed him. Alex reached for her, but she took a step back. At the same time, her hand tugged the robe's belt allowing it to fall open. She shrugged and the robe slipped from her shoulders and dropped in a heap at her feet. Alex was right—Sarah was not wearing anything under the robe.

She held both hands out to Alex and he stood. Sarah untied the belt of his robe and pressed her body against his. Their lips met and Alex lifted her lithe body in his arms. He started for the stairs, and looked down at her body cradled in front of him. Even the scar from an emergency appendectomy did not mar her beauty. Her black, shoulder length hair cascaded back as she relaxed in his arms and let her head fall back. He climbed one flight to the bedroom. He kicked the door closed with his bare foot.

* * *

Since it was dark outside, Caesar knew the door wouldn't reopen till morning. There were sounds from inside the bedroom that caught his attention from time to time, but the door remained closed.

OCTOBER 29th, OFF DUTY, RETURNING TO THE PENTAGON ⬠

Alex was on his way to his meeting with Lieutenant General David L. Watson. As he approached the office, he read the lettering on the door: JCS/J3/DD. The alphabet soup meant the general occupied an important, three-star billet. He was the Deputy Director of Operations, on the Joint Chiefs of Staff. General Watson, then a colonel, was the Wing Commander at Kadena Air Base, Okinawa, when Alex first met him. *Good Lord, has it really been that many years since we met?*

Back then, Alex fought for an opportunity to take his crew on Young Tiger. Headquarters USAF preferred to send seasoned crews to provide air-refueling support for the fighters and bombers in the Vietnam air war. His squadron commander backed him, and he became the youngest crew commander to fly KC-135s in Southeast Asia.

Alex recalled the day that led to his first meeting with Watson. He remembered the day he took his tanker north into Laos, into a restricted area, to rescue a damaged fighter.

OCTOBER 29th, THE PENTAGON, GENERAL WATSON'S OFFICE ⬠

Just before Alex's scheduled arrival, Mildred Harper carried a folder into the general's office. "Here's the file on Lieutenant Colonel Hilliard. He's due in fifteen minutes, but if he's like all you military people, he'll arrive early. That only gives you about ten minutes to read all of this."

"Wow, his folder's getting pretty thick. Don't worry, Mildred, I went through all of it a couple of months ago. All I need to do is refresh my memory."

"Is he aware that you've taken such an interest in him?"

"He's probably guessed it by now."

Mildred was at her desk as Alex entered at the predicted time—five minutes early. He introduced himself.

"Call me Mildred, please," she said and motioned toward a chair. "I reminded General Watson of your appointment, and he should be free shortly."

A few minutes later, the intercom on Mildred's desk buzzed. She hung up and said, "The general will see you now." She escorted Alex into General Watson's office.

* * *

The office was about what Alex expected. It was well appointed without being pretentious. There were many mementos scattered throughout, on the desk, one wall and on the credenza. Typical General Watson. *It looks like him. Utilitarian, a bit sentimental and all work.*

General Watson snapped a quick salute to return the one Alex presented then rose and leaned across his desk with his hand outstretched. "How have you been, Alex? It's been some time since we saw each other. Not to mention the time we first met in Okinawa, how long ago was that?"

"A long time, General. Nearly a career."

"Don't tell me you're getting ready to hang it up and try civilian life."

"No, sir. It's just been a lot of years since Okinawa…and California."

"Alex, seems to me I heard about you before we met. I remember I got a call from that F4 wing commander down at Korat…ah, Ben Sassman, that was his name. Damn fine commander. Told me he was recommending you for a Distinguished Flying Cross. That did come through, didn't it?"

"Yes sir. My entire crew received a DFC."

"I think you were in the Detachment Commander's office there in Thailand when I called. What was that guy's name?"

"It was Lieutenant Colonel Thomas, General."

"Oh, yes. Oscar…I got the impression that dumb-son-of-a-bitch was chewing your ass when I interrupted."

"Yes, sir. His demeanor did change a bit after he spoke to you."

"Head-up-and-locked. Blindly by-the-book. He fit damn near any negative military cliché you can think of. How far north into Laos did you have to go to pull old Chet Monroe's butt out of the fire? I know they reviewed your navigator's log, but I never did see it plotted on a map."

"We were about a hundred miles north of the river, in the neighborhood of Luang Prabang."

"Not a very good neighborhood, Alex."

"That's true, sir, but Major Monroe was coming out of Route Pack 6, somewhere near Hanoi, when he was shot up. That put him way north with damn little fuel."

"Route Packs." The general spit the words out. "I've done my best to forget that term. What a dumb fucking way to fight a war. Divide the geography into sections and only allow certain units to hit targets there. Aw shit, lemme get off my soapbox."

"Well, it did make it easier on the staffs, sir."

"Don't be a wise-ass, Alex." A grin spread across the general's face. "I know what you guys said back then, 'Despite the staff, the crews'll get the job done.' That was it, wasn't it?"

Alex grinned back and nodded. "Don't forget, General, I did have a pair of F4s loaded air-to-air along with us in case the MiGs got nosy."

"I remember that Monroe's call sign that day was Hudson Three. What were the call signs of the F4s who went north with you?"

"I can still hear lead's radio call when he and his wingman were released to go with me. 'Pecan Lead and Pecan Two... burners...NOW,'" Alex said.

"Damn funny how the mind retains bits of information like that. Did you know that Pecan Lead bought it a couple of days later?" The general spun his chair around and muttered as he rummaged through a drawer in his credenza.

Alex thought he heard something like, "Damn, I can't remember his name," and pretended the general's last question was rhetorical.

General Watson punched the button on the intercom sitting on the credenza and said, "Mildred, how about a warm-up on the coffee?"

As Mildred entered and lifted the carafe on his desk, she started to say something, but then she looked at the general with his back to them and said, "Here, I'll just freshen these cups and leave you alone." She turned and left the room without further comment.

The general cleared his throat, spun his chair back around and continued, "You saved a man's life and an airframe, albeit one with heavy battle damage. Did you know they repaired that bird and put her back into the air war?"

"No, sir."

General Watson glanced at his watch. "I still like working with people who take the time to know and understand the risks, and who know when to bend the rules. Okay, Alex, I love trading war stories, but my gut says you have other reasons for this meeting. Shall we get to it?"

Alex looked the general in the eyes and asked whether he could pose a couple of important personal questions. The general's eyebrows and the angle of his head betrayed his confusion, but he nodded consent. Alex said, "General, please let me ask both questions before you reply to either." Again, General Watson nodded. "For some time now, I've suspected that I might have a sponsor in the Air Force. Question one: Are you that sponsor? Question two: If you were absolutely certain in your mind the country was headed for destruction based on the action of civilian authorities—would you be willing to assist in the overthrow of that civilian authority?"

Alex waited for the response—his clenched jaw ached. If he was wrong about the general, he may have signed his own death warrant—at least career wise. It was a short wait. The general leaped to his feet. This time there was no smile on his face. His fists were tight and his knuckles white as he used them for support on the desktop. He leaned forward, face flushed. His voice fairly hissed as he spoke, "Colonel, how dare you. That second part is the most insulting question I have ever been asked. I took an oath that would preclude me from even thinking about such a course of action even if the world was coming to an end." His voice rose to an earsplitting level when he said, "That's sedition. Don't ever ask me anything like that again." He took a deep breath and straightened his stance. "As for the first part, I can guarantee you that you no longer have a sponsor in this or any Air Force. Get out of my office, Mister."

"General, please accept my apology. I was praying for that reaction. If you'll allow me five more minutes, I believe I can explain everything. Please…"

Looking at his watch, General Watson said, "Five minutes—not a second more. Get on with it." He dropped into his chair.

Alex gulped and spoke as rapidly as he could and still remain coherent. Five minutes later Watson glanced at his watch again. Alex was afraid he was losing the battle, but the general did not interrupt, so Alex continued his monologue for another five minutes. The general's eyes were wide with astonishment. Alex wondered if he was convincing him. His heart sank when the general looked at his watch for a third time, but he said "Okay Alex, you've got me hooked. I've heard enough to begin to believe you. I can understand your questions. Got to tell you, that's the first time I've been tested by a junior officer. I've have a meeting with the Chairman in less than thirty minutes. If you can be back here at sixteen-hundred we'll continue our talk. I think we need to."

* * *

Time dragged for Alex. Waiting was not his strong suit. He was back in Mildred's office fifteen minutes early for his second appointment with General Watson today. Again, Mildred offered him coffee and said, "The general's not back from the Chairman's office yet. Those meetings often run overtime. I expect him back in another twenty or thirty minutes."

The lilt in her voice as she spoke of the general, told Alex there was an interest in him beyond that of a secretary. General Watson possessed a fantastic intellect for military and management matters, but Alex wondered whether Mildred's interest went over the general's head.

General Watson entered Mildred's office from a side door that opened on a corridor, which led directly to the Chairman's office. General Watson tossed a small packet of papers on Mildred's desk as he passed. "Those are for the Red File, Mildred…and a cup of coffee, please." He nodded his head toward Alex as he spoke, and Alex followed him into his office.

Mildred brought a fresh carafe for the general and the pot, so she could warm the cup Alex was sipping. "Thanks, Mildred," the general said. "I do appreciate the way you take care of me. It's past quitting time—I won't need anything else this evening, so you can head out if you like."

"Oh, I don't mind staying. I have a bit of typing to catch up on. I'll watch the phones till you're finished for the day," Mildred said as she turned to leave.

"Okay, but don't put any calls through unless it's from the J3 or the Chairman," General Watson said. Mildred nodded to him and closed the door on the way out. "I do appreciate that woman, but she can't tell a fib to my face without giving herself away. The day she needs to stay late to 'catch up on a bit of typing' will be a cold day in hell. On the phone she can spin yarns with the best. I don't care who calls, if it's not my boss or the Chairman, she'll make up the damnedest stories to protect my privacy."

Alex decided nothing went over General Watson's head.

"Okay, back to the subject at hand, my boy," the general said. "Fill me in on the details you skipped earlier."

Alex recapped the highlights and filled in the gaps. "General, I suppose that I have two fears. One, I may be making a mountain out of a molehill which doesn't exist. Two, and this is the worst of the two—the whole damn thing is true and that no one will believe me. There've been times I doubted my own sanity."

General Watson looked at Alex for several minutes. Alex recognized the ploy. Silence provided the general with time to think, and he was processing and weighing the various bits of the information he just received. The silence also worked on the person facing the general. Silence acts like a vacuum and fools tend to enter that vacuum, rushing in with a flood of words, inane and ill-conceived. Alex maintained the silence. He stated the facts as he knew them in a clear and concise manner. He closed with a statement of his current feelings which summarized his position and quandary. Without actually stating it, Alex was asking the general for his opinion and his help if the facts proved to be true.

"Apparently, I taught you pretty well, Alex. Not many folks can stand the silence."

"Yes, sir." Alex grinned.

"How many years ago did I teach you that?"

"More years than I care to remember, General."

"Ever have the opportunity to use it yourself?"

"Yes, sir. I've used it with a great deal of success—many times."

Watson handed the paperwork back to Alex. "You know you've violated security regulations by making copies of those documents and by bringing them to me?" Alex nodded and the general continued. "Good. Looks like you picked another good time to bend the rules." General Watson's voice was lower in tone and volume, "I'm not going to let this go beyond this room. Alex, I find your information intriguing and ominous. At the same time, it's far too general in nature to pursue. I can't see how I could go to Frank Ahern with what we have now. I will go this far—I'll have Mildred put a memo-for-record in my files that will cover what I'm about to order you to do. I will hold you responsible for any classified information that gets into improper hands. I want you to continue to look into this situation and report to me immediately if you get further independent verification. Is my order clear?"

"Yes, sir."

"Now, assuming—and that's a damn big assumption—that there is some sort of a plot, what would your next steps be?"

"General, it's a relief to have some of my basic suspicions confirmed. I'll protect the documents." Watson smiled and nodded agreement.

Alex continued. "I've begun to recruit people I can trust who will be ready to do whatever may need to be done."

"Who have you included?" the general said. He frowned and continued before Alex could respond. "Better the names not go any farther than you Alex. I would appreciate at least one other contact name in the group—just in case"

"General, I think the best point-of-contact for you will be Sarah Crawford. She's Admiral Eastland's secretary in the J.O.C. She'll have all the details, and I trust her—"

"Alex," the general said. "Do you consider it wise to involve a young lady in this? And unless I miss my guess, from the look in your eye, she's more than just an acquaintance."

"You didn't miss your guess, General," Alex said wondering how his interest in Sarah was that obvious. He felt his face flush but continued. "I've considered the risk and when you get to know Sarah better, I'm sure you'll concur with my decision."

"Okay son, press on."

"I'll continue to develop a group of team leaders based on military specialties. I'm well on the way with the first level. Each team leader will recruit three to five additional members. Only the first level team leaders will know exactly what we are facing. Any others we recruit will have to accept us on blind faith. Knowing this group, I have no doubt that they can carry the mail. They've been around long enough to be able to call in markers for whatever we might need." Alex looked at General Watson, who remained silent.

"Beyond that, I need to continue to follow TW developments and get the confirmation you need. When I know the who and when, I can develop the final part of our plan."

"It sounds like you've thought it out pretty well. Just like they taught you at the War College, eh? I'd love to honcho this one, but I think you are in a better position to handle it. Keep me in the loop. You are fortunate in one respect. All aspects of your plan can proceed concurrently, up to a point. There is no absolute consecutive sequence required. As long as your teams are recruited and briefed in sufficient time, there is a reasonable probability of success. Alex, have you considered the fact that if push comes to shove some of your team, even you, may not survive?"

There was a focus in General Watson's eyes Alex couldn't identify. Watson spun around in his chair and faced his credenza again. "General, are you alright?"

"Sorry, Alex," the general said as he slowly turned his chair back to face Alex. "Sometimes I remember too much." He pointed to the symbols of rank on his collar and said, "I hope someday you have at least this many stars on your uniform. As one old warrior to the next generation, I'll share this with you. I hope you don't get there with as many painful memories." Alex cocked his head and frowned. "Too many times I've sent airmen out to do a job, knowing they might not come home. As hard as I tried, they were never numbers, they were people. I think a little bit of me died every time one of my people didn't come home."

"That sounds like a tough load, General—to answer your question, I've got some damn good 'wingmen' coverin' my butt."

"Good enough. Keep me in the loop. That's about all we can do today, but we may need to talk again, soon. Leave your schedule with Mildred and she'll put us together."

Alex saluted and left the office. He left the general with his memories, and he left his schedule with Mildred.

Alex still faced two more days off before returning to the Watch Desk. He decided this would be a good time to get in touch with Staff Sergeant Tufts to see if he could persuade him to join the group.

William G. Tufts was Army with only seven years in, but he gained a unique reputation in the Supply field. He answered to any number of names: Bill, Will or even Sonny after the movie star with the same last name. The main reason Alex needed Tufts on the team was related to the other nickname he enjoyed, and that was Scrounger.

* * *

There was a story about a challenge once issued to Sergeant Tufts. An old time master sergeant bet Scrounger he could not get his hands on a jeep within the next twelve hours. At the time, their unit was on maneuvers deep in the piney woods of Georgia. The closest town and telephone were fifty miles away, as the crow flies. By rutted, dirt road, civilization was nearly twice that distance. This was a survival type operation, so none of the men in the field were issued any communications equipment. Needless to say, the only vehicles in the area were the ones that dropped them off two days earlier. The bet was made about seven in the evening. That gave Sergeant Tufts till 7:00 a.m. the following morning. Master Sergeant Pearson felt that his one hundred-dollar bet was more than safe.

Pearson awoke early the next morning. It was only 5:45 a.m., but there was the smell of a wood fire and of brewing coffee drifting on the damp morning air. He slid out of his sleeping bag and left the two-man tent where he spent a cramped yet uninterrupted sleep. He wiped his eyes and could see Scrounger sitting by the fire.

"Have some coffee, Master Sergeant," said Scrounger.

"No thanks, I'll just take the hundred dollars you owe me. I don't see no jeep 'round here."

Scrounger pointed to the edge of the clearing. Sergeant Pearson turned and saw three large crates past the tree line. Scrounger strained to keep a straight face as he said, "The jeep you wanted is over there in those crates."

"Can't be. None of them crates is big enough to hold a jeep."

Scrounger led the master sergeant into the woods and lifted a lid on one of the boxes. "It's all in these three crates Sarge. You didn't tell me you wanted it assembled. If you'd mentioned that, I would have made the bet at least two-hundred dollars."

Scrounger just smiled while Pearson's mouth hung open in disbelief. He could not believe his eyes, but he handed five, not-so-crisp, twenty-dollar bills over to Tufts. Pearson asked—everyone in the unit asked—how he managed the latest in a long string of unbelievable feats? He never did reveal his secret. It just became another episode that added to the mystique of the Scrounger.

OCTOBER 30th, ARLINGTON, VIRGINIA

Alex knocked on the front door. It was an attractive two-bedroom house just a few blocks off Columbia Pike and about six miles west of the Pentagon. It was a easy commute for Sergeant Tufts. He and Lisa enjoyed a daughter, Christy. Being stationed at the Pentagon was tough on everybody. It was especially difficult for the lower ranking NCOs. The living costs in Virginia were high and the military didn't provide any additional cost of living allowance. The men on the watch team were cleared for high security levels, and Alex marveled the military would put these NCOs at risk. Many barely made it from payday to payday. The offer of large amounts of money would certainly be attractive. He remembered talking to a Communications Security Technician from the National Security Agency several years earlier.

The Tech was conducting an electronic sweep of the offices where Alex was working at the time. Alex asked him if they often found bugs in such a secure area. "Nah, if the bad guys really want to find out what's goin' on in here, they'll just buy a body," he said.

* * *

"Duke said you'd be stoppin' by, Colonel Hilliard. Let's go out to the backyard, so we can talk," said Tufts. "Darlin' this is Colonel Hilliard. You know, one of the officers I work with at the Pentagon. They got a Comm exercise comin' up at work, the Colonel is bringin' me up to speed. We'll be out back for a while," he said and then led Alex through the house. He pulled a beer from the refrigerator and offered it to Alex. It was a bit cool outside, but Alex decided that the beer would taste good. When he accepted it, Tufts pulled a second one from the fridge. Alex noticed that there was a single beer left. "What can I do for you, Colonel?" Tufts said as they settled into a pair of folding lawn chairs.

Alex was getting better at going over the story. For the initial approach, he only hit the highlights something going on, probably illegal, possibly dangerous, could I count on you to lend a hand?

After the first affirmative reply, he reemphasized the danger aspect and told Scrounger about his friend who died under mysterious circumstances. "Are you still interested in helping?"

Again, Tufts nodded. By now he was sitting on the edge of the lawn chair which was in imminent danger of tipping over. Alex covered the entire story in detail. Scrounger offered Alex another beer before they continued their discussion. The first beer tasted so good; without thinking, Alex accepted. He was looking at Tuft's back when he remembered the lone beer in the fridge. Scrounger returned with the beer and handed it to Alex, saying that he drank a couple before Alex arrived and he didn't need another right now. Alex made a mental note to replace the beers.

"Bill, I need you to head up a logistics and supply team. Your job would be getting your hands on whatever we need for whatever is coming. I'll expect you to help develop the Table of Distribution and Allowances," Alex said. "I'd also accept your judgment for recruiting four or five others to help you. Would you be willing to take on that load?"

"Yes sir. I'm proud that you asked me. You can count me in."

"Keep a couple of things in mind. Nobody in the group, other than me, will know the other members of your team. You'll be one of about five team leaders. Team leaders will know one another, but not the members of other teams. I want to reduce everybody's exposure. Pick people you can trust—ones who can help you with the supply efforts, and most of all we'll need people who have an Expert Marksman badge. Besides being able to handle weapons, they need to be able to squeeze off a steady, accurate round if the time comes."

Alex went back over the highlights of the situation to be sure he covered all the details. He reviewed the recognition signals he worked out and told Bill that from now on he would be referred to as Sigma when it came to TW. He also gave Tufts the code names for Duke and Tucker. "Are you available for a get-together tomorrow?"

"Yes, sir. What do you need and where?"

"I want to get a start on the T - D and A. I think Duke and Tuck are available too. Do you know a bar called Roscoe's? Heading west on Columbia Pike, it's just before you get to Little River Turnpike."

"Not one of my favorite watering holes, but I know it."

"Let's plan on twenty-one-hundred tomorrow. The crowd

should be relatively light. Even if it isn't, as I remember the juke box is always loud enough to protect our conversation."

Sergeant Tufts escorted Alex back through the house where they paused near Lisa. They made small talk as Christy raced back and forth looking for attention. Lisa warned her several times, "Be careful and don't run into anyone." But like any four-year-old vying for the attention of adults, she ignored the warnings. She was looking over her shoulder, watching her mom issue the latest caution when she crashed into Alex's leg. She bounced back and plopped to the floor landing on her rear—a lot more startled than injured.

"Whoops" Alex said as he sat down with her. Long ago he discovered that adults were far less intimidating when they were closer to the same height as the small ones they were talking to. "Are you okay, Christy?"

* * *

As soon as Lisa saw her child was okay, her concern turned to the fact her child had caused some damage or—a child crashing into him would upset the Colonel. She was more than a little surprised when Alex dropped down on the floor to talk with Christy. She was even more surprised with Christy's reply to Alex, "I'm okay. Can I hug you?"

"Well, sure you can. I love hugs...Ooooh, that was one of the best hugs I ever got. Thank you, Christy," Alex said smiling at Lisa and Bill over Christy's shoulder.

The look of concern on Lisa's face faded and a smile grew. "She doesn't take to strangers like that very often. You must have children too," Lisa said.

"No, I don't," Alex said with a sigh in his voice. "I wish I did. Children are so much smarter than we give them credit for. Besides, they're a darn sight more fun than most adults I know."

Sergeant Tufts was quiet during the exchange. "Honey, didn't I tell you that Colonel Hilliard was somethin' special? I guess Christy knows how to pick 'em." Turning toward Alex, he said, "and Colonel, are your intentions toward my daughter honorable?"

Alex echoed the wide smile on Tuft's face, "Yes, Sergeant, they certainly are. If I were just a couple of years younger, I'd ask for her hand."

Alex rose and they chatted for a few minutes as he held Christy who was basking in the attention. Lisa sensed that it was time for Alex to leave and reached for Christy. The child wasn't ready to relinquish her current position, but gave in when Alex promised to visit her again.

* * *

Alex stopped at the Pentagon before heading home. He knew Master Sergeant Tucker would be coming on duty to relieve Hillbilly. Long ago, he established a habit of leaving some school papers in the "personal" file drawer they were each allotted, giving him the excuse to come to the J.O.C. to pick up "forgotten" papers. He wanted to confirm the meeting with Sergeant Tucker and Sergeant Pickens. He asked Sergeant Tucker to pass the word to Duke during shift change the following morning.

"Tuck, we'll meet even if Duke can't make it. Scrounger will be there and the four of us should be able to get a good start on a T - D and A," Alex said. He gathered his paperwork and went home. The past couple of days exhausted him He also realized there would, no doubt, be many more like this one over the next couple of months.

OCTOBER 31st, ANNANDALE, VIRGINIA

Roscoe's Bar nestled between other businesses in a strip mall at the junction of two major roads in Annandale. The added rough wood facade of the building was an attempt to make it look rustic and western. C & W music was making a real comeback in the local area and Roscoe didn't want to miss any of the action. He found he wasn't selling much hard liquor, but he could not keep up with the demand for long-neck beers. Case lots moved through the back door, across the bar, and then they were recycled. The liquid went through the restrooms while the bottles found their way into bins at the side of the building. Roscoe also crowded the tables together, so he could provide a small dance area. Deferring to the holiday, Roscoe added a couple of pumpkins to the bar décor and there was a cardboard skeleton tacked to one wall.

* * *

As Alex entered, he noted the feeble attempt to decorate the bar and realized he didn't remember a holiday was approaching. He paused at the bar and left with a large paper bag. A few customers made a stab at a costume, but most seemed to take little interest in Halloween. The majority were wearing their usual uniform: jeans, boots and western hats. Several couples on the dance floor moved rapidly to the "Cotton Eyed Joe." They stomped their boots and shouted rather than sang the only words of the song they knew, "bull shit." Alex found Duke at a table near the rear and as far from the jukebox as he could get and still be inside the building. Alex found Duke was not a country and western fan. Sergeant Tucker returned to the table with five long necks, saying, "I figured everyone would be here in time to get 'em while they were cold. If not, I can handle the extras."

Sergeant Tufts pulled up a chair five minutes later and Sergeant Pickens was right behind him. With everyone present, Alex got down to business. He made notes on a small pad as they began to brainstorm. The general categories came fast and furious, in no particular order and from all of them. They would flesh out the details from the basic list. Duke would formalize that list and get it to Tufts…Alex jotted notes furiously:

Communications: what kind? Walkie-talkie, cellular phones, something else.

Weapons: lightweight, semi-automatic, some automatic, silencers, stun grenades, smoke grenades.

Comm security: how can we talk over phones?

"I've got some help with that last one," Alex said and flexed his fingers to relieve the cramp from scribbling. The group returned to the list of items:

Radios: CB or military, what comm links do we need?

Uniforms: identification, how do we tell the good guys from the bad guys?

Transportation: how do we get everyone there on time? Who'll write the OpPlan?

Alex divided the twenty-five minutes' worth of notes and created a separate page in the notepad for each major heading they identified: Planning, Logistics including Supply, Weapons and Communications. "Each of you is a team leader and responsible for your own part. Duke, you take care of Planning and Logistics. That will include intel and the OpPlan as well as helping me keep everyone informed. Bill, you're the world's greatest scrounger, now it's time to put your talents to work—you'll handle the Supply portion of Logistics. That'll include getting your hands on uniforms, weapons and transportation…and anything else that the others are having trouble getting. Tuck, I want you to identify the very best in communications equipment that will fit the job. The smaller, the better. I've got a couple pieces of CIA equipment that will give us some secure phone capability. I'll go over it with you later." Sergeant Tucker's eyes widened as he leaned forward.

"Hillbilly," Alex said, "you're my weapons man. We'll need all types, and again the smaller the better, as long as they pack some punch. Again, I've got some CIA equipment—a 9 millimeter Beretta, Model 92F with a fifteen-round magazine. It also has an extra magazine—"

Hillbilly gained the floor. "We'll have extra, loaded magazines for all the weapons. Don't want anyone to have to reload a magazine if the goin' gets hot."

Alex nodded and felt as if Hillbilly was reading his mind. He paused and looked at each person at the table to see if there were any questions. As he expected, his group was having no trouble following the flow, so he continued. "Also, each of you will need to recruit four to six people you can trust. I'll trust your judgment on that, but remember, don't give the names to anyone but me. If we keep teams isolated, we can maintain better security. By the way, Tuck, the uniform of the day will have to be distinctive for the sake of recognition. Keep in mind too, we'll have some people who may not be in a position to change to a uniform. We need a distinctive and easily recognizable item, so we stand out to one another. We need to be able to eyeball it instantly from several yards. Don't want us shooting each other. Okay, where do we stand?"

Hillbilly and Tuck were furiously jotting notes of their own. Hillbilly said, "I'm assumin' that most contact will probably be close quarters and inside. That the way you see it, Colonel?" Alex nodded and Hillbilly continued working on his list.

Alex handed Tucker one of the CIA widgets that Mike included in the briefcase. He briefed Tuck as best he could from the comments in Mike's note. Tucker looked like a kid with a new toy as he said, "I've heard stories about these things. Up 'til this minute, I figured that it was just the rumor mill workin' overtime. I guess the Company lab boys done broke the code. If Mike, that was his name wasn't it?—said we have four to five weeks before they break the encryption we should be in tall cotton. To be safe, let's assume we only got three weeks and hold off usin' 'em. When their computer breaks the settings Mike installed, they'll be able to read any traffic they have intercepted. 'Til that time, all they'll know is that somebody may be usin' one. They'll get a line buzz that could be one of these widgets or just line problems. 'Til the computer breaks the code, all they have is a suspicion."

Alex set their next meeting date. Each team leader would complete his portion of the Table of Allowances and get it to Alex prior to the next get-together. Alex would add any comments and pass the rough draft along to Duke. Alex also instructed them to hold off on further recruiting until they could get better confirmation about the plot. "You can put out some feelers, check people's schedules, but let's not bring any more people into the group until we're a bit more confident about what's goin' down. Have a list of potential team members put together by that time—which means everyone has a bit over a week to complete their assignments."

* * *

"Aw shit." Hillbilly said interrupting the conversation. With everyone's attention on him, he said, "That bunch of yahoos at the far end of the bar been eye-ballin' us for some time now. Looks like they done made up their minds. I'd give 'em 'bout thirty seconds before they start this way. Colonel, you best get out the back way. Duke, how 'bout you an' me as the rear-guard detail?"

Duke nodded.

"Haven't been in any barroom brawls, but I think I can hold my own," Alex said.

"Ain't the point, Colonel. We all got jobs to do, this one's not yours, it's mine. Skeee - daddle," Hillbilly said in a tone implying an order. "It's time—two of 'em left, and the other four are closin' the distance between us and them. Guess that makes the odds about even, Duke...two apiece."

Duke nodded again.

* * *

Alex grabbed the paper bag from under the table and with the other two NCOs moved toward the rear exit. As Alex stepped into the alley and closed the door, the sounds he heard told him the donnybrook was in full swing.

Sergeant Tufts was trailing the other two keeping an eye on the door they used to exit the building. Alex and Sergeant Tucker neared the corner of the building as two men rounded that corner at a run. They pulled up short. The look on their faces told Alex they were surprised to be facing three opponents.

"What the fuck you guys doin' out here?" the taller man said.

"Your end run didn't work, butthead," Alex said. He sat the bag on the ground.

The tall guy was in front of Alex and opened his mouth to reply. His words were sucked down his throat as Alex's right fist drove deep into the man's solar plexus. He was gasping and doubling over when Alex's right hand connected again, this time to the side of his face. With a single grunt, he dropped to the concrete.

Alex looked to his right and saw the second man in a boxer's stance, on his toes, dancing left and right in front of Sergeant Tucker. The big Marine shrugged his shoulders, dropped both hands to his sides and stepped forward. The man launched a jab toward the sergeant's head. Tucker stepped forward again, parried the jab and drove a right hand squarely into the man's face. The man was on his knees clutching his nose and moaning as Alex and the NCOs continued down the alley.

Alex retrieved the paper bag and he and the NCOs moved between the buildings and headed for the parking lot. Nearing his car, Alex said, "Tuck, there's a couple of six-packs in here to thank you for the ones you shared with me the other day."

Sergeant Tucker did a sort of aw-shucks shuffle and accepted the bag.

"Do you think those guys were here on purpose, Colonel? I mean...do they know what we're up to?" Sergeant Tufts said.

"I don't know. I hope not, but we've got to find out."

NOVEMBER 1st, THE PENTAGON

This duty tour began on the weekend. With only the typical skeleton crew in the area, Alex found ample opportunity to examine everything in the nearby offices.

The night before, Alex set the wheels in motion to learn more about the men at Roscoe's. Sergeant Tufts was working with an Arlington County police officer he knew to run background checks on the men. The police arrived at Roscoe's Bar, took brief statements and left. The four yahoos decided not to press charges. The police never got around to the other two yahoos in the alley.

Hillbilly was on duty with Alex and was describing the scene from the previous evening with gusto. "Those guys were too embarrassed to press any charges. After all, they outnumbered us two to one, so they'd look like real pussies in front of their buddies if they'd'a pushed it with the cops. Also figured we didn't need any more publicity than we were getting."

"You're right about that. Okay, you get anything besides that bruise on the side of your face?" Alex said.

"Nope, that's it."

"How about the Chief?"

"Man, Colonel, you should have seen the Chief. I thought I was pretty much of a brawler, but you should have seen *him*. He told me later he was top dog in one of the fleet boxing contests...guess that's where his nickname came from—you know, dukes for fists." Hillbilly put his arms and fists up in a John L. Sullivan pose and laughed. "He's put on a couple of pounds since those days, but it sure didn't slow him down. One guy threw a roundhouse punch at him an' the Chief ducked it and came up with an uppercut right that totally cold-cocked the dude." Hillbilly's fists were dancing in front of him as he described the brawl, and his head bobbed side-to-side. "Didn't take him much longer to drop the second one."

The enthusiasm in Hillbilly's voice was infectious and Alex found himself smiling as widely as Hillbilly.

"I was still punchin' away at my two when the Chief steps over and says 'Need any help there, big-guy?' An' I says yeah, so the Chief wraps one guy up in a bear hug an' holds him till I'm done with my first one. Then the Chief lets the dude loose and I finished him off too. Hot damn, Colonel, I ain't had that much fun since I don't know when." He looked at Alex and his face flushed. "Guess a Non-Commissioned Officer ought to be more circumspect than that, Colonel."

"I'd say that was circumspect enough." Alex detailed the encounter in the alley. His gut feeling told him Hillbilly was holding something back and said, "Is Master Chief Eaton alright?"

"Well, I ain't sure how he's goin' to explain that shiner to his wife, but he's sure enough okay."

"Let me know if Tufts calls with anything on our opponents from last night. I'm going to check the area for more Tower Watch traffic," Alex said. He snooped for TW message traffic but found none. The only files he could not get to were the ones that belonged to Admiral Eastland. They were in a separate safe just outside the admiral's office, near Sarah's desk. She was on the access list for that safe. Although Alex would have preferred to keep her out of this mess, that was his heart speaking. His head told him that he needed her help to get the job done.

NOVEMBER 2nd, THE PENTAGON

Alex answered the phone and heard Sergeant Tufts' voice. "Colonel, I heard from my friend in the Virginia PD. You gotta minute to talk?"

"Sure. It's pretty quiet this morning. How'd you approach him about doing background checks?"

"I told him I was concerned about word of the brawl getting' back to my boss an' getting' me in trouble. He did the check an' I don't think he's suspicious of my motives. Anyway, looks like we got nothing to worry about. That bunch of rednecks has rap sheets goin' back a long ways—brawlin' and assaults and such. Police arrested the same six guys four weeks ago for fighting at Roscoe's. That's apparently one of their favorite spots for pickin' a fight. I think we're home free, Colonel."

"Sounds good. I'll pass the word along. If you do get anything more on them from your friend, let me hear ASAP." Alex hung the phone up and left the console under the watchful eye of his NCO as he made another pass around the offices in the J.O.C.

The following morning, he headed for Sarah's office. Alex and Sarah coordinated their lunch breaks and met in the cafeteria. Alex described his fruitless weekend search. He brought her up to date on all the recent events.

Sarah picked up the conversation. "I'll check the admiral's safe while he's gone this afternoon. Another important meeting he said he must attend. The code word I overheard for this one was 'tee time.' He'll be gone for the entire afternoon. If there is anything about TW, I'll make copies. Check for an envelope in your personal file drawer. The afternoon briefing will give me enough cover."

* * *

Later, Alex found the envelope from Sarah. There were copies of about twenty documents and messages as well as a couple of handwritten notes. He put them into his briefcase and took them home with him. He spent the better part of the night going over the papers. Many of them alluded to the Oval Office, but not once did any of the documents directly indicate that the president was issuing any orders. There were more references to "the wrong man" and "polls indicating that the election was going the wrong way," but again, there was no specific information to indicate who or what. General Osborn originated all the documents going to the field. *Who was Osborn's horse-holder?...The one who went to the White House with him?...Richards...Quentin Richards. Yeah, that's the name. Wonder if he's in on this too?*

Both officers were known to Alex, and he held little regard for either. He worked a special project with Colonel

Quentin Richards, the president's military aide. During the project, he learned that "Quent" didn't like to be called Quent—"It is *Colonel* Richards, lieutenant colonel," Alex remembered him saying. On those occasions when Date Of Rank mattered, and two officers with the same DOR were being considered, the tiebreaker for rank fell to your line number on the promotion list. Richards was the type who could recite promotion list line numbers from memory. Alex also remembered asking about the colonel when he was assigned to the project. "He's a great guy. Don't turn your back to him," came a friend's reply. Alex later learned the president gave the congratulations to Richards for the fine report which was submitted. Alex also learned from a person who attended the meeting that "good old Quent graciously accepted the praise and neglected to mention the majority of the input and writing came from you, Alex." At the time, Alex thought, *What goes around, comes around. Someday colonel...someday.*

He met, but never worked with Major General Sherman Osborn, the president's National Security Adviser. From what he learned, Osborn and Richards were from a similar mold. General Osborn was well born, well placed and enjoyed all the money his bride brought to the marriage. He was self-serving and not above standing on anyone's shoulders if it meant more visibility for him.

Alex wondered if the man sending the messages, Osborn, was acting on his own or whether he was carrying out direct orders. The messages only alluded to meetings with subordinates. Most of the detail apparently was discussed at the meetings since so little appeared in the documents. The message routing headers were more significant. Since every message must direct the communications center to a point of delivery, even sensitive traffic contained at least that much information. Alex scanned the list of military units: a Military Police Battalion and a Special Forces Group at

Fort Meade, Maryland—the 82nd Airborne and a Readiness Group, both from Fort Bragg, North Carolina—USAF Airlift Center at Pope Air Force Base, North Carolina—another MP Company at Fort Myer, Virginia—and finally the 101st Airborne and the 5th Special Forces Group located at Fort Campbell, Kentucky. His own duty assignment, JCS/J.O.C. was also included as an addressee.

Identifying individual addressees would be more difficult, because the first line of the message traffic read: TOWER WATCH TRAFFIC, SPECAT EYES ONLY, LIMITED DIS-TRIBUTION. Upon receipt, message center clerks would send copies only to those people on an established list pro-vided to the message distribution center.

Reaching the second to last document, Alex bolted up-right. He was looking at a message they saw earlier—one that quoted an Executive Order. This time, however, there were handwritten margin notes on the document. Alex reread the Executive Order portion. "Should that condi-tion come to pass, it would be the duty of the incumbent president to insure that the nation was preserved. Any and all means would be used to secure the future of the country." In the margin next to those words Alex saw a notation and recognized Admiral Eastland's handwriting. It said: Pres B is ready to go all the way. The word "all" was triple underlined. To this point, the messages were vague—the generalities could be explained simply as concern for the country.

Now, for the first time, Alex felt he knew the depth of the threat. The words indicated a specific threat—those in pow-er believed only a person with the exact same political bent could save the country. At last, it seemed that there was a definite menace to a specific individual and that the threat came from the highest level. Alex still could not believe what the note implied—someone, a group of people, could be plotting to remove an elected official if he happened to disagree with the current president's ideas. *Hell, not only an elected official, but a man elected to the highest office in the country. And "any and all means," could actually mean killing someone as a method of removal? Damn right it could.*

The rest of the message was the usual pep talk, designed to rally the recipients to the cause. It enumerated the perceived threats. It was a list of differences between President Bancroft's policies and those of the candidate. Rather than looking like real threats, they seemed to Alex to be merely a list of disagreements between the current administration and the candidate over economic and foreign policy matters. There was nothing constituting "a threat to the existence of our nation." *There has to be some reason other than those listed here. Maybe someone is just nuts.*

NOVEMBER 3rd, ELECTION DAY

The latest election returns were running nonstop on CNN. Alex and Duke were again sharing the night watch in the J.O.C. It was not looking good for the home team. The sitting president's interviews, earlier in the evening, expressed his good wishes for the candidate of their party, Francis X. Ahern and to Martin Fremont, the opposition candidate, President Bancroft was not his party's standard bearer this year. He served two full terms and was therefore ineligible for a third term. Everyone knew Bancroft, for years, lobbied for the repeal of the Twenty-second Amendment. He believed when a person was doing a good job, they should be allowed to continue in office for as long as they wanted. He also believed he was doing the best possible job.

Candidate Ahern, in another interview, expressed enthusiasm despite the polls. He said he believed he would carry enough states to win the electoral votes needed to secure the office of president. The polls showed the race to be too close to call. Candidate Forbes from the opposing party held about a half percent lead going into the day of the election. With polling errors of two to five percent, it was anybody's guess who would come out on top. Both the candidates and the television anchors expressed the opinion, "It could be a long night." With little to do on this shift, it was fine to have something as exciting as a presidential election to follow on television. Alex cast his vote early in the day—now he wanted to see that vote count.

The night turned out to be a great deal shorter than any of the experts expected. Early exit polls showed a dead heat, but by eleven-thirty in the evening it appeared a bare majority of electoral votes would go to Francis X. Ahern. There would be no landslide allowing the candidate to claim his election to be a "mandate of the people." The percentage of popular vote was as close as the electoral vote won by each man. By midnight, candidate Fremont appeared on television to concede the race. He wished his opponent well and pledged his support to the new administration. President-elect Ahern entered the ballroom of his hotel only long enough to thank all his supporters, and his opponent for his gracious concession. He told the cheering crowd that he would have a full statement in the morning

NOVEMBER 4th, THE DAY FOLLOWING THE PRESIDENTIAL ELECTION ⬟

The excitement of the election was over, so Alex made his run to the NMCC. It was nearly 1:30 a.m. With this trip plus one more about 6:00 a.m., he would be well prepared for the morning brief. He made his way to the Cab to check with General Watkins. As he entered, he noticed the general slide a file folder over a message lying on his desk. Alex could see the large rubber-stamped letters at the top, EYES ONLY, LIMITED DISTR. Watkins handed the usual clipboard to Alex and excused himself saying, "Jake, I'll be in the latrine for a while. The damn chili I ate for supper gave me the trots.

Send the runner out for me if anything happens." Watkins left through a back exit.

"Yes sir," Colonel Jacob Townsend said to the disappearing back. Alex liked Jake. He enjoyed swapping war stories with someone from another branch of the service. From previous discussions, Alex learned Jake was only eighteen when Jake enlisted in the Army. He was one of the few who came up through the ranks, from buck private, to NCO, to Officer's Candidate School and then from second lieutenant to full colonel. He was approaching the mandatory retirement age for his grade, and probably would not receive another promotion. Jake enjoyed his job as well as his rank. He came so much farther than he ever expected when he raised his right hand as a teenager. Alex liked the way Jake just enjoyed life. They spent any number of lunches together swapping yarns and trying to out-lie each other.

"Jake, suppose the general will mind if I use his desk while I read through this stuff?" Alex said.

"He'll probably be gone for at least fifteen minutes. He hasn't made it back in less than that all night. Just be out of his seat before he checks back in. When I see him on the monitor from the guard station camera, we'll have about forty-five seconds warning. I should know, that's when my feet come down off the desk."

Alex eased into the general's chair. He swiveled the chair and his clipboard to block Jake's line of sight to the desktop. He pretended to leaf through the messages while sliding his fingers under the file folder, which rested on top of the EYES ONLY message. Alex's heart leaped into his throat. It was a short message, so Alex would never forget a single word. He sorted the numeric addressees into order and formed an acronym for the rest and memorized the list. He wanted to compare them with the message he read at home the night before.

11/04/0500Z TOWER WATCH TRAFFIC - SPECAT
EYES ONLY

LIMITED DISTRIBUTION

FROM: TOWER WATCH ONE

TO: TOWER WATCH DISTR:

101ST AIRBORNE, FT CAMPBELL

5TH SPECIAL FORCES GP, FT CAMPBELL

USAF AIRLIFT CENTER, POPE AFB

82ND AIRBORNE DIV, FT BRAGG

READINESS GP-BRAGG, FT BRAGG

11TH SPECIAL FORCES GP, FT MEADE

519TH MP BATTALION, FT MEADE

MIL DIST WASH/MIL POLICE CO, FT MYER

JCS/J.O.C.

WRONG SUBJECT IN. OPERATION TOWER
WATCH IS A GO, REPEAT GO. ALL MEANS
AVAILABLE. STAND BY FOR DATE ALERT.

WARM REGARDS

END

* * *

Alex slid the file folder back on top of the message and leaned back in the general's chair. He put his feet up on the desk to emulate Jake's posture when the warning came. "Heads up, Alex, he's on the way in," Jake said as he dropped his feet off the desktop. Alex did the same and quickly stood. General Watkins came through the door, and Alex was standing in the same spot as when the general raced out. Alex leafed through the last message on the clipboard and thanked the general. As he headed back to the J.O.C., his body began to tremble. He realized he was coming down from an adrenaline high. *I'd make a lousy spy. Too damn honest, I suppose. I'd better practice keeping the adrenaline pumping if I'm going to survive.*

* * *

"Duke, I just saw a message over on General Watkins' desk. Help me get it down on paper before I forget any of it." Alex knew he needed to concentrate on the address list. He and Duke both scribbled notes as Alex recounted how he could see the message and what it said. A couple of times, when Alex's memory stalled, Duke's suggestion spurred the process.

He and Duke considered other actions which needed attention. Alex would see if his J3 contact was available. He had decided to keep General Watson's identity secret for now. Duke would alert the other team leaders and get an update on their portion on the T - D and A and their recruiting efforts.

Alex completed the morning briefing to Captain Bedford and Admiral Eastland. It was 7:00 a.m., and he also completed the change-over briefing for his relief, Commander Lawrence. Alex knew he needed to see General Watson as soon as possible. "Mildred, this is Lieutenant Colonel Hilliard." After the usual pleasantries he said, "I wonder if the general has some free time. I'd sure like to chat with him again—as soon as possible."

There was a short pause before Mildred replied, "Sorry about the delay, Colonel. I was checking his calendar for openings because the general told me you had top priority. He's out of town until this evening, but he has Oh-seven-hundred tomorrow morning available. If you'd like, I'll leave a note on his desk to let him know. When he returns from a trip, he always stops by his office before going home."

"That would be fantastic, Mildred. I'll be available at the general's office at Oh-seven-hundred even if he decides he doesn't have time for me."

"That won't be necessary, Colonel. General Watson will leave me a note, after he sees the message. I'm always here by six, so I can give you a call to let you know what he says."

Alex found Mildred was as good as her word and lived up to General Watson's high opinion of her. At exactly 6:00 a.m., his phone rang. "Colonel Hilliard," she said, "General Watson will be happy to meet with you this morning at Oh-seven-fifteen. Will that be convenient?"

"That would be fine, Mildred. Can I look forward to a cup of that great coffee you make?" *That's not empty flattery, she does make good coffee. And it's always a good idea to be on the proper side of a secretary at her level.* Long ago, Sarah taught Alex the value of knowing the right secretaries. In the Civil Service, they were the equivalent of military NCOs. Secretaries and NCOs were the backbone of the service and the ones who finished the job even when the high ranking "experts" were failing.

* * *

Alex eased into a chair in Mildred's office at 7:00 a.m. sharp. She provided him with a cup of coffee, which began to fill the void a skipped breakfast created. At ten past seven, General Watson flew through the office door at slightly below Mach 3. "Good morning Mildred," the general said. "Come on in Alex, bring that cup with you if you'd like…a cup of coffee for me too, please, Mildred."

Both men settled into chairs at the conference table in the general's office. "Alex, what's going on? You must have something, asking to see me on such short notice." Alex brought the general up to date. He described the handwritten note from Eastland and the last message he saw in the NMCC.

"Son-of-a-bitch. Alex do you realize the impact of what you're saying?"

"Yes sir, and I'm not sure what my next step should be." Alex felt the knot in his stomach again. This time it was not a matter of not knowing. Now he knew, at least in general terms, what was happening. The knot came from the knowing. "My next major hurdle will be getting to the president-elect. Once in touch, I need to convince him, and possibly his inner circle of the reality of the situation. If someone I didn't know came to me with this story, I'm not sure how much credence I would put in it. Assuming the president-elect can be convinced, I'll need to develop a counter-plan. In order for it to work, we'll have to get as much information about TW as possible. The biggest obstacle is not knowing who the actual bad guys are. If we had that list, we'd have a better idea who we could talk to. Without it, every step in the process will be painstakingly slow." Alex looked to the general for his input.

"As for setting up a meeting with Frank Ahern," Watson said. "I think I can make it happen. I've known him for a long time. Same Academy class, but he decided to leave the military after about six years. We've stayed in touch. He got himself a law degree, Georgetown here in the District, I think, and went into politics a few years later. From then on, as they say, 'It was just a matter of history.' If he'd stayed in the Air Force, he'd probably be Chairman of the JCS by now.

"If I can get through to him on the phone, I'll convince him to give you some time. He'll have to accept my request on faith, but I think he will. Take a look at your schedule and I'll put a call in. Better do it while you are off duty, don't want to bring any undue attention to yourself. You're right, Alex, we need a detailed list of the participants. The Army handles most of the Joint message centers and those centers would have the individual addressee lists. Have you got any Army comm specialists in your group?"

Alex winced. "Why didn't I think of that? Yes sir, I've got just the man to put on that job. He's Marine Corps, and he's been in the comm field long enough to have contacts all over. With a bit of luck, we should have those lists in a flash," he said, using the name of the second highest precedence that could be assigned to message traffic.

"Alex, if your puns don't get better, I'll have you replaced with that guy from the late show," the general said smiling.

NOVEMBER 8th

The three days following his meeting with General Watson dragged. Waiting for word of an appointment kept him on edge, and every time the phone rang he started. No call came. Alex knew the general would contact him as soon as a meeting was set. No word, no meeting. He called Cindy Reilly to arrange a visit with her and her children.

NOVEMBER 9th, OFF DUTY

The trip to Mike and Cindy's home took a little over an hour. Alex always enjoyed the drive to this part of Maryland, and thought they picked a near perfect place to live and raise children. Their two-story, red brick home was just southeast of Potomac, Maryland in a beautiful wooded section. They were barely a mile outside the Beltway, which made the commute to most places in D.C. easy. Alex left home southbound and joined the Capital Beltway. From there, he headed west, and then north. He crossed the Potomac River at the northwest corner of the Beltway and took a state road. As usual, the last part of the drive through the woods was peaceful and helped prepare him for this visit with Cindy.

* * *

Alex knew it would feel strange to visit Mike and Cindy's home without Mike there. Always before, if Mike didn't answer the door, it was Cindy telling him to head for the backyard where Mike was barbecuing or playing with the kids. This time, when Cindy responded to the door chime, he could see the redness around her eyes. "Cindy, I wish there was something I could say that would ease your pain. I know there isn't, except to tell you that I know how you are feeling and that I'll miss him too."

In an instant, she snapped the words out. "How could you possibly know how—" The tears in her eyes welled as quickly as the ill-conceived words escaped her lips. "I'm sorry Alex, of course you know. How did you survive?"

"The same way we all do, Cindy. One day at a time."

"Thank you for saying you'll miss Mike," she said, putting her arms around Alex and kissing him on the cheek. "Mike felt the same way about you. He always said you were someone he could trust. Mike didn't give that kind of trust to many people."

"Hi, Uncle Alex." It was Bobby, passing through the entrance foyer at a high rate of speed. "My Daddy's in heaven, did you know that, Uncle Alex?"

"Yes, I did," Alex said and found himself looking at Bobby's receding back. He saw Liz standing in the same doorway Bobby disappeared through. She said nothing, but looked like a lost soul. "Liz, I could sure use a hug," Alex said kneeling down. She didn't say anything as she approached, then she put her arms around Alex's neck and began sobbing. "Oh, Uncle Alex. I miss my Daddy so."

"I know you do, darling. I miss your Daddy too." Alex held her until her sobs began to subside. Then he took her hand and followed Cindy into the family room. They were all halfway through milk and cookies when Liz said, "I'll go look for Bobby, so you and Mommy can talk, Uncle Alex."

"You don't have to leave, Liz. You're always welcome to stay," he said. Liz excused herself and left the room.

"Are you getting along okay? I mean, money problems or anything?" Alex said. "Mike's benefits should be coming through."

"I'm doing fine. The checks are coming and I'll be getting Social Security and the veterans' benefits straightened out soon. Just to make sure that I get everything I should, the Company has two men checking to be sure Mike's death was considered 'line of duty.' I thought it was nice of them to make a special trip out here just to talk to me," Cindy said.

"Oh, they made a trip clear out here, did they?" Alex led the conversation until it became natural to ask about the two men.

Cindy chuckled as she recalled the visit. "I could just see Mike describing this pair. He loved to use jargon, and these two were a pair of doubles. He could have called them a Mutt and Jeff pair as well as a Salt and Pepper twosome." The hair went up on the back of Alex's neck. No sooner were the words out of Cindy's mouth than he recalled the description in the accident report of Mike's death. The trooper's description of the two witnesses—tall white guy and a shorter Black man—who disappeared from the scene matched Cindy's. He also remembered the two men in the black Ford that he and Sarah spotted on their way to Mike's funeral. Now he was positive—these two were popping up too often to be a coincidence. He was also sure the names the two gave to Cindy would be of no value.

Alex led her further into the details of the visit. They asked if she knew where Mike was going when the accident occurred. Did he tell her who the meeting was with? "Mike didn't tell me anything that day before he left and that's what I told them. Alex, Mike was acting strange for a couple of days before the accident. Did he talk to you? Do you have any idea what was going on?"

"I'm sorry, Cindy. I don't have a clue." Alex felt the lie was justified and hoped it didn't show on his face. "If I learn anything, you can be sure I'll let you know." They talked for another hour. Small talk, the weather—and about important matters, Mike. "Cindy, I want you to count on me as a friend. I want you to know that if you need anything, or if the kids need anything—you can call me. I know people say the words in times of sadness, and later the words fade and the actions fail to materialize. I promise I will not let time dim my commitment. One last thing, Cindy. Mike always wanted to rest at Arlington National and I'm going to do everything I can to see that his wish is fulfilled."

"Mike would appreciate that, Alex," she said. "And, thanks for your concern."

Alex made his way to the backyard before leaving. He felt sure that Bobby would be there playing under the ever watchful eye of his sister. He was right. Liz was sitting near the barbecue grill, in the chair that her father usually occupied. They talked for several minutes as they both kept an eye on Bobby. "Come on, Bobby," Alex said, "let's go on in now." He led them both by the hand, back into the house and into the arms of their mother. Alex said his good-byes and headed back to Alexandria. He would need time to prepare for tomorrow's meeting with his team leaders.

NOVEMBER 10th, OFF DUTY ⬠

Alex answered the phone in the study of his home and heard, "Colonel Hilliard, this is Mildred Harper, General Watson's secretary. The general wonders if it would be convenient for you to stop by his office today."

"Of course, Mildred. Was there a particular time that would be best?" Alex said.

"The general indicated he would be in his office all day and the matter would only take a few minutes. So he left the time up to you."

"Mildred, please let the general know that I'll be there in about an hour. That would make it about...ten," He could meet with General Watson and still make the team leader meeting he scheduled for fourteen-hundred today.

* * *

A cup of coffee waited for Alex as he entered Mildred's office right on time. "I can always count on you to be prompt, Colonel. There are so many young men who do not have that quality today. Please go right in, the general is expecting you."

"Sit down, Alex," Watson said pointing to the more comfortable chairs at the small conference table. Watson poured himself a cup of coffee from the carafe on his desk and joined Alex. "Frank Ahern called me back. He's a bit put out that I won't go into the matter on the phone. He's also got his nose out of joint over asking him to meet with an unknown lieutenant colonel. Sorry, Alex, but he's been around generals too long, and can't imagine an officer of lesser rank with the sense to pour piss out of a boot. Trouble is, a lot of the generals he knows couldn't accomplish that feat even when you tell them the instructions are on the bottom of the sole. Damn, I must be getting old if that's the best line I can come up with. Well, I did convince him you knew what you were talking about and could handle the brief just fine. You have any problems with that, Alex?"

In the back of his mind, Alex hoped the general would decide that it would be politically wise to brief President-elect Ahern himself. Of course, Alex planned to be on hand to fill in the details. Now he was being handed the entire project— meet with the president-elect of the United States, tell him a wild story that his life was in danger and then convince The

Man that he, a mere lieutenant colonel could take care of the plotters and protect his life.

"No sir. I don't have any problem with that. When is Mr. Ahern, excuse me, President-elect Ahern available?" Alex said. Watson told him that Ahern would like to meet with Alex in two days. "That may cut it close, sir. Where would the meeting take place?"

"Ahern wants you to brief him at his home in southern Virginia. It's on the peninsula—are you familiar with the area?"

"Yes sir. In general, at least."

"It's quite a drive from here. Let's see, you get off shift at nineteen-hundred hours—got to be a four to five hour drive. It'll be early morning by the time you get there."

"Yes sir. I have a day shift on the 11th, and I have to be back for a night shift on the 12th, but I can make it."

"Sure you can you handle that schedule and still stay awake for a night shift the following day?"

"Yes sir."

"Okay then, Alex. I'll get in touch with Ahern and lay it on. I'm sure he'll go along with this. If not, it may mean a long delay in getting the information to him. Either way, I'll call you at the J.O.C. tomorrow. I won't mention Ahern, but I'll let you know whether you'll be driving all night or going home to sleep."

* * *

Alex made a fast stop at home to change from his uniform into civilian clothes. A uniform would attract too much attention in midafternoon at Roscoe's. He and Duke were able to get word to all the team leaders that they needed to meet. The only one who could not attend was Tufts since he was pulling a day shift. Duke would bring Tufts' part of the plan and would fill him in on the meeting details later in the evening.

Alex told the assembled group he would be meeting with the president-elect within two days. "I hope I can convince President Ahern to take this story seriously. I've also been giving some thought to the time frame we may be facing. I believe we have until at least the middle of December before anything happens."

In the face of furrowed foreheads and knitted eyebrows he continued. "I figure they'll wait until after the Electoral College votes on the president and vice president. That's scheduled for December 14th. The folks involved in this scheme want the elected officials out of the way, so they can put someone else in office. Ahern and Ryder only have a majority of the electoral votes—they aren't confirmed until the Electoral College votes and sends the tally to Congress. Actually, they are not fully confirmed until the Congress, both houses, convene and count the votes on January 6th. If something happens to Ahern, Ryder, or both before that vote, it's anybody's guess what might happen. The College could get a wild hair up their ass and elect someone else president and vice president. After all, they're not actually committed to vote for any specific person. It could be up for grabs. If that happened, our conspirators would have to go after whoever the College elected, and that only increases the body count. Does that makes sense?" Alex tossed the idea out to the group. They discussed other possibilities, but Alex's scenario held water.

Looking toward Alex, Duke said, "Is there any benefit for them to fake the votes that are sent to Congress?"

"I doubt it. Too damn many copies of the votes floating around—every state, the National Archivist, and one's sent to the Senate. The votes are a matter of record by that time, but I think they'd want to be certain Congress has confirmed the votes. It makes sense they wouldn't wait much past January

6th, the date of the vote count," Alex said. "I think that gives us a rough idea of when—we still need more information on where. They'll need access to both the president-elect and the vice president-elect at the same time. They need some privacy to do the job. Some way to isolate the two men from their protective staffs. Let's see if we can pin down the *where*."

Again the team leaders tossed various ideas and times around, proposing, then shooting them down. The germ of an answer began to grow. Each of the men contributed and came to a consensus regarding time. For two reasons, the week between Christmas and New Year's Day evolved as a suitable time frame. First, both men would probably be in the D.C. area for the holidays. The president-elect used a family home in southern Virginia and the vice president-elect lived in Maryland, just outside Annapolis which was his home-away-from home. The second reason was a COMEX, planned for the NMCC during that week. Even though it was a holiday season, the Chairman of the JCS directed that the World Wide Military Command and Control System would run a communications exercise. The WWMCCS needed some bugs worked out.

"Some of my contacts told me the Chairman made a personal visit to talk to the Whim-icks folks." Sergeant Tucker said. "He told 'em to plan to work their asses off over the holidays."

Alex smiled and said, "Not a bad solution for a committee decision. The date's a bit early considering the congressional vote on January 6th, but it certainly meets all the other criteria. I think we're right on target. There'll be a lot of exercise traffic floating around—great cover for actual Tower Watch messages. It could also cover the movement of units while the exercise is simulating similar moves. Okay, now let's get back to the *where*."

Brainstorming bore another seed, which began to flourish.

It would be tough to coordinate two separate attacks, one on each of the elected officials. One attack where both men were present would be an easier scenario. "Where would both men be at the same place at the same time?" Alex said. "We don't have any detailed itineraries for either man, but their general schedules were a matter of public record. I've checked and both would be in the local area during the holidays, and—"

"That one's easy, Colonel," Sergeant Tucker said. "I saw the first of the COMEX messages being put together in the Comm Center just a couple of days ago. There was one of those 'Warm Regards' messages from the Chairman going to the White House. He was inviting President Bancroft to attend the exercise and suggesting the newly elected president might want to attend as well."

"Tuck, you're fantastic," Alex said slamming his fist down on the table. "Yes. I think you just nailed down the *where*. Everyone keep your eyes open and see if we can confirm it from this end. I'll ask President-elect Ahern to let us know if he and the vice president-elect get an invitation."

Next, Alex covered his ideas on how they would carry out their part of the operation. "We're shift workers. I'm assuming many we recruit will be in the same boat, and we can't control their schedules. To cover the bases, I want four complete teams. I'm hoping we can field two of the groups when the time comes. If there are extras from the other two, we could use them to augment the available teams, or I'll form a third team. Now let's see how we are doing on the Operational Plan."

Duke began this phase. "I've got the easy job at this point. All I gotta do is put the OPLAN outline together. As soon as the Colonel goes over the details, I'll plug it into my outline. We've managed to get our hands on more TW traffic, but we didn't find anything new or startling. What we need is the

'Limited Distribution' list for these messages. Any chance you can dig that out, Tuck?"

"I'm not sure, Duke," Sergeant Tucker said. "I'll get to work on some folks who owe me favors. Since I got the floor, I might as well cover my part. I can get my hands on a half dozen mini-radios. They are capable of transmitting and receiving on four separate channels if we need it. We can give each team a separate channel or we can put them all on the same frequency. They are so small that they hardly set off the metal detectors at the Pentagon entrances or the ones at airports. Besides, I have a lead on headset transceivers for each team member. They're like the ones SWAT teams use. We'd have a hands-free ability to transmit and receive, and they're compatible with the mini-radios as far as frequencies go. I think we could have about two dozen people in constant contact. I figure we need that many units, so we can pre-position them. I don't want guys trying to get just a few sets in the right hands at the last minute. I figure when the time comes, we ain't goin' to have much time to get our asses in gear."

"I think you're right Tuck," Alex said. "I hope all of us are thinking along those lines. How goes the arms race, Hillbilly?"

"I got a lock on that one, Colonel. I been thinkin' the same as Tuck. I'm planning' on gettin' enough weapons, so everyone can get familiar with them and bring a friend to the party. Don't want some pistolero showin' up at the last minute with a scatter gun—might forget to aim good and shoot ma butt off." Hillbilly slipped into his West Virginia twang, and left everyone at the table chuckling. "I've got a list of weapons I think will do the job. Team leaders'll pack a 9 millimeter Beretta or Glock, dependin' on what I can get. In either case you got over a dozen rounds before you have to change magazines. I want two guys for heavy support—one will use a riot type shotgun, a 12-gauge pump and I'm' lookin' at a Calico for the other guy. It's fairly new and the Test and Eval folks over at the Aberdeen Proving Grounds put me on to them. They take a 9 millimeter round and carry a crazy lookin' magazine that can hold either fifty or a hundred rounds. Damn thing comes in pistol form or in a carbine. The Aberdeen boys have done some mods on 'em and they can go full automatic, single shot or three-round burst. I'm goin' to check them out this weekend and make a decision. Extras'll carry a 9 millimeter pistol. We'll have at least two extra magazines for each handgun. I'm checkin' to see if we can get all the 9 millimeter's silenced. Should call 'em sound suppressors 'cause it's damn near impossible to kill all the sound. The 9 millimeters are okay, but they're still pretty damn loud. I plan to get a smaller caliber for you, Colonel, and for the team leaders. A suppressor on a small bore makes it as close to noiseless as it gets. A sound suppressor sure would help if we need to stay covert for a while. On top of that, I figure a couple of smoke grenades and some stun grenades per team. That's about it, Colonel."

Alex looked at Pickens shaking his head in disbelief. "We'll be able to arm the whole East Coast by the time you're through, Hillbilly. Can we get our hands on that much firepower without calling attention to ourselves?"

"I don't think it'll be a problem, Colonel Hilliard. There's a couple of guys hereabouts who owe me big. I pulled their butts out of a firebase one night back in the Nam. Matter a fact, one of 'em will be comin' along with us when the shit hits the fan," Pickens said.

Duke picked up the conversation again. "Scrounger passed these notes on to me and asked me to cover for him. He says the uniform problem is solved. He'll be supplying all of us with a set of Army Class B greens, with sweaters. For easy recognition, he said he is working on a florescent yellow ID patch for the sweater and the shirt. Each ID will have a blank Velcro patch on top. Then, all you have to do is pull the top patch off and the yellow will leap out at you. There's Velcro on the back of the ID patch too, so it'll adhere to most fabrics. He also said to call him about anything you're having trouble getting your hands on. He has several people in mind who can reach out for whatever we need. Transportation shouldn't be a problem and he's in touch with a couple of guys at the Washington Navy Yard. With two hours notice, he could get his hands on up to ten trucks, each of which is large enough to transport two teams, a staff car and a Navy launch that could drop a team from the water around the D.C. area. If we were headed for the Pentagon, a team could land on the west shore of the Boundary Channel. That's about two hundred and seventy meters from the River Entrance."

Alex thought for a moment, then said, "I hadn't considered using a water approach, but we can certainly keep it in mind. We'll need a strong Communications Annex in the OPLAN. Getting the word to everyone in time to deploy to the proper location will be critical. We'll need assembly points identified so that the military transportation can pick us up. We can hold our cover longer by arriving in military vehicles. Duke, make sure that Tufts has a handle on that aspect too." Duke nodded and Alex said, "I'll go over these notes, add my ideas and get them to you at the morning change-over, Duke. Anyone else have anything to add at this point? Hillbilly?... Tuck?...Duke?... okay. This round's on me, let's relax for a couple of minutes." Twenty minutes later, they began to exit Roscoe's. Alex pointed to Tufts, who rose and headed outside. "Make it five or six minutes between us getting out of here," Alex said. Five minutes later, Alex left Roscoe's. To anyone watching, they looked like several individuals leaving rather than a single group.

* * *

Alex went straight to his home in Alexandria and reviewed the notes each man gave him. He decided to put the information on his computer. That would be a time-saver for making revisions. *No sense leaving a copy of the plan on the hard drive. If someone decides to go through this place it'd be too easy to find. I'll keep it on a floppy. Duke can make notes on the printout. Once he has a shot at revisions, we can update the final document at the J.O.C. or here.* His word processor was the same as the one installed on Sarah's computer. He had used the one in her office on a number of occasions to complete school papers. He could make some of the updates during night shifts while on duty. One more floppy disk in his briefcase would not stand out. The guards were used to that "picky colonel" who didn't trust the X-ray machine or the metal detector. They kept telling Alex the manufacturers said neither machine would affect computer disks, but Alex insisted they manually inspect his briefcase. All the guards ever saw were newspapers, yellow pads, computer disks and his lunch, so they gave it only a cursory glance when he opened it for inspection.

As Alex entered information from his notes into the computer, he tore the notes into small pieces. When I get all the notes transcribed, I'll burn the scraps. *Hmm, what about this draft copy of our plan?* he asked himself. *No problem with that. I'll use the shredder at the J.O.C.—they'll look like any other classified documents in the burn bags.*

Alex finished the first draft of their OPLAN by 11 p.m. and laid out his uniform and a small travel kit for the coming day. *One more day, and with luck, I'll be on my way to meet with the president-elect. I wonder what you're supposed to call a president-elect. Is he, 'Mr. President-elect' as if he was already in office? Suppose I'll find out tomorrow. If I make a social gaffe, I'm sure there'll be someone around to correct me.*

Alex arrived thirty minutes before his scheduled day shift was due to begin. He slept well, but awakened early with the sure knowledge he would not fall asleep again before the alarm buzzed. He used the extra time to go over their plan, adding margin notes to areas that needed corrections, updates, and added information. He passed the document on to Duke saying, "You can mark this one up. I've got a second copy with me. I've already started with the revisions."

The hands on the clock imbedded in the watch console moved—but *so* slow—Alex kept checking its accuracy against his wristwatch. Sergeant Pickens relieved Duke and was staffing the NCO position. "Go easy, Colonel. It's natural to have the jitters at a time like this. Every time I went to step out that chopper door in a hot LZ, I was never sure I was goin' to be able to hold ma water."

Alex chuckled and said, "You are one hell of an NCO. I bet you used that same line on the F-N-G's just to take the edge off before the newbies got their baptism of fire."

"Yes, sir. I reckon I did," Pickens said, understating his own abilities as usual.

The hours crawled by. Alex and Sarah met for lunch and spent a pleasant half hour. She pried him away from the phones after Hillbilly swore he would locate Alex if the general called, "I'll be on your scent like a Blue Tick Hound, Colonel. Don't you worry yourself 'bout that."

The lunch was even more enjoyable because they talked of everything except the impending events. Later, as Alex put his notes together and checked the wall maps in preparation for the afternoon briefing to Admiral Eastland, the phone rang. Hillbilly answered, "Joint Operations Center, Sergeant Pickens speaking...Yes sir, General. He's right here, one moment please." He placed his hand over the mouthpiece, and he nodded toward Alex.

Alex finished the call, returned the handset to its cradle and turned to Hillbilly. "Looks like I'll be going for a drive tonight. Get the word to the rest."

The balance of the day was a blur. He committed an outline for the presentation to memory. He went over the notes, added detail and memorized it using a mnemonics technique Mike taught him years ago. Alex spent the final two hours of the shift reading. He put his thesis research material aside, and opted for his favorite light reading. He opened the paperback to his bookmark and continued with the latest murder mystery he was halfway through.

* * *

Duke arrived at half past five, a good forty-five minutes early. He would be on the night shift relieving Hillbilly. Duke showed Alex copious notes he added to the plan he wanted to go over. They used the copy machine in the J.O.C. to duplicate the copy Duke was editing. Then they fed the extra copy into the shredder. They divided the strips and placed them into two different burn bags. Hillbilly was caught up in the excitement of the hour and stayed until the normal end of the shift. Ray Sanchez arrived at five minutes till seven. It was a quiet evening and there was no sense boring Ray with unimportant details. Alex briefed his replacement in a couple of minutes.

Alex picked up his briefcase and looked toward Ray and Duke. "Keep the world safe." He turned and started for the door.

Hillbilly said, "I'll walk out with you, Colonel." The two left the J.O.C. and headed toward the River Entrance. Outside the building, Hillbilly stopped and looked Alex in the eye.

"Lock and load, Colonel, lock and load. I know if anyone can make a believer out of The Man, it's you. Push has come to shove, and it's time to rock and roll." There was emotion in Hillbilly's voice that Alex never heard before. He wanted to thank Sergeant Pickens for the confidence but didn't have the opportunity. Hillbilly snapped the most military salute Alex had ever seen and without waiting for the salute to be returned, he executed an about-face and marched off toward the parking lot.

Alex took a minute to appreciate the cool breeze coming from the river. His thick brown hair was cut to a length that barely met the dress regulations, and the wind off the Potomac blew a hank of hair down over his forehead. Alex unlocked his car and placed the briefcase on the floor behind the driver's seat. He slid into the Mustang and locked the door. Alex brushed the strands of hair back from his forehead and made sure the seat belt and shoulder harness latch was secure. He checked the rearview mirror and the side mirrors. All these motions were slow and deliberate. Alex found himself going through these actions in such a methodical way, he wondered if he was trying to postpone the inevitable. He shrugged, settling into the bucket seat and took in a long breath. In another deliberate move, he let the air out. Then he started the engine, flicked the headlights on and eased his two-door coupe toward the parking lot exit. *How could anyone believe they could get away with this? Well, here goes nothing. Nothing, hell. Here goes everything.*

BOOK 2

THE OPPOSITION
(EARLIER THE SAME YEAR)

🏛 MARCH 5th, THE OVAL OFFICE

The primary campaign for President Bancroft's party was developing into a bitter contest full of infighting and backstabbing. The original field of thirteen candidates narrowed to seven. The president was lamenting this fact to his longtime adviser, Ray Howland. "Ray" was a shortened version of his first name, Reynard, and President Bancroft was virtually the only person who used the nickname. All his acquaintances from school and in business used his initials, R. J. All his life, Howland insisted on this form of address since he didn't like either of the names his parents gave him.

* * *

Many wondered if his parents, in some infinite wisdom, chose the name Reynard because they anticipated his adulthood, or whether he grew and developed into the person the name best described. Tracing it back to its French origins, it meant "fox" and the Germanic root was "mighty." Reynard Jarl Howland was the epitome of both meanings. He was always able and available to participate in the glow of wealth and power. When things went wrong however, Ray was never in sight. The media often referred to a Teflon this or a Teflon that—if the term was applied to those behind the scenes, Ray would have taken home an Oscar.

* * *

Ray Howland was summoned to the Oval Office. "Ray," President Bancroft said. "This election is going to hell in a handbasket. At this point, I'm not even sure if old Cliffie will even get the nomination." The president referred to his vice president, Cornel C. Clifton. The vice president from Bancroft's first term suffered from serious health problems. In the previous election, and at the last minute, President Bancroft dumped that vice president in favor of Clifton as his new running mate. Clifton, a lackluster Congressman, did bring a Midwestern constituency to the ticket the president considered a necessity. "At least, if that twit gets into office, I have a commitment from him. He'll create a new advisory post here in the White House and appoint me to that position. That way I can still run the country from behind the scenes."

"Well, that's good for you and the country, Mr. President." Even as he seemed to agree with the president, Ray was already assessing his role in the next administration. *If the "twit" becomes president and Bancroft is the power behind the throne, what is left for me? I need to make sure I have a strong position in the next administration. Do I want to be the third in succession behind the power or should I try to approach Vice President Clifton? No, at this point that would be dangerous. If he doesn't get into office, and Bancroft learns of my attempt, I'll be out in the cold. Better wait to see how the wind blows.* "Sir, you know I'll always be here to serve you in whatever capacity I can," he said, hoping his delay in answering would be construed as deciding what was best for the president.

* * *

President Bancroft didn't notice the delay. He was too immersed in his own thoughts. His deepest fear was being removed from the seat of power. He longed for a third term and believed he deserved one. He had campaigned for years to repeal the Twenty-second Amendment. *What a stupid law. I cannot imagine any one of these people in my party being able to run this country. Good Lord, what if the opposition gains control? That would be the ruin of our entire way of life. I don't think the country could survive four years, hell, maybe eight years, under their rule.* "Ray, I think we need some sort of contingency plan, just in case."

"Just in case of what, Mr. President?"

"Damn it, Ray. Haven't you been paying attention?" Bancroft said in a roar not realizing he began his conversation in the middle of his thought process. Ray often reminded his old political ally of this shortcoming.

"Yes, Mr. President. I have been paying attention," he said. "We were discussing the primary campaign, and you were remarking that if someone other than the vice president were to be elected, you would not be in a position to continue directing the country. Now just what contingency would you like me to begin planning for?"

* * *

Lamar Aurelius Bancroft was fighting his own demons. He felt he was violating the inescapable commandments conferred upon him by his parents. Simon and Wilma Bancroft aspired to a status they could never hope to attain—they possessed neither the financial nor the intellectual capacity. In ongoing harangues, his parents impressed young Lamar with the need to excel, to achieve, and to never abandon any of his progress. Young Lamar's only rebellious act was to ignore his middle name. He hated it so much that when faced with forms requiring a *Middle Name*; he would enter "A. (initial only)." He excelled, he achieved and he still retained the first dollar he earned in business. Following that first dollar, his rise to the top of the world of commerce was nothing short of meteoric. His business acumen was above average, and his ability to be in the right place at the right time was invaluable.

The fact he was a multimillionaire assured his success when he turned his aspirations to politics. In a few short years, this tall, distinguished man with silver-gray hair endeared himself to many, especially to the intellectually immature. "Daddy's going to take care of us." Following one and a half terms as a popular, if not a successful state governor, the move to the White House was the next logical step in his mind. He didn't have to pay his dues in the political arena—he moved into the Oval Office just as easily as in the past he moved into the CEO's chair of the corporations he acquired. Following his parent's admonitions, he excelled, and he achieved. Now the greatest problem he faced was relinquishing his seat of power.

* * *

"I'm sorry, Ray. It's just that I'm coming to the end of my final..." The president pronounced the word "final" as if it were related to a funeral rather than to the conclusion of a term of public service. "I mean, where does an ex-president go? Oh, I know I can travel the world and charge a fortune for appearances, but I need to be in the middle of things. I need to be at the hub of power. If Clifton makes it, I'll be here for at least another four years. Who knows, I could run for president again after that. But if any of those other assholes get in, I'm out in the cold. Even worse—what if the opposition gets in? Worst of the worst—if Frank Ahern gets in, I wouldn't even be asked to advise him on the color of the lawn…and he's from our own party. God, Ray—figure out something to keep me here."

"Don't worry Mr. President. I'll look at the possibilities and see what we can do. Now if you'll excuse me, sir, I have business to attend to elsewhere. After all, we need to keep your face in front of the public even if you're not running for office. We want the rabble to remember how well the economy is going. And it is totally your doing, isn't it?" Ray Howland always knew which buttons to push. Little did it matter the president's party was the minority in Congress. Little did it matter most of the economic triumphs were due to his own minority leaders in both houses selling their plans to the majority party. The president appeared to be basking in the glow of his accomplishments as Ray left the office. Ray knew the glow would not last long.

SUPER TUESDAY, MARCH 10th, THE OVAL OFFICE

In the week preceding the Super Tuesday primary elections, two more candidates from President Bancroft's party called it quits. Vice President Clifton, along with four other candidates remained in the race. The vice president was lagging in the polls with little support from the public or from his own party. Bancroft's blood pressure rose every time he saw the poll numbers.

Bancroft consigned the late edition of *The Washington Post* to the trash, and then he was using the control panel in his desk drawer to switch from one evening television news program to another. There were five monitors installed in the armoire. When he moved into the White House, he insisted on the huge piece of furniture housing them. His advisers pointed out there wasn't enough room in the Oval Office for all the furniture. "Well, lose one of the sofas," the president said. "The other sofa and the armchairs will hold five. If there are more than that in here, hell, they can stand or sit on the floor for all I care. Besides, the location of the armoire will give us much better pickup for the cams."

Previous presidents used audio recorders in the Oval Office. President Bancroft opted for the latest technology. Recording in the past was considered immoral, if not illegal and led to the resignation of one White House resident. Bancroft ignored the warnings from his close advisers. He insisted the only problem in the past was—too many people were aware of the installations. He told his immediate confidants to get the job done and hold the information close.

Now he enjoyed audio and video coverage of the Oval Office from two adjacent walls. "I've got anyone in this office in a virtual cross-fire," he once said.

He surfed through all the news shows and settled on two of the major networks, CNN and two local independents. He busily muted the volume on one and brought up the sound on the next set. He managed to catch poll information on four straight tries. His face grew redder with each report.

All the newscasters were telling the same general story. Vice President Clifton was still in the running, but two other candidates from the president's party were the front-runners. One of those front-runners was Francis Ahern. The opposition party's choices dwindled to two.

President Bancroft could have summoned Ray Howland with the simple push of a button on his communications control panel. Instead, he leaped to his feet and reached the door in a few long strides. He ripped the door open with such force that he startled the Air Force officer seated outside the office. "Are we on our way out, Mr. President?" the colonel said, regaining a bit of his composure and trying to judge how much effort it would take to keep the briefcase he carried within reach of his Commander in Chief. Old habits die hard. The Cold War warmed—but there were still enough nuclear weapons in the world that the military services, on a rotating basis, provided an officer as the president's horse-holder. He was the man who carried the "football" with the codes—the codes capable of launching a nuclear arsenal. He remained close to the president, knowing there was a maximum of fifteen seconds to be within arm's reach with the large briefcase open.

"Sit down, Colonel. I'll just be down the hall in Ray's office," the president said moving rapidly past the officer.

* * *

Ray heard his first name shouted as the door to his office burst open. It was a favorite trick President Bancroft enjoyed. *Shake up the staff time*, he called it. For the most part, it worked. Many on the staff were reduced to a quivering mass following the slam, and the shout, and the menacing approach of a scowling president. Howland was startled, but learned long ago to control his body language and display a calm exterior no matter his visceral response.

"What can I do for you, Mr. President?" he said with his usual calm voice.

"Have you been watching the news? Have you seen the numbers? What the hell is happening to this election?" Ray knew Bancroft was into phase two of his "shake 'em up" routine. If the abrupt entrance didn't faze the recipient of the indignity, he would hurl enough questions at them to throw them off track.

"Which of those questions should I assume has priority, sir?" Ray said.

"Damn it to hell, Ray. Can't I ever shake you up? You're no damn fun."

"If you're just looking for fun, Mr. President, there are a couple of new staffers about four doors down the hall. Bust in on them like that and I almost guarantee they'll turn white as flour before they shit their pants and slide under their desks." To reinforce his apparent unflappability, Ray replied to President Bancroft's questions. "No sir, I haven't seen the news this evening—I have seen the poll results and I don't know what's happening with the election. I think you need to have a long talk with Clifton's political adviser. He needs to get the campaign on track or get out."

"It may be too late. My gut says Cliffie's train is already off the rails. If it is, only Forbes, Ahern and the other two piss-ants are left. The polls say Ahern is on top. Again, my gut says they're right."

Ray Howland was too smart to participate openly in campaigns or attempt to suggest strategy. He was good at it, but even a world-class strategist can't come up a winner every time. He reminded himself on many occasions, Ray, stay behind the scenes. Fall on your face just one time as a campaign manager and the power brokers will bury you. Behind the scene, you can stay on top forever.

"Mr. President, you know I don't pretend to be a campaign strategist. I'll rely on your gut instincts...it does look like Frank Ahern will be the candidate for our party."

Pressing on, the president continued his diatribe. "I'd like to get my hands on that Ahern and strangle him. Did you hear how he's been attacking me for the past week? He's not concentrating on the opposition—he's after me. He thinks he can tie the rest of our candidates to me and sink them."

Seems like he's doing a pretty good job of it, Ray thought.

"Doesn't he realize how popular I am because of the economy?" the president said. "How can he hope that strategy could possibly work?"

"Mr. President," Ray said, "Let me repeat, I'm no campaign strategist, but...it seems to me that these attacks by Ahern are taking their toll. Sir, you must keep in mind the public accepts you because the economy is reasonably prosperous. On the other hand, acceptance is not necessarily indicative of popularity or trust. Whether Ahern has any good ideas or not, whether you like him or hate him, the public seems to like him and trust him."

"But Ray, how about those groups who came out for me for a third term?" the president said.

"Mr. President, again, don't confuse a highly vocal minority with popularity. Those groups are valuable and we may be able to use them but…there are not enough of them to get you or a handpicked successor elected."

"Yeah, my handpicked successor…first I give my support to my own vice president. I know he'll let me be the power behind the office—after all, Clifton gave me a commitment. But, even with my initial support, he couldn't get enough votes to be elected dogcatcher. Then what happens?"

Howland waited patiently for the president to answer the question; he knew was rhetorical.

"I drop Cliffie and throw my support to Forbes. I support him over my own vice president." The president spat out the words as if trying to get a foul taste out of his mouth. "I gave Forbes a shot at the most powerful office in the world…and what does he do with the chance?"

Again Ray said nothing.

"I'll tell you what he did. He pissed it down the toilet. Damn him. After all the support I gave him, I figured he owed me. But no. He turned me down flat on that special White House post that Cliffie agreed to…And there's not a chance in hell that Ahern would ever go for anything of the kind." Bancroft inhaled a deep breath and blew the air—in a long, slow fashion—out through pursed lips. "I suppose it doesn't make much difference either way. Forbes isn't even going to win the primary battle let alone the White House. It looks like I'm left out in the cold." He paused again, but his face grew redder. "Damn, damn, damn," he said pounding his fist on a desk to emphasize each word.

Ray waited for the president's rage to subside. "Mr. President, I believe you could easily win a presidential election this time or four years from now. It's an unfortunate situation. The first choice is unconstitutional. Since it is a virtual reality Clifton will not be the next president, the second choice leaves you out of the loop for four years."

The president dropped into one of the two overstuffed armchairs next to Ray's desk. He stared down at his lap for several minutes. Ray knew better than to interrupt. The president was either gathering his thoughts or was so mad that he was about to explode. Those in Bancroft's inner circle learned that no matter which was happening, it was not a good time to interject one's own thoughts. If President Bancroft was thinking, you were bound to get a new undefined task. If he was angry, you could expect your flesh to be flayed no matter who was present.

At last, Bancroft looked up and said, "Ray, I asked you to look into ways I could stay in power. Come up with any ideas?"

"Sir, I can review your options," Ray said, "but I can't say that I have a definitive solution." Ray began ticking off the points on his fingers. "One, you are facing a Constitutional limit on your term in office. Two, you are not currently involved in the primary elections. Three, you will have a position at the seat of power only if Clifton is the next president. Four, Clifton is trailing in the primary. And five, even if Clifton were to win the primary, his chances of beating whoever runs for the opposition are nil. Mr. President, your only opportunity to remain in power is to remain in office... and that is constitutionally prohibited."

The president again heard the admonition of his parents, "Never give up ground gained." He always translated "ground" to mean progress and advancement—power and position. This was the guiding premise for his rapid business and political advances. Over the years, he found he needed to escalate the stakes to gain each successive goal. So this decision, this seed took root—a plan that involved the murder of elected officials—was no giant leap. It was merely one more small escalation to achieve a goal.

"Ray, I think you've just given me an answer. Get two copies of the Constitution and all the amendments. Get one copy to me by this evening, and I want you to study the other one. Keep the thought 'Constitutional crisis' in mind. When do I have some open time tomorrow?"

* * *

Ray consulted his copy of Bancroft's schedule for the following day. "You don't have much of anything available, but…if we cancel the photo op with that farmers' group we could squeeze out an hour or so."

"No, I don't want to piss off the farm vote. What else?"

Ray scanned the schedule again. "We could set up a working lunch and get just over an hour together. Will that do?"

"That'll do fine, Ray. Between now and then, go over the Constitution. Then get together a list of heavy hitters from that 'vocal minority' you mentioned earlier. Also, begin getting the names of military commanders who fall in that same category. Keep it quiet Ray. We don't want any outsiders getting wind of what I have in mind. The military guys should be Airborne or Rangers or Military Police…units which are used to getting unusual requests and are ready to move on very short notice. Can you do that, Ray?"

"Yes sir, I can handle that. Do you want to give me an idea of where we are going with this?"

"Not now, I've got some details to work out before lunch tomorrow. Just do your homework and come prepared to get under way. I'd better get upstairs and change. I think I'm scheduled for a black tie dinner."

"That's correct, Mr. President," Ray said looking once more at the president's schedule. "I'll see you at lunch tomorrow." *What the hell are we in for now?* he thought.

🏛 MARCH 11th, THE OVAL OFFICE

His mind was still racing—formulating and revising the plan that he was sure would allow him to retain the White House. The president arose early this morning, even before his normal wake up call. The previous evening's black tie dinner went like he was slogging along in slow motion. On several occasions aides rescued him as he neglected the scheduled activities of the evening or forgot the name of the recipient of a toast. His mind raced over the points he gleaned from the copy of the Constitution Ray Howland left him. He formulated a plan and was going over the details. He was devising solutions and reviewing answers for the questions he knew Ray would pose.

He met with the delegation of farmers from some Midwestern state. He nodded and mumbled platitudes at appropriate intervals. His mind still wasn't attuned to anything except The Plan. *Why didn't I let Ray cancel this stupid Photo Op with this bunch of stupid yokels from...from where?...I don't even remember where.* What a waste of my valuable time. "Why yes, of course, sir, and I hope you enjoy the rest of your tour of the White House and the halls of Congress," he said pumping the hand of the delegation leader.

President Bancroft made it through a morning full of scheduled meetings with little regard for content or substance. When the noon hour arrived, he gathered the red folder full of scribbled notes he completed the evening before. Precious little time was available the previous evening, so the notes were not much more than a sparse outline. *Never mind, I can fill in all the details I need from memory.*

* * *

Ray Howland opened the door to the Oval Office and poked his head in. "Get in here, Ray," the president said from his desk. "We've got a busy hour ahead of us...Gilbert, you can bring in lunch and a coffee carafe now. After that, I won't be needing you here."

The mess steward departed and returned shortly. He placed the luncheon plates and coffee on the small table where Bancroft and Ray Howland were seated. As the steward left the room, President Bancroft said, "We don't have much time, and we've got a lot of ground to cover. I hope you don't mind—I ordered for you."

A lot of good it would do if I did mind. Ray smiled and nodded to the. "Mr. President, what is—"

President Bancroft sat bolt upright, his eyes wide. "Ray, I have a plan to keep me in office following the November elections." Ray's mouth went slack, but he knew better than to interrupt his boss. "I want to go over the basics of what I have in mind, and as I do, I want you to play devil's advocate and try to shoot the plan down. If I don't have an answer for any point you bring up, I'll find one...but I warn you, I've got all the bases covered."

Ray was becoming nervous. He was about to become a party to a plan that must be illegal. "But Mr. President, there is no way you can legally serve a third term. The Constitution and the amendments clearly…" His voice trailed off as he faced the angry scowl on the face of the president. Ray was sweating because he didn't intend on becoming an accomplice before the fact. "Mr. President, I'm not sure I want to hear this. If I am privy to anything illegal, then I'm—"

"Ray," the president said, "I'll make sure that you have ironclad deniability. Will that make you happy?" Without waiting for a reply, he launched into his plan. "Here's how it lays out, Ray. First we—excuse me, *I*—will take a look at the election results. Of course, if Clifton makes it in, and the odds against that are only about twelve million to one, I'll just melt into the background and fill the position he'll make for me and the problem goes away. But that's not likely, so by the end of the year, I need all assets in place and we'll—excuse me *I'll*—be ready to press ahead. Now you know, on January 3rd, the Senate will reconvene following the year-end recess. They will vote to remain in session only until the sixth and then to adjourn until January 21st, the day after the inauguration. On the sixth, the electoral votes will be counted and verified. The election results will be certified and they can adjourn. Then on about the 7th of January, I'll call Congress into session and get it to vote to delay reconvening until the first week in March. It's vital Congress is not in session during the second and third weeks of January, and it'll be good if they're not around for several weeks after that. Any questions up to this point, Ray?"

Ray saw the crinkle near the president's eyes indicating he was just lying in wait for an obvious comment or question. Ray decided to oblige, "Since you say it is vital that they not be in session, what happens should they decide not to adjourn during the first three weeks of the year?"

"Good question, Ray. I've got enough markers I can call due to get the job done. But just in case—got your copy of the Constitution? Okay, take a look at Article II, Section 3. I'll simply find an 'extraordinary occasion' and adjourn them 'to such time as he shall think proper.'" The president continued quoting portions of the Constitution he pulled from the red folder. "Don't worry, I'll find something which will suffice as an 'extraordinary occasion,' so the plan tracks. This must occur after January 6th when the electoral vote is confirmed. There's no problem here as long as they adjourn immediately after that. At that point we'll have a president-elect and a vice president-elect. I must have specific *targets*."

Ray winced at that last word. He was becoming more and more suspicious. And nervous. He wondered whether the sweat he felt trickling down his sides under his starched white shirt was as obvious as it felt.

"Now, Ray, the two or three days after January 6th will be critical. The timing must be down to the minute and the players must be ready to carry out the game plan. The president-elect and the vice president-elect will die on January 7th. If nothing else, deaths will suffice as the 'extraordinary occasion' I can hang my hat on. If necessary, I'll call Congress into session during the early morning hours of the eighth. The leaders will suggest that they vote to come back early in March. As I said, I think I have enough markers to get the job done. If not, I have enough to constitute 'a dispute' and that would allow me to invoke Article II, Section 3 again and tell them to go home. I'll bar entry to the House and Senate buildings on grounds of national security. That should be easy enough based on the deaths of the recently elected leadership."

President Bancroft paused. "Ray, are you uncomfortable with any part of the plan so far?"

"No sir. I guess...I guess I am wondering how you can be so sure the president-elect and the vice president-elect are going to die on a date specific."

"Well Ray, I guess that'll just have to remain a mystery for a while. You wanted deniability didn't you? Next, I'll fill the vacancies—I'll name myself and Cliffie. I'll quote..." The president consulted his notes. "...Article II, Section 2, Part [3] if need be, which says that I can fill 'commissions.' These vacancies should qualify. This may be the weakest of my Constitutional arguments, but I don't think it will make much difference. Remember...two elected leaders have just died."

"Mr. President, what happens if the Congress decides to ignore your directions to stay in recess? What if they should somehow reconvene and pass legislation preventing you from carrying out your plan?"

"I have that covered, Ray. If there is legislation to deal with, I'll simply veto the bill. We don't have a majority, but I should have enough votes in both houses to sustain the veto. If the veto fails, or if they try some type of judicial maneuver, I'll use Judge Ralston. I'll have him issue an injunction to stop whatever they try. Remember, Ray, the up-front details don't have to hang together forever. I'll only need time to consolidate my position and convince the public that what I am doing is in their best interest."

"Mr. President, what about the amendments that designate presidential succession? It seems to me that there are several...the normal sequence of succession in the Twentieth Amendment gives that power to Congress—the Twenty-fifth Amendment spells out how the president can appoint a vice president. Also, Mr. President, don't forget Title 3 of the U.S. Code where the law specifies the order of succession through the president's cabinet members."

"Good thinking, Ray, but I believe I have an answer for all those and more. Check me out on these theories. I can defeat most of the arguments because they are written to cover a president or vice president after they are in office. Also, the Constitution and laws assume only one vacancy at a time. In the case at hand, two vacancies will exist at the same time, and both parties died before being sworn into office. The Twenty-fifth Amendment is primarily designed for a time when the president is incapacitated. Remember it was instituted after Eisenhower's heart attack. It also allows the president to name a vice president. Nixon exercised that amendment. When Agnew resigned, Nixon simply named a replacement. When Nixon resigned, Ford assumed the presidency based on the same amendment and again named a new vice president. The whole amendment is moot since it applies to individuals who are already in office, and in our case the new ones will not have been sworn into office. As for the Twentieth Amendment, you're right about Congress having some authority in naming a president if the elected person is not available to begin his term on inaugural day. That's the main reason Congress must not be in session until I consolidate my position. Ray, Title 3 doesn't come into play. It assumes the president has confirmed and sworn cabinet members, and that couldn't happen until after an inauguration. How does it track up to this point, Ray?"

"Looks like you do have the bases covered, Mr. President. I believe you'll have to agree that the covering is pretty thin in places. What do you plan to do if the opposition gets their backs up and just refuse to go along with your plans?"

"Ray, that's where the military units come into play. You've got a list of heavy hitters with an outlook similar to ours, haven't you?"

"Yes sir, I have this short list." Ray handed President Bancroft a handwritten note containing six unit names along with their commanders.

"This is not good enough, Ray. I'll probably need twice that many. You are on the right track with the type of units, and the commanders fit right in—just beef up the numbers. We'll have a working dinner—back here—six tonight. Have a complete slate by then. Tell Richards and Osborn to be here," the president said. "I've already felt them out, and they prefer to stay on in the White House rather than go back to their regular military duties."

"One last item, Mr. President. How can you be so certain the president-elect and the vice president-elect will die on a particular date?" Ray pressed the issue one more time, praying for deniability, but wanting the president to admit his culpability. *I need something I can hold over him for my own protection. Legal or illegal, I'm part of this whether I want to be or not.*

"Ray, I'm disappointed in you. That's one question I was sure you wanted deniability on. I'll leave it at this—I have a hunch that there will be an unfortunate accident on that date. Beyond that, you don't want an answer. Another thing and I cannot stress this strongly enough, neither Osborn nor Richards must know of this part of the plan. They need only know they must pull the military units together and make sure they are ready to go into action. They do not even need to know the date specific, only that any units needed must be ready to go by the first of the year. Let's keep it compartmentalized for security. Do I make myself clear, Ray?"

"Yes, sir, and I'll have a complete list by six."

🏛 EVENING, MARCH 11th, THE OVAL OFFICE

As the plan developed, President Bancroft suggested a code name for the operation. His military aide, Colonel Richards, and Major General Osborn, his National Security Adviser, both warned the president, for security reasons, the computer should be used to select the name on a random basis. They were both overruled—the president prevailed. The operation was thereafter referred to as TOWER WATCH.

The name having been decreed, the discussions began. Bancroft didn't take long to get to the subject at hand. "You boys want to stay on in the White House rather than going back to regular military duty, right?" Both Richards and Osborn nodded. Without a pause President Bancroft put them both on the spot, "How far are you willing to go toward that end?"

As the ranking officer, protocol dictated Osborn should reply first. He didn't like putting his head in an unknown noose without knowing where the rest of the group stood. The pregnant pause was noticeable to everyone. He cleared his throat twice before he began. "Mr. President, I'm not sure what you have in mind, but you know I support you in whatever you decide."

"C'mon now General, that sounds like a bunch of non-committal bullshit. How far out on a limb are you willing to crawl? If I told you I mean a long climb on a weak limb, would you be willing to risk everything? We will be treading on thin ice, on the very edge of legality if I am to remain in office after the November elections."

"Mr. President, if you believe you can remain in office, I am willing to do everything in my power to help you," Osborn said.

"How 'bout you Richards?" The president fixed his stare on his military aide. "Are you ready to let it all hang out to help your president stay here in the White House?"

* * *

Richards used the time it took General Osborn to respond, to make his own decision. "Yes sir, Mr. President. I'm ready." He was not at all happy with the decision he made. He didn't want to risk anything, let alone everything. *Then why in hell did I just say I was ready to agree with whatever harebrained scheme this nutcase has hatched. I'll tell you why, Quentin old boy—if you had given anything but an unqualified yes, your next tour of duty would be Thule, Greenland. With the* problem in his mind resolved, Richards brought himself back to the conversation. "And what, may I ask Mr. President, do you need from me?"

* * *

"First, Ray have you finished the expanded list?" President Bancroft scanned the sheet of paper Ray handed to him. "Good…good…excellent…Ray, this is good work." Turning to the other men in the room, he said. "Here's how it lays out gentlemen." He handed the list to General Osborn. "Sherman, Quentin," the president said, using their first names to draw them into the conspiracy on a personal level. "Check the list. I need both of you to formulate a plan. It should include how you will contact the men on that roster to enlist them in our cause. Next, the plan will provide a cover story. A story that will bring their units to a full state of readiness by the end of the year. Notice, the orders must only go to these specific men, and must not go to their superiors. Only these people will be authorized to read Tower Watch information. The plan also will coordinate troop movements to Washington, D. C. and two or three other major U. S. cities. Don't forget the logistics needed to make the moves. These units are capable of seizing strategic targets and holding them. Above all, no one will know their destination until you tell them to move. Troops will be briefed while airborne, en route to their targets." President Bancroft paused for effect and to judge their reactions.

Osborn's mouth was still agape as Colonel Richards spoke. "Mr. President, getting the units ready for deployment should be a breeze. It's the secrecy that I have a problem with. That much message traffic may cause a stir."

"What do you recommend to alleviate that problem, Colonel?" the president said.

Osborn, feeling left behind in the conversation, jumped

into the discussion. "First, Mr. President, I'll designate Tower Watch as SPECAT, EYES ONLY traffic. As Special Category messages they'll be transmitted only by the most secure means. As 'Eyes Only' traffic, the fewest number of people possible will see the decoded versions. Will that handle it, Colonel?"

"Yes sir. I'll coordinate the 'Eyes Only' list. I suggest that it include only the commanders of the units on this roster, plus just one Senior Watch Officer in the NMCC. General Osborn, I would suggest the cleared NMCC Watch Officer be General Watkins."

Osborn nodded, "Yes, I believe General Watkins would be supportive. Go ahead, Colonel."

"Obviously, General Osborn and I, as well as you, Mr. President, and Mr. Howland will be cleared for the Tower Watch traffic. The clearance list should also include the head of the Joint Operations Center. It is quite possible that we may need his assistance with message traffic, and I believe he would support your position, Mr. President."

Richards paused for a moment. Since there were no objections, he continued. "As for the message traffic itself, we should use short code phrases. I'll prepare a Key List of a couple dozen or so phrases and their meanings. A copy of that list will be hand delivered to each unit commander involved. The messages themselves can contain innocuous phrases even when decoded. Only those with a Key List will know the actual meanings of the phrases. When we need an outgoing message, I'll prepare the communication tape and send the message myself—"

Osborn interrupted, "Good plan so far, Colonel, but I will personally send all these messages. Now continue."

"We'll use the communications center here in the White House. We can route the messages through our dedicated circuits to Fort Huachuca in Arizona. It's a high-speed communications center, which can handle the highest classification levels through their automated system. Few people will see the actual messages."

Although the president agreed that Colonel Richards' idea was an excellent one, he would not accept the idea of minimizing the text in the traffic. Both officers objected, but the president said, "I'll decide the contents and the length of the Tower Watch messages. If I feel the need to go beyond your Key List phrases, I will." He looked back to Richards.

"I also propose the initial briefing and any later, substantive briefings for unit commanders be conducted in person. That will reduce the volume of Tower Watch message traffic to a trickle. Mr. President, with your concurrence and authority, and considering the geography involved, I believe I could personally brief all unit commanders in roughly three to four days. If you could spare General Osborn for a few of the nearby units, I think we could bring the briefing time down to two days or less."

"Give me a minute to digest that, Colonel," the president said. Bancroft looked toward the ceiling while tapping one index finger on the fingers of the other hand—as he looked toward Richards he nodded agreement. "I like the idea of the personal briefings. General Osborn, you could brief the three units here in the local area. Colonel, I'll see that you have a VC-140 from the Andrews VIP Squadron at your disposal. You'll have damn near the same priority as Air Force One, so you shouldn't have any ground or airborne delays between briefings. I'll personally okay it. When you need the bird, contact Colonel Bennett at Andrews, he'll be expecting your call. What else needs to be covered?"

Not to be left behind in the planning phase, General Osborn held his hand up, palm toward Colonel Richards and said, "Mr. President, I'd like to go over the points of your plan again. One, how to contact the units is resolved. Two, coordinating the unit movements will take minimal planning. I'll have Richards determine the numbers of aircraft required and departure times. Three, the units involved are prepared for rapid deployment and will take only a few hours to mobilize and embark. Once at their destinations, they are fully capable of securing and holding nearly any type of installation or facility. You indicated that units will be briefed on actual targets at the last minute. That leaves the fourth point, a cover story for the build-up period. Did you have any thoughts about that, Mr. President?"

"As a matter of fact I do, General. Initially, they'll be preparing a simulated scenario to defend against simultaneous terrorist attacks on the seat of government, and against major centers for communications and commerce. That should keep their planners busy. We'll designate targets which will match actual targets only in travel time. When they are airborne, timing will not change, but destinations will. I'll give you the targets, you select the bogus locations. I believe we have the bases covered. Thank you gentlemen. Get busy."

The president rose and left the room for his private quarters. As he left the Oval Office, he made a mental note to contact Trevor Quincannon. Quincannon was third in line on the Operations side of the house at CIA. *I'll call Trevor first thing in the morning and have him stop over here as soon as possible tomorrow. His help'll be vital for the ultimate task.*

🏛 MARCH 12th, THE OVAL OFFICE

Trevor Quincannon and President Bancroft were close since their college days at Harvard and shared similar political philosophies. Quincannon owed his current position to the president and was more than willing to keep him in office. He could already picture his name in large gold letters on the Director's door at CIA. He gave Bancroft the names of two men and explained, "They're no longer on our payroll, officially. Unofficially, I keep them on retainer through a special part of our black budget."

* * *

President Bancroft knew sub rosa budgets existed, but never pressed the issue to the point of knowing any dollar amounts. He preferred to maintain deniability on many subjects—and this one was at the top of the list. Now a secret slush fund was mentioned in his presence, and he didn't want to know any more of the details. He told Quincannon whoever was chosen must be capable of terminating with "extreme prejudice."

Quincannon explained these two were more than capable. They would also prefer prison to revealing their mission or their controllers, assuming the pay was right.

Bancroft told Quincannon, "I want you to remain out of the loop once you have briefed these two. Direct them to report only to me—they will discuss their assignments with no one. When their assignment is complete, they can expect a bonus and a vacation."

* * *

Quincannon gave the president a quick rundown on the two men he was planning to recommend. "Both are CIA and FBI trained in weapons and self-defense. They've also finished Agency training in assassination methods and weapons. Dickie Brocklin is a short, stocky Black man, capable of snapping necks and relishing it. Physically, Corbett Chapman's the opposite. He's tall, thin, and white. That's where the differences end. He also enjoys his work although he's a bit more quiet and circumspect about it. Lamar..."

Quincannon switched to a first name basis indicating President Bancroft's debt to him was personal, and the obligation was a large one. "These two will do the job for you, whatever needs to be done."

* * *

The meeting with Quincannon was over by 1:00 p.m. The president was feeling confident. He paused, and then said, "Trevor, I'll probably bring you in at the last minute to handle one of the final details."

🏛 MAY 13th, THE OVAL OFFICE

The polls looked bleaker than two months ago. The president directed Colonel Richards and General Osborn to brief the military commanders on the Tower Watch roster. He told the two this would be a good time to check out the geography involved and the timing required for briefings. He directed the trips simulate a short fuse trip later on. "Lay on the transportation, and cover the territory. Brief the commanders on the basic outline. You may tell them they are working for me, but all contact will be through you two. Do not allow my name to be recorded or written down. You have only thirty-six hours to get the word out," he said. "How do we stand on the plan and the commanders?"

"Of course we haven't been able to go over the details with them, but from all appearances, everyone on the Tower Watch list is ready to participate," Osborn said. "We have the geography and timing generally covered. We know what assets we'll need from Military Airlift at Pope Air Force Base to get all the units in place. We need to have your specific target list in order to select bogus sites for the units."

"Okay, General, here are the actual targets. Washington D. C., the House and Senate buildings—New York City, the

United Nations buildings. The broadcast centers for the four major networks plus CNN in Atlanta and New York City. Now, lay on your initial unit briefings for next week. Start on Tuesday, but don't call for any transportation or contact any of the units till Monday. I want to see how fast you can get the job done. Brief me on the results…make it Saturday, the twenty-third."

▥ MAY 23rd, RAY HOWLAND'S OFFICE, THE WHITE HOUSE

General Osborn and Colonel Richards briefed President Bancroft while Ray Howland lurked in the background. They recounted their successes and recapped the results, which elated the president. "So, all the commanders on the Tower Watch list will support my efforts. Only one was lukewarm, eh? Keep an eye on this Lieutenant Colonel Martinez. The Special Forces unit at Fort Meade is important, but…Since he's in the local area here, I think we can keep him under control. Can always threaten his career. Great list you put together, Ray. Fourteen out of fifteen are ready to wholeheartedly support my bid for another four years in this office."

"Thank you, Mr. President. I just hope we don't have to test the theory of your plan."

"Ray, you know we'll have to do it…or haven't you been watching the primaries and the polls? I know better—you've watched them as closely as I have. There've been about twenty states decided since Super Tuesday. And they're all pointing the wrong way. I'll see you tomorrow, Ray," the president said as he rose and started to leave. "Whoa, wait a minute. Ray, stick around. General, Colonel, please excuse us, I have something further to discuss with Ray." He paused until the two left Ray's office and added, "Get word to Chapman and Brocklin that I want to see them here within a day or two.

Set up the meeting. Make the arrangements quietly. Nobody but you is to know I've met with them. For all intents and purposes, they are here to meet with Richards—he's my stooge. So be sure he is here and available for this and any subsequent meetings. He won't actually sit in on any of my briefings with these two. Good night, Ray."

The president left and moved with a slow gait along the path from the West Wing toward the main part of the White House. He took the elevator to the second floor and his private living quarters. As he walked, he considered parts of the plan. *Now, if any part of this goes south, or Brocklin and Chapman are caught, I can roll it up and hang it around Richards' neck. He'll be the one swinging in the breeze.*

🏛 MAY 26th, COLONEL RICHARDS' OFFICE, THE WHITE HOUSE

President Bancroft met with the two ex-CIA agents. He didn't bother to shake their hands, but he was civil enough to offer them a chair. He told them nothing of the plan, but did recite a list of people they were to research. The president made sure these men were not tied to him in writing. The list was extensive and included Ray Howland, General Osborn, Colonel Richards, General Watkins, Admiral Eastland, Francis Ahern, and a number of other presidential hopefuls. When the agents asked what their research should include, he said, "For national security reasons, I need to know if any of these people have any financial difficulties, have unexplained income, or any opening through which they could be exploited or subverted. I cannot share the reasons for my concerns. Suffice it to say you come highly recommended and I know I can count on you. All reports are to be handwritten; I want no computer records to exist. Seal all reports in double envelopes and hand deliver them only to Colonel Richards. He is the officer you met on the way in here. Any questions?"

The agents shook their heads, muttered, "No sir," and rose, ready to get on with their tasks. The president buzzed for Colonel Richards' secretary. She was nowhere around. Colonel Richards was cooling his heels at her desk. When he opened his office door, the president thanked the two agents and said, "Colonel Richards will see you out."

▆🏛 JULY, THE WHITE HOUSE

The summer was hotter and more humid than most in the capital could remember. The unseasonable weather did nothing to improve President Bancroft's disposition. His mood, combined with the latest primary results and political polls, energized Bancroft's writing juices. He generated Tower Watch messages at a feverish pace. At first they were short, using the Key List prepared by Colonel Richards. In a short time, he found these key phrases too limiting. He also hated researching the phrases from his copy of the Key List. He much preferred to write and speak extemporaneously.

He wrote out messages in longhand and gave them to General Osborn to send. Over strenuous objections from Richards and Osborn, the messages became more frequent and grew in length. One message in particular, a "pep talk for the boys," Bancroft called it, became a four-page tirade.

▆🏛 EARLY AUGUST, THE WHITE HOUSE

The primaries came and went. The president's mood suddenly swung toward the positive side. Ray Howland seemed puzzled and deigned to ask President Bancroft about this change in his outlook. "Mr. President you look like the cat that ate the canary."

Bancroft took perverse pleasure in scapegoating. Putting someone down gave him a superior feeling to the object of his scorn. Howland's observation gave him a perfect opening. "Ray, there you go again. You must think you're back teaching at Georgetown University."

* * *

"I'm not sure I understand Mr. President." Ray said, as he realized the opportunity he was handing the president.

* * *

"You haven't forgotten your nickname, have you? You know the one, about the clichés you use...Ray the Cliché. Is it true your students created CPH pools for your lectures? That they bet on how many Clichés Per Hour you would use on a given day?" The president leaned back in his chair, paused and wondered if Ray would attempt to answer the questions. Bancroft mentally rubbed his hands in glee. If Ray remained silent, Bancroft's point was made. If the man attempted to answer, he was open to a second, more painful attack.

Ray Howland remained silent.

The president dropped the attack and continued, "Ray, something hit me last week like a ton of bricks." He smiled inside. *Just raked your ass over the coals for clichés and I hand you one right back. Got any balls, Ray?*

Howland's face remained impassive, and he said nothing.

I thought not. Bancroft continued. "The way the primaries have gone, Ahern will have all the votes he will need for the nomination. If he gets our party's nod, he'll be a shoo-in for president."

"Yes sir, I agree. But how does that help your plans?"

"Think about this, Ray. I want to stay in office. Ahern is or will be the president-elect and he's from our party. Now, Ray, who's the Speaker of the House?"

"Charlie Burnside, of course. How does he help you?"

"Is Charlie from our party, Ray?" He continued without waiting for an answer, "No, he isn't. What's the sequence of succession if there is no president and no vice president? The Speaker of the House. The rabble elects a man from our party as president. If he and his vice president are not around to take office, the office devolves to the Speaker. Since Charlie is part of the loyal opposition, I can claim leadership of the country is going to the opposition…against the will of the people." The president's face glowed with enthusiasm. "See how it reinforces my remaining in office in the face of the loss of our party's standard-bearers?"

OCTOBER 21st, LANGLEY, VIRGINIA

Jim McKee had been Mike Reilly's boss for nearly a year and genuinely liked Mike. Now he wasn't sure about him. Mike was nosing around looking for information on Tower Watch. Quincannon briefed McKee to be on the lookout for anyone asking questions on that subject. McKee didn't ask about the subject matter, but still he wondered. And now the word came down from Quincannon—Mike might be a security risk. He knew Mike was on his way to meet someone—he signed out with the notation "informant meeting." Friend or no friend, McKee was not about to let anyone track shit on the carpet of his office where Quincannon would notice it.

McKee caught Mike just before he left CIA Headquarters. He ordered Mike to attend a "conference" on the subterfuge that Mike might be assigned to some local action. It worked. Mike missed his meeting with Alex.

* * *

Even though Mike would not be able to meet with Alex, he knew he should get some of the information to him. He remembered the large panel in the restroom near the J.O.C. and the NMCC. *That'll be a damn good spot for this briefcase. I can leave a note for Alex that'll lead him to it.*

* * *

I need to see what Mike's been up to. McKee decided to pull the CIA duty at the NMCC the next day. *It'll give me a chance to check around the place and see who the inquisitive ones are.* He directed his deputy to make the necessary schedule changes.

OCTOBER 22nd, ALEXANDRIA, VIRGINIA

Chapman and Brocklin were working solo and splitting their time between surveillance subjects. They saw little of each other for a week. Today they decided to ride together, so they could compare notes. During McKee's search of Mike's home, he copied all the names in Mike's address book. Word moved quickly from the CIA, through the White House, to the rogue agents, and Alex was their subject for the day.

Chapman drove while Brocklin briefed him from a small notepad. Brocklin finished his notes and said, "Do they really think this Hilliard is a problem? I mean how much weight can a lieutenant colonel carry? He must love his work, looks like he's heading toward the Pentagon and this is one of his days off."

"Yeah, sure does." Chapman yawned. "Wonder if I'm gettin' too damn close to him. Got any idea whether he suspects we're on him?"

"Nope, but don't take any chances. Yep, he's pulling into the North lot. Whoa, he's acting kinda' hinky…watch it—he's stopping. Don't pull in, go on by."

Chapman had slowed the black Ford sedan planning to follow Alex into the parking lot. Heeding Brocklin's warning, he accelerated down the street and said, "We can pick him up later."

* * *

Alex shook off the feeling that someone was tailing him and cruised the Pentagon's North lot looking for an empty parking spot. Inside the Pentagon, he checked out the NMCC. He noticed a new face at the CIA desk and introduced himself to Jim McKee.

Alex hoped his story about needing to find Mike was holding water, but he noticed McKee's raised eyebrow. He stopped at the J.O.C. and talked with Sarah Crawford. The note from Mike she gave him led to the briefcase hidden in the restroom cache.

* * *

McKee didn't like coincidences. He also didn't fully buy the story Alex told him about needing to locate Mike. Later he used the secure phones to contact Brocklin and told him to tighten up their surveillance on Hilliard.

OCTOBER 23rd, THE GEORGE WASHINGTON PARKWAY

The black Ford sedan stayed about five car lengths behind Mike's car until they entered the GW Parkway. There was little traffic on the road and Brocklin accelerated to within two car lengths of Mike.

Chapman was sitting in the middle of the backseat. He selected a special shell, from the bandoleer on the floor, and loaded the shotgun on his lap. The Shok Lock, metal-ceramic round was designed to disintegrate on impact. "Usin' this shell, there shouldn't be any evidence left after it blows out a tire. Uh-oh, I think he's made us. Oh well, we got the word to do him, and this looks like as good a spot as any. Get up on his right side, just leave room for him to swerve right when I take out the right rear tire."

The shotgun blast tore a chunk from the tire's sidewall. Mike's car swerved in front of them and went off the right shoulder of the road. Brocklin slammed on the brakes and as the car slid to a stop he shoved the shift lever into Park. Both men were out of the car before it stopped sliding— running at top speed toward the tree, which caught the full impact of Mike's car.

Chapman hunched over the driver's door. "I'll be able to block anyone's view if they come this way. Get in back and check him out. Is he dead?"

"Not yet," said Brocklin. He reached forward with both hands. Mike's head was turned to the right and he was slumped toward the steering wheel. Chapman pulled Mike upright in the seat and cupped Mike's chin with his right hand while he placed his left hand at the base of Mike's neck. In an instant, the man's hand tightened on Mike's chin and jerked the head to the right. There was a sickening cracking sound, and Mike died. Chapman reached over the seat and pressed the release button for Mike's seat belt. He kept Mike's head turned to the right as he slammed it forward against the steering wheel. Chapman scooped up the envelope lying on the front seat and slipped out of the car.

Rubber-neckers began to gather. Brocklin and Chapman edged back toward their car. "Looks like he died when he hit the tree," Brocklin said loud enough for people to hear but to no one in particular.

By the time the State Trooper verified Mike was dead, the two were back in their car and accelerating down the Parkway.

OCTOBER 27th, ARLINGTON, VIRGINIA

Brocklin and Chapman tightened their surveillance on Alex, devoting more time to him since the word came down. Chapman was driving today and muttering about the traffic. "Damn, Route 50 sure is crowded today."

"Okay, so it's crowded," Brocklin said. "At least we got a good idea where he's headed. Even if we have to drop back and lose him, we should be able to pick him up at the cemetery. He's got to be on his way to that CIA guy's funeral."

Chapman kept his position two cars behind Alex and they could see both occupants with ease. It was Chapman's turn to wonder aloud. "That broad is sure spendin' a lotta' time on her hair. What a waste of time, the CIA guy ain't gonna care. Shit. She ain't doin' nothin' with her hair—she's usin' the mirror to check behind 'em." With that, Chapman decelerated and changed lanes to the right putting an additional car between them and Alex. "Them two sure spend a lotta time together, I wonder if she's into this caper too?"

By the time Alex exited the Lee Highway and turned into the cemetery entrance, both men in the black Ford were sure Alex was spooked. He went out of his way to arrive at the cemetery. Brocklin said, "Let's drop off here. We don't need to watch his funeral—we were there when he died. We can pick Hilliard up on the way back or later at his place."

▥ OCTOBER 30th, ARLINGTON, VIRGINIA

Chapman and Brocklin trailed Alex to a private residence in Arlington. Alex was in the house long enough to pique their curiosity. As Alex left the house, Brocklin said, "Let's check out the dude who lives here. Might be another person we should be interested in."

Brocklin spoke in a precise manner enunciating each word clearly and correctly. Chapman was intelligent enough, but paid little attention to his English teachers and had even less use for correct grammar. He made no effort to cover the accent the ethnic neighborhood of his youth gave him. His speech was clipped—he seldom pronounced words correctly and continuously chopped "g's" from the end of words.

Brocklin cringed as Chapman spoke. "You're right, I got the address, shouldn't be too tough findin' out who lives here."

Later the two learned the house Alex visited was the residence of one Staff Sergeant William G. Tufts. Chapman said, "I think we add him to da list. He's gotta be part of it—ain't no other reason some officer is visitin' a sergeant's house."

▥ OCTOBER 31st, ANNANDALE, VIRGINIA

For the second day in a row, the pair of rogue agents followed Alex. Chapman was cautious but stayed with him through an off ramp-on ramp maneuver that brought him back onto the expressway. "We need to be careful, he's gettin' spooked again," Chapman said. "Maybe we oughta' ditch this Ford." As Alex took a second overpass Chapman decided it was time to end the tail for today. "He's just too damn hinky. I'm droppin' off. Let's do some more checkin' on that Tufts guy."

* * *

If Brocklin and Chapman's decision included continuing the tail, they would have guessed Alex was meeting with others involved in the plan. At the very least, they would have photographed everyone entering and leaving Roscoe's tavern around the time of Alex's visit.

▰▥ NOVEMBER 2nd, THE WHITE HOUSE

The secure phone on General Osborn's desk rang. He picked up the red receiver and said, "Osborn."

"Sherman, Eastland here. Are you alone?"

"Yeah, what's on your mind Ted?"

Eastland lower his voice to a whisper. "I think we may have a problem with some Tower Watch traffic. Nothing is missing, but I have a feeling someone went through the entire stack of my Eyes Only messages—"

"What makes you think so?" Osborn said.

"Not sure, they just seem to be out of order, or...I don't know really. If they were out of the safe, someone could have read them, or even made copies before returning them."

"What's your damage assessment, Ted? Who do you think's involved?"

Eastland said, "I've got three names: my secretary, my number two and a watch officer. Damn, I was sure I could trust my secretary. Sarah Crawford has the best access to my office, so she's at the top of the list. If she's involved, I doubt she did it on her own and I know she's thick with the Watch Officer—Alex Hilliard, Air Force, lieutenant colonel. The other person with the safe combination is my deputy, William Bedford, captain...Navy."

"Okay, Ted. I'll take it from here," Osborn said.

* * *

The buzzer on President Bancroft's desk went off. Someone in the outer office wanted to see him. His secretary said, "General Osborn is here to see you, sir."

"Okay, Jennifer. Send him in."

Osborn entered. "I can only give you about five minutes, Sherman." Bancroft said.

"That should be plenty, Mr. President. I have some disturbing news regarding Tower Watch." Osborn outlined the call from Admiral Eastland and added, "I've taken the liberty of updating the surveillance list you gave the dynamic duo. I added the secretary and Bedford to the list. I told them to step up their activity regarding the watch officer. He was already on their list."

The president's inner group decided to use Batman and Robin as nicknames for their ex-CIA agents. Brocklin was Robin since he was the shorter of the two, and Chapman would be Batman.

Osborn said, "I was a bit surprised, Batman says he's been on Hilliard's tail for over a week. Hilliard was apparently nosing around about the CIA guy that Batman did in."

"What damage has been done, General? How much could anyone know from the messages, if they saw them?"

"Mr. President, I'm having Eastland messenger copies of all traffic which might have been compromised over to me. It's possible there was substantive information in them. I hope not, but at a minimum the messages could have aroused some curiosity or suspicions. I'll report back to you as soon as I have anything definitive." Osborn started to rise from his chair, but hesitated.

"Was there a second subject?" the president said.

"Yes sir, yesterday Colonel Richards reported to me that he believes someone has been talking to the people at Fort Huachuca about Tower Watch messages. It sounded like they were trying to find out who is on the Tower Watch, Eyes Only distribution list."

"Did they get the information?"

"To the best of our knowledge, they didn't. But there are no guarantees," General Osborn said.

"Keep me posted," the president said as he swiveled his chair around and gazed out the windows of the Oval Office.

Osborn left having used only four of his allotted five minutes. Bancroft rose and stepped from behind his desk to continue his daily schedule. As he approached the door of his office, his cheeks puffed out from the breath he refused to release—his face was red. Then, with an explosive burst of air, he muttered a curse, and reached for the doorknob.

🏛 NOVEMBER 3rd, THE OVAL OFFICE

The results were going as the president feared they would. Francis Ahern wrested the presidents' party nomination from Forbes during a contentious convention. He preserved a slight lead in the polls throughout the campaign. It was Election Day and Ahern found himself about a half point behind. Due to the typical margin of errors in polling, everyone was saying the race was too close to call.

* * *

Near midnight, the president fiddled with television controls and watched three sets at the same time. They all told the same story. Election results trickled in on the networks all evening. The pundits began forecasting winners across the nation. Along with state winners, the networks were now predicting a presidential winner. It was Francis X. Ahern.

There were two men in the Oval Office. "Shit," said the man behind the big desk. After several minutes of silence, the same man said, "Ray, tell Osborn to get the word out. Tower Watch is a go."

BOOK 3

THE BRIEFING

NOVEMBER 11th, ALEXANDRIA, VIRGINIA

Alex knew his briefing was excellent, yet dozens of details flitted in and out of focus. *Well, here goes nothing. Nothing, hell. Here goes everything.*

At home, Alex made sure Caesar's timer-dish was filled with dry food and then popped the top on a can of cat food. The sound brought Caesar around the side of the counter where he eyed Alex and the distance to the countertop. He unleashed the exact amount of energy required and in one graceful motion make the transition from seated on the floor to standing on the counter. He kept a watchful eye on Alex as the moist food was spooned into one of his dishes.

Alex sat down and smiled as the cat attacked one of his favorite meals. He wanted to go over the timing for the next twenty-four hours one more time. "Okay, Caesar, here's how it lays out. I can get nearly four hours of sleep before I leave. That'll put me on the road about midnight. I'll drive below the speed limit to keep an eye out for cars that might be following. That'll give me about an hour for breakfast. Should put me in the area around six a.m. It'll be getting light by then. Then brief the president-elect and come on home. Damn, wish the last part could be that easy."

Alex looked down at Caesar, whose dish was empty now. "What do you think? Will it be easy?" Caesar didn't reply— he just licked a paw and swiped his whiskers. Alex rinsed the food dish and headed for his bedroom.

NOVEMBER 12th, ALEXANDRIA, VIRGINIA, JUST PAST MIDNIGHT ⬠

He awoke at the first buzz of his clock radio alarm. It took him fewer than twenty minutes to shower, shave and dress. Downstairs, he checked Caesar's food dish and said, "Well, Caesar, this is the big day. Keep the faith, old boy." He added a bit more to the cat's food container. "Here's some extra Caesar, just in case I don't have time to stop by here tonight on the way to work." Caesar looked at Alex as if to thank him. "You're welcome," Alex said, remembering how much company this cat was over the years, and how often he talked to Caesar as if he were human.

Alex entered the garage and checked the backseat of his car. He knew it was safe, but he needed to confirm the briefcase was still on the back floor. He disarmed the security system, opened the garage door and backed the car out into the street. Using a remote control, he closed the garage door and rearmed the anti-intrusion unit.

Southbound on I-95, Alex checked for tails. Twice he used the exit ramp, straight back onto the highway maneuver and once he doubled back to the previous interchange. The eye he kept glued to his rearview mirror during these maneuvers didn't reveal anyone with an interest in him. *But just to make sure.* He pulled onto the shoulder of the interstate and rolled to a stop. He watched a half dozen cars pass by. Again satisfied, he accelerated back up to highway speed. Shortly, he slowed to fifty miles per hour and set the cruise control.

Alex followed the directions General Watson provided. They would take him to President-elect Ahern's retreat in Northampton County, Virginia.

He left the interstate on the north side of Richmond taking U.S. 64 southeast toward the coast. About halfway between Richmond and Hampton, Alex pulled into the parking lot of a large truck plaza. He eyed the restaurant wondering if the maxim about truck drivers and good food was true and could really outweigh the sign, "EATS."

I'm too keyed up to taste the food, but enough coffee will wash it down. It'll also give me a chance to see if anyone follows me into the lot.

* * *

Alex emerged from the diner nearly an hour later. He didn't see anyone follow him into the lot or the restaurant, and he enjoyed the meal more than he anticipated. He reentered U.S. 64 and stayed on that road past the Langley Air Force Base exit and through Hampton, Virginia. Alex saw an overhead sign indicating there were only two more exits before reaching the Hampton Roads Bridge-Tunnel.

West County Street—the route we took to old Fort Monroe. He remembered a far more pleasant time. Sarah and Alex were on a sightseeing adventure to Civil War battlefields. As they enjoyed a picnic lunch at Fort Monroe on a warm, sunny day, they discussed the history of the Civil War fort. They tried to imagine the battle between the Ironclads, the Monitor and the Merrimac, which took place in the waters nearby.

With all that's happened recently, that trip seems like a lifetime ago.

The bridge-tunnel took him into Norfolk. On the east side of the city, he found the exit to U.S. 13 and headed northeast. As he approached the tollbooth on the Chesapeake Bay Bridge-Tunnel, he dug his hand into his trouser pocket. His fingers withdrew some change and several crumpled bills.

The route Alex picked kept him in Virginia all the way. He weighed the possibility of an alternate route back to the Pentagon. Mileage wise, the other route was a bit shorter, but there was far less interstate available.

Well, I'll keep it in mind. Should be getting close to his home now.

* * *

Two Virginia counties are isolated from the rest of the state. The peninsula separating Chesapeake Bay from the Atlantic Ocean is home to three states, or parts of them. All of Delaware occupies the northeast third of the geography. An arm of Maryland surrounds Delaware on the west and south leaving only the southern tip of the peninsula for those Virginia counties.

President-elect Ahern purchased a home in this isolated part of Virginia some years ago. Several acres facing Chesapeake Bay near Bridgetown remained in the Ahern family for at least three generations. Shortly after Francis Ahern inherited the property he had the good fortune to buy nearly four acres of adjoining property. This acquisition brought the size of the compound to thirteen acres of wooded property with a thousand feet of coastline on the western shore of the peninsula.

During the campaign, the compound facilities expanded to accommodate security and communications personnel. The morning after the election, dozens of experts swarmed over the property. The Secret Service moved a full detail into the compound to provide security for "TopHat," the code name assigned to the president-elect.

Since the election, it was a beehive of activity. Much to the horror of his neighbors, the Secret Service applied their full effort to the land which was now referred to as the Presidential Compound.

The activity around the Compound in this quiet landscape caught Alex's eye. He noticed men in cars parked on the shoulder of the road. Even in the dim light preceding sunrise, he saw several figures moving through the woods near the road. He slowed enough to see them with ease. They all wore the telltale wires emerging from under their collars and terminating at the protrusion plugged into their ears. They also carried a communications device.

Must be getting close. No mailboxes to check, but the unusual entrance gate General Watson described should be coming up. Alex recognized the gravel road leading from the highway to the president-elect's home. The columns bracketing the road were rough flagstone and over three feet square. There was a large "A" in the center of the ornate wrought iron that arched the span between the columns.

NOVEMBER 12th, 6:00 A.M., PRESIDENT-ELECT'S COMPOUND ⬟

As Alex eased his car onto the gravel road, a man behind the column to his right raised a transceiver toward his mouth. Alex was sure his arrival was being announced. Thirty yards from the entrance gate the road made a ninety-degree right-hand turn. As he negotiated the turn, two people stepped onto the roadway and blocked his progress. A woman held up a hand signaling Alex to stop. The second figure stood far enough from the first to put him in a different field of fire, just in case. Alex noticed the second agent provided cover for the first while maintaining a clear view of Alex and his car. He also saw this man's right hand buried deep in his overcoat pocket—probably through the slit behind the pocket giving him access to the grip of a fully automatic weapon.

Alex was well aware a warning from the agent with a raised hand would signal the second agent to act—and in a split second reveal his weapon aimed at Alex. Then if threatened, the agent could put up to fifteen rounds through his windshield in less than a second. With those thoughts swirling in his mind, he took a deep breath and swallowed hard.

The actions of these two agents reminded Alex of his visit to the FBI's tactical training range. There, he saw firsthand teams of agents from the FBI, the Secret Service, and other agencies put through their paces. The team members took turns leading and covering, reacting to various situations and determining risks. Even when someone shouted the threat warning "gun," they could not immediately open fire. Their task was to identify and evaluate the threat as well as insuring a clear fire lane.

Alex braked his car and made sure his hands remained visible on the top of the steering wheel. The "raised hand" agent was now standing by the driver's door. She leaned down and said, "Please lower your window and identify yourself."

His window responded with a whir as he pressed and released the auto-open switch. "Hi, I'm Alex Hilliard. My ID is in my left hip pocket." The agent nodded and Alex eased his wallet from the pocket and removed his driver's license. The agent inspected the document, compared the photo ID to Alex and returned it to him. "Colonel Hilliard, please continue along this road. Turn left and park at the near end of the trailer you will see. Engine off, gearshift in Park and set the hand brake. Leave your car unlocked and leave the keys in your vehicle." Without waiting for the inevitable question, she said, "Your car will be quite safe there, sir. Enter the trailer through the door on the end. The security detail will escort you from there."

As he drove off, Alex saw the agent use her transceiver to pass along information about him to those in the trailer. *She knew exactly who I was before she looked at the license. I didn't use my military title and it's not on the license. Was that a slip up or was she letting me know just how sharp they are?*

He followed the instructions to the letter. He retrieved the briefcase from the floor of the backseat and entered the trailer. The agents inside watched as he came through the door and passed under a framework which appeared innocuous, but one he concluded was at least a metal scanner. They asked his permission to inspect the briefcase. He gave it to them knowing the request was only a semblance of politeness. They would inspect it with or without his consent.

As the Secret Service agents conducted their search, Alex observed the interior of the trailer. He wasn't sure if the trailer was a rebuilt commercial model or a custom-built unit. It was mobile because it stood on wheels, but that was its only similarity to any standard trailer. A heavy door with a padlock barred entry to a wire mesh door of an arms locker. *With the firepower these guys must have, I wouldn't be surprised if they had a bazooka in there.*

There was a door at each end of the trailer. A narrow hallway led from this room to the opposite end. To one side of the hall were doors. In the main area where he stood, a bank of television screens lined the wall above the primary security position. The agent at the console was not distracted from his duties as Alex entered. He continued to scan the monitors and speak softly into the microphone on the end of the small arm that curved from the earpiece toward his mouth. Alex managed to overhear, "Roger that, Hawkeye Nine" and saw the agent flip a switch on his communications panel and glance toward the agent inspecting the briefcase. The agent closed the briefcase and nodded to the man on the communications console who said, "Hawkeye One this is Hawkeye Two, briefcase and car are clean, Hawkeye Five's ETA is three minutes."

Alex realized in the few minutes since he entered the trailer, a team of agents including someone called Hawkeye Nine inspected his car and reported an "all clear" to the trailer. The "briefcase inspector" handed the briefcase back to Alex and said, "Thank you very much, sir. Please exit the trailer." Pointing to the end opposite the door Alex entered, he said, "The agents outside will transport you to the main house."

Two new agents were waiting for Alex as he left the trailer. The first led Alex toward a government-issue plain black sedan parked nearby. The agent following Alex stepped around him, opened the right front door and ushered Alex into the front seat. One agent drove while the second agent sat in the backseat behind Alex. Alex wondered if the "Hawkeye" number related to specific individuals or just the security position they filled at the time. *No sense asking... they wouldn't tell me.* The ride was brief and Alex was sure they beat the "three minute estimated time of arrival" Hawkeye Two had passed to the main house.

The relay of information being passed from one agent to the next must have continued. As the car stopped in front of the house, another agent descended the steps from the porch. He approached the door next to Alex, opened it and said, "Mr. Hilliard, the president-elect is expecting you." Without hesitating, the agent turned and started back toward the porch.

Alex was hard-pressed to snatch his briefcase and catch up with his usher before the agent reached the front door.

"Please wait here in the foyer, Mr. Hilliard. I'll let the president-elect know you have arrived," the agent said. He disappeared through a nearby doorway.

Alex nodded and glanced at his watch. *Six-fifteen, damn good timing. Better fifteen early, than one minute late for a briefing like this.*

Standing alone in the foyer, Alex ticked off the main points of his briefing in his head. He went through the list a second time before the door to his right reopened. The same agent said, "The president-elect will see you now."

Good grief, I've rehearsed the briefing till I have it down pat, but I didn't give any thought to the introductions. What do I say to him first?

NOVEMBER 12th, PRESIDENT-ELECT
AHERN'S DEN ⬠

His thoughts echoed in his mind as Alex entered a room that looked like a comfortable and well-used den and saw seven people. "Well Alex, it's a pleasure to meet you. I've heard a lot of good things about you," President-elect Ahern said, breaking the ice. He continued. "Yes, sir, General Wa—"

"Mr. President-elect." Alex shouted. Ahern stopped with a startled look on his face. "Please excuse me, sir, but I've gotten rather paranoid over the past few weeks. Would you mind, sir, if we didn't use any names until I'm sure of my surroundings?"

At least two people in the room gasped and the president-elect looked surprised as well. After a moment of recovery, Ahern said, "Well, he told me you were outspoken, and blunt, but trustworthy. I'll honor your request."

The president-elect introduced the other six people in the room. Alex assumed they were being presented in roughly their order of rank in the president-elect's mind. Jerome Fowler, Ahern called him Jerry, was an old friend and adviser. He held no formal position or title, but Alex was sure his access to Ahern was special.

Ahern introduced Reston Whitman as his political adviser.

"My right hand man and campaign manager," were the words the president-elect used for Dexter Shelby. The fourth on the list was Ahern's press secretary, Ted Montgomery.

The president-elect lavished the most praise on the next person saying, "I know the old military axiom, 'Good NCOs run the show.' Well, in civilian life if you haven't already learned, it's secretaries and this one is a world-class champ. This is Joyce Maxwell."

Joyce blushed a bit as she extended her hand to Alex and thanked the president-elect for his compliment.

"Oh yes, Mr. President-elect," Alex said, "I've worked with enough civilian agencies to come to the same conclusion."

"Don't be bashful, Luke," the president-elect said, addressing the remark to the final person in the room. "Alex, this is Luke Cutter. You've probably heard him mentioned over those communication what-cha-ma-call-its." Then, lowering his voice, as if to be conspiratorial, the president-elect winked and continued. "You no doubt heard his 'code name,' Hawkeye One."

Luke Cutter stepped forward, extended his hand toward Alex, and said, "Mr. President-elect, you know I'm not bashful. I was getting a perimeter update through my earpiece."

Alex assumed Luke was the Secret Service team leader for President-elect Ahern's security detail.

The president-elect continued. "There were several others I wanted to attend this meeting, but we had schedule conflicts. I thought Vice President-elect Ryder should be here, but these Secret Service guys like to keep us separated. Also, I wanted my foreign policy adviser, Doris Newman, and my domestic policy adviser, Martin Gilchrist here."

Alex took Ahern's pause as the opportunity to voice his concerns. "Mr. President-elect, I can certainly understand your wish to have all these people present for our meeting. As I mentioned earlier, I'm a bit paranoid about this. I hope no one is upset at the suggestion I'm about to make, but it's imperative the group I brief be reduced even further. With your approval Mr. President-elect, I would like to brief you, Mr. Fowler, Ms. Maxwell and Mr. Cutter."

"Damn, blunt hardly describes it," the president-elect said. "I'm not sure I agree, but I'll go along with you."

Alex could tell by the president-elect's tone of voice he was not pleased with someone else setting the agenda.

"My apologies," Ahern said. "Resty, I'm going to ask you, Dex and Ted to leave us for a short while." The trio rose and left the room without uttering a sound.

When the door closed, the president-elect turned to Alex. His voice took on the quality of a snake's hiss as he said, "Colonel, you better have damn firm ground to stand on. I've just insulted three people who are close to me."

"Mr. President-elect, I have nothing against any of the three—and please convey my apologies to them. I'm doing my best to lessen the odds. The fewer who know, the less chance for slips. In a moment, sir, I'll tell you about a good friend I lost and then maybe you will begin to see why I'm so cautious."

"Very well, Colonel, let's get on with it," the president-elect said.

* * *

Alex recalled his briefing points and began covering them. He started with his suspicions when he saw the first Tower Watch message and the fact it disappeared from the briefing book. Next he described how his friend Mike Reilly gathered information which seemed to point to some type of plot and how Mike died in an auto accident.

At this point, the president-elect interrupted Alex. The knot on his jaw disappeared and Alex knew his teeth were no longer clenched. The expression on his face turned to one of disbelief. "Alex, do you really believe that this CIA employee, this friend of yours, was killed because of his investigations into, what did you call it…Tower Watch?"

"Yes, Mr. President-elect, I do believe that. I believe Mike died because he looked into a subject someone didn't want him or anyone else to know about." Alex noted the president-elect was again using his first name rather than his title. *Here's your opening,* Alex told himself. *You'd better make some big points while he's receptive.*

Alex continued covering his rehearsed points. He described being followed when he attended Mike's funeral, and also believed he was tailed on other occasions. He assured everyone in the room the precautions he took today made him certain he was not followed to this destination. From the corner of his eye, he saw Luke Cutter's furrowed brow and near imperceptible head movements. Alex hoped the nods meant approval of the actions, but it didn't look like it. The next briefing point was the Tower Watch messages he brought along today. They were still divided into two packages—the one from Sam Cooke and those provided by Sarah. He omitted their names and the roles they played.

"As you can see from these messages," he said, handing the first stack to the president-elect, "the unit address list is extensive and widespread. There is a common element to the units on that list. Each unit's mission statement includes crowd control, seizing targets, and rapid deployment." Alex paused to give Ahern time to examine the documents and pass them onto the others in the room.

As the president-elect passed the last of these Tower Watch messages to Jerry Fowler, the first of the documents reached the last in line to see them. Luke Cutter digested them rapidly as they reached his hands. Alex was sure that a high percentage of the exact content was being stored in this man's gray cells. That guy didn't get to be the head of a presidential security team by being dumb. *Hope he's on my side. I need the help.*

"Alex," Ahern said, "does this list of units do us any good without knowing the individuals who may or may not be involved?"

"Mr. President-elect, the same thought occurred to me, so I put one of my acquaintances to work on it. He has an extensive background in the communications field. Through his contacts at Fort Huachuca, he was able to obtain a list of the fifteen individuals who are authorized to see Tower Watch messages. That was no easy task since this message traffic is designated SPECAT or Special Category, with Limited Distribution and EYES ONLY headers. The subject matter is closely held and only the fifteen people identified are authorized to see the material. I'm sure you have been briefed on similar subjects since your election, sir." The president-elect nodded and Alex continued. "In every case, the messages are not going to the commanders of the major organizations shown on the message itself. They are directed to commanders of subordinate units. Here's the list of the individuals actually receiving the Tower Watch messages."

President-elect Ahern took the list from Alex. He looked at the names for a moment and said, "Do we know anything about these people? Do I need Luke here to get more information on them?"

"Mr. President-elect," Alex said, "I've done a bit of investigating on my own. It would be good if Mr. Cutter could verify what I discovered. From what I was able to learn from friends in the Pentagon, these men all seem to share the same political leaning as President Bancroft. Nearly all of them have been censured or reprimanded for being politically outspoken when representing the military."

Ahern turned to Cutter. "Luke, get me everything you can on this bunch. Just be low-key about it. I don't want anyone to be aware of our activities until we can be sure we're on firm ground." He handed the list to Luke and without waiting for a reply turned back to Alex. "What do you see as the next step in our course of action?"

"Mr. President-elect, I've assembled a group of people I can trust. They are divided into several teams…for two reasons. First is security, the fewer people who know the entire operation, the fewer who could compromise it. Second, most of my people are shift workers. That means they may not be available when push comes to shove. Each group has similar abilities, so we will not degrade any activity we may need to carry out. Team leaders know the other team leaders and me. They will not know the members of any team other than their own. I am the only one with that knowledge. For contact purposes, I selected 'Beta' as a code name."

"Hmm, Beta. Are you a test phase of new computer software or is that part of the Greek alphabet?" the president-elect said.

"Once again, sir, you're ahead of me. I did pick letters from the Greek alphabet as code names for team leaders. My people are experts in communications, weapons, intelligence and several other military specialties."

"Alex," the president-elect said, "Since you're Beta, can we assume there is an Alpha involved? And if so, who is it?"

"With all due respect, sir," Alex said, "I must decline to give you Alpha's name at this time." Hoping to diffuse the potential problem this response might elicit, Alex decided a change of topic would help. He hit on the "widgets" Mike included in the briefcase left in the Pentagon. "Mr. President-elect, I have a communications device, thanks to my friend Mike Reilly, which will give me secure communications. The only problem is that I must initiate the phone calls and the device is only good for a few uses—anyone monitoring the line could decipher the messages based on volume. Here's a list of phone numbers where your people should be able to find me. The call should sound like a wrong number, and ask for any name other than mine. When I tell the caller that person is not there, your representative should respond,

'I'd beta look it up in the white pages.' I'll assume you directed the call and I'll return it from a safe phone using my device. I should be able to respond within fifteen minutes or so."

"Good Lord, Alex. You've put a great deal of thought into this, haven't you?" said the president-elect. "And…why in God's name did you decide to get so involved?"

"Sir, I believed the situation warranted the attention. Why me? I'll tell you up front, sir that I do not agree with most of your platform and policies. At the same time, I couldn't allow anyone to subvert the Constitution, which I remember from the time I raised my right hand and accepted my commission." Alex hoped there was sufficient rapport with the president-elect to be this plainspoken. "When I first became aware of this situation, it did occur to me to let it slide—and let others get involved. Even if it's a natural reaction, it flies in the face of everything I've learned from every significant mentor and teacher in my life. Someone else would discover the danger and be here now. I could either accept the responsibility or be responsible for putting that other person in harm's way. If I opted for the latter, I'm afraid I'd need to give up shaving in the morning, sir."

"Well, I'm damn glad you feel the way you do, Alex," the president-elect said. "Perhaps over time, I can change your mind about my politics. In the meantime, let's get on with the business at hand. Luke…" He turned to his Secret Service team leader. "What do you think of the Colonel's ideas and plans?"

"On the surface, top drawer, Mr. President-elect. To this point, he has the bases well covered. I have reservations, but I would like to work with him coordinating the next steps that we may need to take. If I might make a suggestion, I think I would be the best point-of-contact for Colonel Hilliard. If you need to reach him, I'm always nearby. I can place the call to him and when he returns it we can use one of my lines. That would make it more difficult for anyone to trace or intercept."

Alex watched Luke Cutter as he spoke. He noted Cutter looked people straight in the eye as he talked to them. Alex made a gut level decision to trust this man. Now if he could resolve Cutter's doubts.

When the president-elect asked Alex how he felt about the suggestions, Alex accepted them without comment. As he spoke, however, he hoped he wasn't placing his head in the wrong noose.

"Great," said the president-elect. "Unfortunately I have to meet with my campaign staff, but I would like you to have a working lunch with Jerry and Luke. Please go over all the details, and Jerry, I'd like a follow up briefing around 2 p.m. today. Joyce, I'd like you to take notes and I'm sure I don't have to remind any of you that no one outside this circle is to be aware of these discussions." Ahern's secretary nodded. The president-elect stood and reached out to Alex. Alex leaped to his feet and accepted the president-elect's hand. "Alex, I want to thank you again." He turned and left the room.

The abrupt departure caught Alex off guard. There was no opportunity to introduce the second package of documents—the ones from Sarah—the ones with the margin note by Admiral Eastland implicating President Bancroft. He reached for them when Jerry Fowler said, "Colonel, if you would excuse us, we have some points to cover. Please wait for us in the foyer. If we need you again, we'll call for you."

Alex felt a lump in his stomach the size of a bowling ball. He moved to the door with the documents still in his hand. As he pulled the heavy door closed behind him, he was sure his one chance, to convince this group the plot was real, had disappeared.

NOVEMBER 12th, FOYER, PRESIDENT-ELECT'S HOME ⬠

The only furniture in the foyer was a mahogany parson's bench. Alex sat on the hard wood leaning toward the door to the den, and wishing the decorator placed this seat closer to the den's entrance. He could hear voices, and he could distinguish between the voices. Cutter and Fowler were arguing—both on the verge of shouting but not loud enough for him to make out the words.

Damn it to hell. Alex old boy you really screwed the pooch. I planned to hold that message with Eastland's note pointing a finger at Bancroft for a closer—the inescapable proof that...

"What did Fowler say? 'If...*If*...we need you again.'" He glanced at the package in his hands and at his watch for the twentieth time. He screwed up his courage and rose from the bench. "Bullshit. I didn't come here to fail." Alex was one step from the door when it opened.

"No, I don't suppose you did," Cutter said in a low voice—he also winked. Then in a conversational tone he said, "Come back in, Alex. We've got some more questions for you."

Alex joined them at the table and Fowler began, "Don't mind telling you, Colonel, I have some real doubts about you and this tale of yours."

"I can appreciate your feeling that way, sir. I think you need to look at these," Alex said. He handed the new pile of documents to Fowler.

Fowler and Cutter reviewed the new evidence, and the reservations began to melt. The conversation continued for another thirty minutes. They discussed Alex's plan in detail—further efforts they could take to identify and isolate all the individuals involved, and the possibilities of countering the plot against Ahern. And if any attempts were made against the president-elect, he could field a team to provide armed resistance and protection. He would need only thirty to forty-five minutes notice to deliver coverage anywhere in the District of Columbia.

Fowler was still shaking his head. "Even if this wild plot turns out to be true, I'm opposed to using an Air Force lieutenant colonel and a rag-tag band of military people as a first line of defense."

Luke Cutter intervened asking Alex a dozen rapid-fire and pointed questions about the qualifications of his recruits. Alex provided concise and detailed responses in the same rapid-fire manner. When Luke finished, Fowler's expression turned from a scowl to a reluctant nod.

Alex was feeling even more confident about his decision to trust Cutter. He had the same gut reaction to this man as when he first met Mike Reilly. "Thanks for the vote of confidence, Luke. I'll be happy to work with you as a liaison to the president-elect."

Alex glanced at his watch realizing the briefing and discussion took over three hours.

Luke Cutter took charge of the meeting. Since security was this man's occupation, everyone deferred to him. The three men covered a wide range of possibilities—try as he might—Luke could not budge Alex when it came to the identities of his team members. With a sigh, Luke said, "Alex, I understand your reluctance to give ground on this subject. But, and it's a big but, what happens if the opposition takes you out?" After the question, Luke used one of the oldest sales techniques known, the one General Watson taught Alex. He kept his silence and stared at Alex.

Alex thought, *whoever speaks first, loses.* He also knew he would have to speak first. After an interminable period of time, Alex broke the silence. "Luke, I admit I didn't consider the possibility…I'm not willing to commit the names of my people to paper, but I will give you a name." Looking around the table, he said, "I will give one name to Luke only, and with the promise that he will not reveal it to another soul. Do I have your word, Luke?" Cutter nodded and Alex continued. "One of the ways I've survived a career of flying is by being paranoid. By anticipating what *might go wrong* and preparing for those eventualities. Now I must have another promise." With that, Alex looked at Joyce Maxwell and Jerry Fowler in turn and said, "I insist the very fact Luke has a name must remain between the four of us. Not even President-elect Ahern will be briefed on this." Alex waited for the looks of astonishment to dissolve.

Jerry Fowler broke this silence. "Why, in the name of all that's holy, do you insist on that?"

"Mr. Fowler," Alex said, "I see it this way. If the name I give to Luke is compromised or the person is harmed, I have only three suspects to go after…the three of you. If anything happens to Luke, I only have two suspects." He paused to let this threat penetrate. After looking at each of them, he said, "I happen to like those odds. Now do I have your word?"

Before either could respond, Luke said, "Mr. Fowler, I know how tough it will be for you to omit this fact from your briefing to the president. I also believe that Alex is right—he needs to keep the odds in his favor by minimizing the number of people with information about this problem."

Joyce Maxwell spoke first. "I will respect your position, you have my word, Colonel. I don't mind telling you though—I think you are more than paranoid. I have never kept anything from President-elect Ahern and this will be extremely difficult."

Alex looked Ms. Maxwell in the eye and said, "I can appreciate your loyalty and I admire you for that. Now, Mr. Fowler, do I have your word?"

Jerry Fowler nodded his head and said, "Yes, you do."

Alex leaned toward Luke Cutter and whispered in his ear. Alex gave Chief Eaton's name and a code word to the Secret Service Agent. "That will identify you to that team leader." Then to avoid giving even the gender of the person, he continued, "That team leader will know your name and hearing the code word will know you're the representative of this group. Now what other ground do we have to cover?"

Agent Cutter again took charge of the discussions. Alex gave him the background of the planning meetings he held with his team leaders. Luke wanted exact numbers, but Alex evaded direct answers. Luke pressed him for more details on the grounds it was vital for his own planning. Alex apologized for remaining vague but held his ground. "I have at least three teams and that's conservative," he said leaving them wondering how many more teams might be involved.

Luke pushed Alex further for details—this time about the arms available and the team members' qualifications with those weapons. Again, Alex remained vague. "I can assure you that each team member is well qualified with firearms. I established weapons as the second criteria I gave my team leaders when they began recruiting. The first criteria I insisted on was each team member being mature enough to know when to use the weapons. Anyone can be effective, and do something right. It takes maturity to be efficient and do the right thing. The third criteria I insisted on was experience, preferably combat experience."

Luke again pressed hard for details. "That's all well and good Alex, but how about the types of weapons you have available. What types of situations are you prepared to face?

"You don't give up easy, do you, Luke?" Alex continued his description of the teams within the bounds of his own limits. "Each team is staffed with enough members to handle anything short of facing a full platoon of Rangers." Alex decided to exaggerate a bit at this point. He did not anticipate having to face more than a dozen opponents at one time. He expected when the time arrived, the opposing force would be fairly small—two or three—at the outside, six. He was confident that his teams could handle that number. "I'll also tell you this much about weapons. Each team will be equipped for anything from long-range sniper activity, to one-on-one with silenced weapons, to a close-in fire fight requiring a heavy field of fire."

Alex saw the surprised expressions on the others. It was Luke's turn to look incredulous. He said, "Where did you get hold of all those weapons? It sounds like a cross between a military and a civilian agency armory."

Alex smiled as he thought of the gyrations Hillbilly and Scrounger went through for those guns. Hillbilly knew what weapons they needed. Scrounger's ability to get his hands on what they required was invaluable. The two of them called in a large number of chits. Alex figured that they would all owe a few favors before this project ended.

"What's so damn funny, Alex?" Luke asked.

"Nothing I can share now. When this whole affair is over, I'll be proud to introduce you to each and every team member."

Luke said, "You seem to be well prepared, but judging from that unit addressee list on the Tower Watch messages, you could be up against very large-scale units. How would you plan to handle that situation?"

"I'm not planning on a large-scale engagement. I can't imagine the bad guys using those units for the actual attack. They would be in place and in reserve for controlling the population. No, I think a small group will carry out the initial attack, possibly as few as one or two. My plan is to provide direct protection to President-elect Ahern. I've given this some thought, using the "means, motive and opportunity" criteria. Motive seems to be a man in office—the sitting president—who prefers not to leave his position. Regarding means, I'm not positive, but it would not be difficult for the president of the United States to have enough contacts to come up with an assassin." Alex paused to let the word "assassin" soak in, and then continued. "Yes, I do believe that the plan involves killing the president-elect and very likely the vice president-elect at the same time."

Jerry Fowler jumped into the discussion and shot a question at Alex. "Why do you think both the president-elect and vice president-elect are targets? How in the world could any sane person think they could get away with killing both of them?"

"Mr. Fowler, I don't think we can assume the person behind this conspiracy is sane. For the plan to succeed, I believe both are to be killed. If one survives, then the Constitution and applicable laws spell out the succession to the presidency. And the sitting president is nowhere in that line. I've also given a great deal of thought to the opportunity aspect. I believe that the act will be committed before the inaugural. It seems to me the most vulnerable period will be between the vote of the Electoral College and Inauguration Day."

Alex probed for more answers. "Prior to the electoral vote there are enough confusing factors which might lead the members of the Electoral College to cast their votes for people other than President-elect Ahern and his vice presidential candidate. There's no requirement they must vote for the ones the people elected. That could complicate the matter beyond hope. For the actual opportunity, I would look for a time when both the president-elect and the vice president-elect are scheduled to be in the same place at the same time. I know you work to avoid those situations, but is there anything on the calendar that seems to fit?"

Fowler turned to Joyce Maxwell. "I don't have anything like that planned. Joyce, do you have any appointments on the president-elect's schedule fitting this scenario?"

"No sir. There have been two or three requests that fit. Typical fund raisers and political meetings, but they were all declined."

There was a knock on the door to the meeting room. A steward entered and took lunch orders. The interruption gave the four the opportunity to stretch and walk around the room. The meeting continued after the meals were delivered and centered on future coordination and communications. Alex described the telephone gadgets that Mike Reilly passed on to him. He said Mike warned about using them too often lest an eavesdropper break the built-in encryption. Luke agreed and told the group he would limit calls to an absolute minimum. The agent also indicated they could be used even if Alex did not initiate the call. For the encryption protection to kick in though, the calling party needs to be using a secure line. They also discussed strategies regarding the Tower Watch distribution list. They looked at options they might use to obtain details about each unit commander on the list.

* * *

The door to the den burst open without warning, and each of them started. Ahern poked his head in the door. "Sorry to interrupt, folks. How's it going?"

Jerry Fowler spoke for the group, "Everything is fine, Mr. President-elect. I think you will be pleased when I brief you."

"How's the security side, Luke?"

"Sir, I believe that we are on 'firm ground' here," he said, borrowing a phrase from the president-elect's vocabulary. He knew it would let Ahern feel comfortable. "For the time being and considering we don't know exactly what we're up against, I would cast my vote for Alex and his Baker Street Irregulars. From what I see, he has an excellent mix of military specialties and experience to handle what he proposes. I would feel more comfortable using my own counter-assault team, but at this point we'd be involving another twenty or thirty people, and explaining why to any number of others. Alex is right, we don't know exactly who or how high up in various agencies this might go. I'll vote again with Alex to limit the number of people on our side who know about Tower Watch."

"Great," said Ahern, a smile dancing across his face. "Alex, I'm going to be tied up for a good while. In case I miss your departure, I want to say thanks again. I spoke with your mentor over a secure line a few minutes ago and he gave me a bit more of your background. I want you to know that I trust you and I am counting on you, lad. Oh, by the way, President Bancroft called. He says there's an important and, in his words, 'a very interesting exercise' scheduled in January I should attend. He also invited the vice president-elect. It was originally scheduled for the last week in December. I was invited to it, but couldn't fit it into my schedule. Anyway, Bancroft says its been postponed till January—I should be free then. Sounds like an excellent opportunity for me to work with the transition team to see what goes on in the White House, the Situation Room and that five-sided puzzle palace. I'm planning to go, so Joyce, please get the details and work my calendar around those meeting times on January 4th through the 7th."

Before Alex could reply, Ahern disappeared again and the door slammed shut.

Alex looked at the group and said only one word, "Opportunity." After a pause, he added, "Luke, the president-elect missed some of the meat of our talks. Be damn sure he's aware we're talking about death threats and that the plot goes to the very top of the government."

"I'll make sure of that. That gives us less than eight weeks, folks," Luke said.

The Tower Watch messages again became a subject of discussion. Each person reviewed the entire file one more time. They all agreed that a copy of the file should remain with the president-elect's staff. Ms. Maxwell gathered up the papers, excused herself and returned several minutes later with a duplicate file.

Jerry Fowler probed Alex for the source of the documents. "Since these are EYES ONLY messages, you certainly didn't have access to them. Who made the copies for you, Colonel?"

Alex looked Fowler in the eye and said, "I don't know how a name could possibly help you in your deliberations, sir." Alex caught the slightest hint of a suppressed smile on Luke's face and smiled in return.

The group finished their meal and ended the meeting. Alex thanked the others and asked, "Luke how do I get back to the trailer?"

Luke just nodded toward the door and led the way for Alex. They walked through the foyer and onto the large shaded porch. Alex marveled at the quiet beauty of the vista before him. A beautiful, wide lawn sloped down to the waters of the bay. There was also a large white circle painted on the lush grass that gave the pilot of the president-elect's helicopter a target for landing. Alex was surprised when he saw his own car parked at the bottom of the steps. "How the hell did you do that, Luke? You haven't been out of my sight since the meeting began."

Luke pursed his lips and nodded again. "We all have to have our own little secrets, don't we?" Then he broke into a large smile and said, "It's not all that big a secret. I'll bet you figure it out before you get back to the highway. Good luck, I'll stay in touch."

Alex loaded his briefcase into his car and pointed the nose of the little coupe back down the gravel road. The drive took him past the trailer and the pair of agents guarding the road. He saluted them as he passed and they nodded in response. He also saluted the agent at the front gate as he passed between the flagstone pillars and turned left. His decision was to take the peninsula north to Annapolis for the return trip. *Hope I don't have to make this trip again. But if I do, might as well know how long each route takes. Luke was wrong. I still haven't figured out how he contacted his people to bring up my car.*

1:00 P.M., NOVEMBER 12th, PRESIDENT-ELECT'S COMPOUND

The figure walking near the water struggled getting the bulky cellular phone from a jacket pocket, pulled the antenna up, and dialed a private number at the White House. When General Osborn answered, the caller spoke in a rapid-fire staccato. "General, you know who this is, don't you?"

Osborn said, "Yes. Why the hell are you calling? It's not our regular time."

The figure continued. "We just had a visitor at the compound. A Lieutenant Colonel Hilliard—works at the Pentagon. He's got some wild hair about a plot. I don't know much of the detail because I wasn't allowed to sit in on the briefing, but I did hear one bit of interesting information before I was asked to leave the meeting. I heard a name—at least part of a name."

"What name?" said Osborn, raising his voice.

"Well, Ahern started to name someone when this Hilliard interrupted him. All I really heard was the rank of general and that it sounded like a name that began with a 'W.' Maybe like the 'wa' in water. Does it mean anything to you?"

"Never mind what it means to me. Are you sure that's all you heard?"

"Yes, sir, as I said, I didn't sit in on the meeting."

General Osborn said, "Why weren't you in on the meeting? Are they onto you? Have you compromised any of us?"

"No, sir, I don't think they know anything about me or our arrangement."

"They damn well better not. At the first hint of that, your pay stops and that would be the least of your worries. Do I make myself clear?"

"Yes, sir, I understand. I'll be very careful."

"Is there anything else?"

"No, General. I'll get back to you at our regular time." With that, the figure put the phone into a pocket and started up the wide lawn toward the main house.

🏛 1:05 P.M., NOVEMBER 12th, THE WHITE HOUSE

General Osborn snatched the phone from its cradle and stabbed the intercom button marked: Richards. "Quentin, get down here to my office right away." He slammed the receiver down without waiting for a reply.

Colonel Richards entered the office. The general was in a rage—the veins on his forehead were bulging.

"Quentin, here are the facts. Think carefully and give me an answer. Someone who is on the inside of Tower Watch. Someone who could give Hilliard an introduction to Ahern. Someone whose name starts with a W and possibly with W-A."

Richards thought for a moment and replied, "Sir, I can only think of one person who fits that profile. You must be describing General Watkins."

"Get Batman on the secure phone for me right now. I've got a delicate job for him."

Richards made the connection and handed the phone to the general. "That'll be all, Colonel."

Osborn waited until his office door closed and then spoke to the ex-CIA agent. "Chapman, I've got two jobs for you. They are vital and the first one must be handled tonight."

6:30 P.M., NOVEMBER 12th, THE PENTAGON

The drive from President-elect Ahern's compound back to the Pentagon took most of the afternoon. Alex used U. S. Routes 13 and 50 through Maryland. He stopped at a small seafood restaurant in Cambridge. He wasn't particularly hungry, but it was time for a stretch and a good place to check for anyone who was overly interested in him. As he reached the restaurant door, he noticed a silver Camaro pull into the lot and park at the side of the building.

He selected a table that gave him an outstanding view. Not only could he see the Choptank River, but he could also observe the front door and the parking lot at the same time.

The waitress looked like she had seen better days, but her demeanor did not suggest any such attitude. Her smile plus her manner earned her a generous tip even before she took the order. He decided on a fried clam roll and kept his eyes peeled as he waited for his meal. The young man from the Camaro came through the door and moved toward a booth at the back of the restaurant. That put him at Alex's back.

He replayed the day's events in his mind. Alex decided everything went well, up to this point, and was more productive than he expected. He twisted in his seat trying to see if the interloper was watching him. He didn't have a clear view of the man, but he did seem nervous and kept glancing toward Alex and the door.

The front door opening caught Alex's attention, and an attractive older woman entered. She scanned the entire room and then with a brisk pace went to the back of the restaurant.

Alex gave the couple several minutes together—then he started for the restroom. His path took him by their booth, and his observations appeared to go unnoticed. His conclusion—large diamond on her left hand—she was married. Her tablemate was either unmarried or didn't wear a ring. They were not married to each other—among the few whispered words Alex overheard her say were, "…but my husband would…"

The two were dealing with their own problems and nobody seemed to find him interesting, so Alex finished his meal and eased his car back onto Route 50. He crossed the Chesapeake Bay into Annapolis and followed Route 50 into the District of Columbia. It was just a short stint on I-395 and across the Potomac River to the Pentagon. With about an hour till he was to be on duty, Alex decided to skip the drive home, and used the facilities at the Pentagon to shower. He selected a fresh uniform from his locker and relieved the day watch officer a bit early.

* * *

Very few day workers were still in the J.O.C. Alex saw Hillbilly was already on duty and Duke was still there. "I suppose you both want a briefing on the day's events."

Both men nodded. Alex gave them a rundown on the entire day and finished with, "I think I convinced them of the possible dangers and they're on our side. I'm especially pleased with the Secret Service team leader." Alex described his discussions with Luke Cutter. He told them Duke would be a backup contact for the teams if anything should happen to him. "For both of you, the contact code is 'et tu Caesar?' From Shakespeare's *Tragedy of Julius Caesar*, but I changed it to honor my cat."

Chief Eaton was the first to break the silence. "Colonel, I'm not sure if I'm happy or sorry the Secret Service and the president-elect agree with us."

"Master Chief, I know what you mean," Hillbilly said, "but hot damn, now we can get down to some serious planning. Like I told you last night Colonel, it's time to lock and load." A grin expanded across his face.

"Well, I'm out of here. I'll be back soon enough and my family hasn't seen much of me the last few weeks." With that, Duke left the J.O.C.

"Hillbilly, what's on the schedule for tonight and who's the NMCC duty general we'll be briefing in the morning?"

Sergeant Pickens ran down the mission schedules then said, "General Watkins is due on at midnight, so he'll be in for the morning brief."

"Hillbilly, let's go over the Op Plan and see where we are and what we still need to accomplish," Alex said.

BOOK 4

PREPARATION -
THE DEVIL IS IN THE DETAILS

6:15 A.M., NOVEMBER 13th, J.O.C., THE PENTAGON ⬠

The buzzer from the security door to the J.O.C. sounded and Alex looked toward the small TV screen. He saw Colonel Jake Townsend standing in the glare of the spotlight. He punched the button that released the lock on the door and turned to Sergeant Pickens.

"I thought General Watkins was on duty this morning?"

"He's on the schedule, Colonel. Maybe he's just tied up with something else," Hillbilly said.

Alex met Jake halfway down the hallway to the briefing area. "What's up, Jake? It's not often we're graced with the second in command from the NMCC."

"I thought you guys always knew the scuttlebutt. Haven't you heard?"

"Heard what, Jake?"

"They're scrambling to find a replacement for General Watkins' shift today. As of now, I'm it. The old man blew his brains out last night. I tried to cover for him for a while—called his house and couldn't get him. I had to report him overdue for duty. They started a search and found him about twenty minutes ago. Guess it was a hell of a mess. Damn good thing he didn't live with his family."

"Son-of-a-bitch. He sure didn't seem down the last time I briefed him."

"I know. Just yesterday, we were talking about what we were going to do on this upcoming break. I told the general I didn't have much scheduled beyond yard work, but he had all kinds of plans. He seemed to be looking forward to the time off. It's a real shocker to me."

"Me too, Jake. If you hear anything else, give me a shout. Damn, let me see if I can get my mind organized and back on business...here's what's coming up for today." Alex covered the events scheduled for the day, but it was hard to concentrate. He kept thinking it was strange—one of only two men with Pentagon duty who were on the Tower Watch list just committed suicide.

Alex scribbled a few words on a notepad and handed the paper to Sergeant Pickens. "Hillbilly, on the way out I want you to use a pay phone and call my home. Leave this message on my answering machine."

Pickens read the note. He frowned and looked up at Alex. "Colonel, I guess I don't need to understand what this means, but didn't you say you suspected that your home line was being monitored?"

"You've got that right. I'm banking on the fact someone will intercept this message. I'm not keeping you in the dark. I'm just adding a new twist to the game—hoping the 'bad guys' will waste time."

"Well, I got the right gizmo for that job." Sergeant Pickens pulled two disks from his pocket and handed one to Alex. "Just put this thing over the mouthpiece on any phone and talk normally. This little doo-dad alters your voice. Even if someone hears the words, they can't figure out who said it based on a voiceprint comparison."

"Where in the world did these come from?"

"Well, Colonel, we ain't just been sittin' on our butts while you was briefin' the Prez," Hillbilly said. "Tuck pulled in a few more chits and got a half dozen of these gizmos from some friends of his."

"How many? Who has them?"

"By the end of the day, all your team leaders will have one. I already gave one to Ms. Crawford. I've been told they even help disguise the caller's gender as well."

"Good work, Hillbilly. Pass the word on—meeting tonight at seven. I think it's been long enough that we can use Roscoe's Bar again. How does that sound?"

"Everybody's off duty. I'll get the word out, and have them there, Colonel."

Chief Eaton and Commander Jim Lawrence relieved Sergeant Pickens and Alex for the day watch. On the way out, Hillbilly patted the pocket containing Alex's note and nodded as he headed for the phone bank just inside the subway entrance to the Pentagon.

* * *

Thirty minutes later, Alex was home. He hit the "Repeat Last Message" button on his answering machine and heard what must be Sergeant Pickens' voice, "Beta, this is Alpha. Meet me, today, 1 p.m., G-town." Alex looked for Caesar, but didn't see him. The cat always heard the garage door opening and was on hand to greet Alex as he entered the townhouse.

He located the big old cat in one of his favorite resting spots. Just off the kitchen, in the utility room was a good size cardboard carton. The box began life transporting products to a supermarket. Next it became a storage box for items Alex intended to donate to charity. The first items which went into the box were several rather rag-tag towels and well-worn shirts, but Alex started another collection box because Caesar appropriated this first one.

"Well, there you are, Caesar. How come you weren't at the door to greet me?" The cat looked up at Alex and mewed in a voice that sounded like pain to Alex. He reached down and petted Caesar on the head. As he ran his hand down the cat's back, Caesar winced and pulled away. It was then Alex noticed that Caesar's side appeared to be swollen. He gently placed his hand on the affected area and Caesar tolerated his probing. "Damn, how did this happen, old guy? That must hurt like hell."

* * *

An hour later Alex was back home. In the interval, he made an appointment with his vet, and took Caesar to Dr. Frasier's office for an examination.

The vet knew Caesar as a normally calm animal, but in pain even Caesar might become violent. The doctor prodded and probed Caesar with as much care as possible. Caesar accepted the exam with only a few verbal complaints.

"Alex, if I didn't know better, I'd say someone kicked Caesar here in the side. He couldn't have fallen and injured this area. It looks like his ribs have been bruised. Any idea what might have happened?"

Alex shook his head. "Not a clue, Doc. I thought I saw some blood on his right front paw, but I've got no idea what happened."

Dr. Frasier examined the paw more closely and announced, "You're right. I think one of his claws is missing. Like he latched onto something or someone, and the claw was pulled out as the other object ripped free. Alex, I'd like to keep Caesar at least overnight for observation. Is that okay?"

"Sure, Doc. You know me, anything he needs, you give him. I'll give you a call later today."

* * *

Alex looked around his home for anything suspicious. He checked all the doors and windows on the ground floor looking for signs of forced entry. He didn't find any. Next, he checked the alarm panel. When he moved to the D.C. area, he knew he would be keeping odd hours. Security systems were a priority when he went shopping for a home. He liked this townhouse even before the real estate agent told him the previous owner was a security nut. They included a built-in system, with several extra whistles and bells. There were motion and pressure sensors on all three floors. These were in addition to the normal ones at every door and window. All the sensors fed information to a central control panel connected to the security company's monitoring office.

He used the cell phone Scrounger *procured*, to call Castle Security. He identified himself with his password and asked if they were notified of an alarm on his system last night. "Yes, sir, we got one about 3 a.m. this morning. Did you check your answering machine?"

Arriving home earlier, Alex noticed the message light blinking on the machine, played the one from Sergeant Pickens and then began looking for Caesar. He assumed it was the only one. Now he looked more closely, and saw that two messages were recorded. He punched the Play button and heard the message from Castle Security, the first one on the tape, as he listened to the security officer on the line. "We had a signal from your home and called to verify. We didn't get an answer, so we dispatched one of our cars. Our officer arrived and did a complete perimeter check of the premises. He was not able to detect any activity inside or any apparent attempt to enter. He made several trips around the block keeping an eye open for any lights inside. We figured somehow your cat set off the alarm. I know the sensors are set high enough to preclude false alarms, but sometimes things happen. I hope everything is all right, Colonel Hilliard."

Alex thanked the security representative. *I've got to get a couple of hours sleep before my big outing for lunch in George-town. Sometime today, I need to give Sam Cooke a buzz.*

12:30 P.M., NOVEMBER 13th, ALEXANDRIA, VIRGINIA ⬟

Alex was up and ready to leave for the appointment the false message from Sergeant Pickens appeared to set up. He backed his car out of the garage and headed north. He decided to drive a short distance and then take the Washington Metro the rest of the way. He would catch the subway at Crystal City. The amount of parking space there was reasonable. The prices they charged for parking were far from reasonable. Alex saw the black sedan enter the parking lot three cars behind him. *I think I've got the tail I want.*

He deliberately parked toward the rear of the lot and started toward the Metro station. He saw the black sedan pull into an open spot three rows nearer the Metro. He was halfway to the station when he made a motion with his hand and snapped his fingers as if to say, "I've forgotten something." With a disgusted look on his face, he wheeled around and started back toward his car. There was the driver of the black sedan, twenty paces away and walking directly toward him. *Gotcha. If you do anything except walk straight ahead, you'll stand out like a sore thumb. If you keep on walking, I get a good look at you. Not too tall, must be 'bout four to five inches shorter than me. Makes you about five-eight...five-nine, Black, muscular build, maybe as much as 170 pounds. The jacket doesn't fit the bulk very well—you need a better tailor, friend. No other significant details—at least no permanent ones. The bandage on your left hand really does stick out like a sore thumb.* Alex smiled at his own pun. *I'll know you next time, Mister One. Since you're the first one I've seen up close and personal you get that handle.*

The man continued walking straight ahead. Alex took his time, then concentrated on fumbling in his pocket for his keys. He retrieved the morning paper he deliberately left behind and headed for the Metro again.

* * *

This guy is good—I don't see him. Bet he pops up when the train comes. He caught a glimpse of Mister One from the corner of his eye as he boarded the northbound train. Mister One slipped into the car behind the one Alex entered and took the seat nearest Alex's car. He pretended to be reading a paper, but was more interested in Alex. Alex didn't bother with his paper and spent his time gawking in all directions. He glanced at the overhead advertising and did some peo-ple-watching, but every few seconds he turned his attention toward the car to the rear. Several times he caught Mister One peering back.

The subway train crossed under the Potomac River and lurched a bit as it swung to the right to head eastbound in the tunnel. Alex stood as they approached the Foggy Bottom station. He smiled as he caught sight of Mister One making his way toward an exit.

Alex was headed for a restaurant on the north side of the George Washington University campus. It was a popular watering hole for both graduate students and many of the Pentagon denizens who could afford a long lunch hour. A few blocks and a short time later, Alex was seated at a table toward the back of the *Chez François*. It didn't hurt that François, the owner and maître-d' of the restaurant had a brother who owned the garage that did all the work on Alex's car. Since Alex patronized both brothers, his standing with each was enhanced. As they reached the table, Alex whispered to François, "Good thing you're quick with the table. If not I'll start calling you by your real name, Frankie."

"Mais oui, monsieur." He leaned close to Alex and dropping the French accent said, "If you do, you'll never get another table here." With a wink, he said, "Anything you need, Alex?"

"As a matter of fact, there is. Don't look at him, but there's a Black guy, the one at the end of the bar waiting for a table. Make him wait at least fifteen minutes for a table and then delay his order for another fifteen minutes. I don't want him to enjoy a meal, so I'll leave in a hurry. He'll be leaving right behind me."

Alex's meal was served well before Mister One was even seated. He nodded greetings and spoke to several people he recognized at adjacent tables. Mister One kept a sharp eye on him, looking for any approach that could indicate a message being passed. Since no one did, Mister One concentrated on the waiter every time he approached Alex's table. Finally the meal Mister One ordered arrived and Alex thought, *now it's time to give you some indigestion my friend.*

Leaving enough money on the table to cover his luncheon bill, a good tip and the damage he was about to create, Alex tensed his body. He waited for the situation he wanted. Mister One was just putting the third bite of his meal into his mouth when Alex found his opportunity. A group of about eight military officers entered the restaurant. Alex stood up and as he did, his hand brushed the nearly full glass of wine standing on the table. It flew across the table, the wine spreading as a dark red stain on the white tablecloth and splattering onto the opposite chair. Alex muttered an audible curse at himself and headed toward the exit. On the way to the door, he pushed through the group waiting for a table.

He made sure he brushed close to several in the crowd. *That ought to give you food for thought Mister One. Try to figure out if one of these guys is the one I'm supposed to meet.*

Alex left the restaurant—he saw Mister One digging through a wad of bills as he tried to pay his lunch tab. Alex blended into the sidewalk traffic and strolled back toward the Metro station. *Well, it didn't take you too long to catch up. Now I'll lose you at the Pentagon.* He figured there were enough entrances to the building he could leave without the tail following him. He planned to catch a taxi back to the parking lot in Crystal City.

Alex left the subway station, displayed his security badge and entered the Pentagon. He stopped inside near an information kiosk, which gave him a clear view of the guard station he passed through. *Damnation. That son-of-a-bitch has security access to the building.* Alex spun around and started toward up the escalator toward the J.O.C. *I know he doesn't have access there.*

* * *

Two hours later, Alex departed the J.O.C. through the normal entry point. Mister One was nowhere in sight. *Might as well grab the subway back to Crystal City.* He spotted Mister One browsing at the newsstand. Alex stood near the edge of the platform on the southbound side of the waiting area. He could hear his train approaching from the north and moved closer to the yellow warning line at the platform's edge. Mister One dropped the magazine he was leafing through and also moved toward the same yellow stripe. He was about three car lengths north of Alex's position. Alex could also see that a train from the south was nearing the station. *Maybe I can sucker Mister One onto the southbound and then grab a northbound. That should torque his jaws.*

Alex waited until the last minute, and as the doors of the southbound train were closing, he stepped into the waiting car. Mister One waited for Alex to make his move before boarding. At the last second, he ducked between the closing doors and looked to his left in time to see Alex jump back onto the platform. Trapped on the southbound train, he watched Alex moving toward the other train. Alex glanced back and smiled inwardly as he saw Mister One pass by.

The northbound train stopped at the next station and Alex got off. He emerged into the sunlight, and hailed a cab, which dropped him back at the Crystal City station. Walking to the parking lot, Alex was certain he would spot Mister One. He did. *Plenty of free time to have met with "Alpha," Mister One. You'll have to wonder who and where.*

* * *

The first thing Alex did after arriving home and setting the security system was to use his cell phone to call Dr. Frasier's office. The vet assured Alex Caesar was going to be fine. He also told him he was certain someone kicked the cat in the side and he was also just as sure Caesar retaliated. "Alex, that cat of yours gave somebody fits. Caesar does have a claw missing on the right front paw. We both saw the blood, but since then, he let me check his claws and there is definitely one missing. My hunch is that he left it in someone's clothing or their flesh. Personally, I'm hoping for the flesh. I can't abide buttheads who abuse animals."

"I'm with you, Doc. When do you think I'll be able to pick him up?"

"Give me another day to keep an eye on him. Day after tomorrow'll be fine—anytime you can make it. If it's going to be after office hours, just give us a call and we'll make arrangements. Oh. By the way, that blood I said was on

Caesar's paw…wasn't all Caesar's. Some of it was human… that's why I'm certain about an abusive son-of-a-bitch."

"Doc, keep a sample of the blood on ice. I'll have a friend of mine stop by and pick it up for analysis."

"I could run some basic blood tests right here, Alex."

"I appreciate the offer, but this guy has some high-powered connections and access to labs that would make us all jealous."

"Hope you can trace the bastard who did it, but who's going to expend that sort of effort over a cat? I didn't know you had that kind of clout."

"Doc, let's just leave it at this—the guy is a real cat lover. Someday I'll share the story with you over a beer."

* * *

Alex walked to a small strip mall about three blocks from his home and used a public phone. Moving down his list of numbers and several quarters later, he reached Sam Cooke. "Sam, I need a couple of favors."

"You got 'em. How can I help?"

"I'd like you to come by and figure out how someone broke into my house. Somehow they bypassed the entry point sensors. One of the interior monitors picked them up and sent a warning to my security company. Oh, also on the way over, could you pick up a blood sample at my vet's office? If you can, I'll let them know what time you can make it. How's your schedule for tonight?"

"This sure blows the game I was going to watch on TV, but 'break-in' and 'blood' got my full attention. I assume the vet's in your area, so I could be there around…five-fifteen."

The two exchanged directions and times and hung up. Alex used his last quarter to make arrangements with Dr.

Frasier's office for Sam's stop. His growling stomach reminded him of supper. He told himself it was going to be a long evening. He stopped at a nearby deli for take-out.

🏛 4:30 P.M., NOVEMBER 13th, THE WHITE HOUSE

General Osborn made his way to Colonel Richard's office and directed the man to leave his office. Chapman called earlier to set a time to report on the previous night's events. Osborn sat drumming his fingers in Richards' office waiting for Batman's arrival.

Brocklin and Chapman were ushered into Richard's office. When the door closed, Osborn said, "What the hell are you both doing here? We asked for Batman to come in."

Without being invited, Chapman dropped into a chair next to the desk and began his report. "Huh? Shit, I can't get used to them nicknames you're usin' for us. I jus' figgured it'd be good if my buddy came along as well. Well, anyways, everything went fine at General Watkins' place. He believed me when I told him you sent me."

"Why in the hell did you tell him that? You might have compromised me."

Chapman's smirk showed most of his teeth. "Why the hell not? He was going to be dead in a few minutes. Well anyways, I got him talkin' 'bout guns and he pulls out this big old service pistol of his and unloads it. 'Good,' I think. 'Now I'm sure his prints are all over the thing.' Well, I ask him for a drink and while his back is turned, I slip on gloves, reload the piece, take off one glove and put the gun behind my back...you know...keepin' it in the hand that still has a glove on. Then the only thing I have to clean later on is the glass. Man, it was jus' like that scene from that movie...ah, oh, yeah—*Three Days of the Condor*, d'ya ever see it? Well,

anyways, he hands me a glass of whiskey and sits down behind his desk. Gawd, that sure was a big desk—"

"Damn it, Chapman, I don't need every last detail. Are you
sure it will hold up as a suicide and that you didn't leave any
incriminating evidence behind?"

"If ya d'in interrupt so much General, you'd get the full
story. Yes, I'm damn sure 'bout how it will look and double
damn sure I didn't leave any fingerprints or nothin' else.
Now let's get to the second chore you had for me—that Air
Force guy, Hilliard. I decided not to waste him last night.
Good thing, too, 'cause early this mornin' we picked up a
call goin' to his place from some guy called 'Alpha.' You
know, they been usin' them Greek letters for names. We
ain't never heard of this 'Alpha' before. Anyways, I decided
to see if I could find out more before I did Hilliard."

Brocklin broke in and related the details of the message
on Alex's answering machine and his attempt to tail Alex to
the meeting. He also outlined his break-in of Alex's home.
"That's where I got this." Brocklin said, displaying his ban-
daged left hand. "Hilliard has a big damn cat that took a
dislike to me. Could be he was pissed off because I gave him
a swift kick."

"That doesn't seem very bright to confront an animal. Did
it attack before or after you kicked it?"

"Damn thing came after me right after I booted him. Hit
me on the leg with his feet and chomped down on my hand.
Anyway, after that I tried to kick him again and he took off."

The general leaned back in his leather chair. "Well, beyond
that, it sounds to me like Hilliard saw you on his tail and
pulled the stunt at the subway station."

"Naw. Don't think so. I'm pretty good at this. That's a trick
anyone might use just to try to shake a tail if there is one. I
don't think he saw me or knows about me."

"If you're so damn good at tailing people, why don't you know who Alpha is?"

* * *

"Sometimes ya just gotta let the subject go 'cause ya don't wanna 'tract no attention." Brocklin covered his anger—he knew he'd blown the tail, but he wasn't about to admit it to this overblown flunky of the president. Handing a double sealed envelope to Osborn he added, "This is our handwritten reports. Can you get it to President Bancroft?"

Osborn took the envelope and left Colonel Richards' office. He headed toward the Oval Office leaving the two agents on their own to find a way out.

5:30 P.M., NOVEMBER 13th, ALEXANDRIA, VIRGINIA ⬠

Alex welcomed Sam Cooke to his home. Sam was carrying a small thermal cooler containing the blood sample he retrieved from Dr. Frasier's office. He also carried a large catalog case in the other hand though he made no mention of its contents. Sam switched the stereo on and increased the volume to an unbearable level. Alex outlined the events of the day and his encounter with Mister One. He also explained the meeting he needed to attend, and briefed Sam on the apparent break-in. Alex gave Sam the current security codes and phone password to use with the security company.

"Not a real good idea, Alex—giving away your security codes."

"Sam, Mike reminded me I could trust you. I remember back then—it's all I need to know."

"I appreciate the confidence in me, Alex. Nevertheless, change the codes tonight and change the password as soon as possible."

Alex nodded in agreement. He told Sam about Caesar's condition and his suspicions about what happened while the intruder was in the house.

"By the time you get back, I'll have a good idea of how the break-in was accomplished. Hopefully Caesar created enough of a diversion there may even be a clue as to who it was." Even with the stereo blaring, Sam put a forefinger to his lips and patted the catalog case he arrived with. Sam scratched out a note that read, "I'll do a sweep of the place and check for bugs."

Twenty minutes after Sam's arrival, Alex was on his way to the meeting with his team leaders.

7:00 P.M., NOVEMBER 13th, ROSCOE'S TAVERN ⬟

Alex allowed forty minutes for his drive to Roscoe's, which gave him ample time to double back looking for a tail. Now, aware of the opposition's profound interest in him, he was far more cautious than the last time he headed for this location. He was the second of the group to arrive and took a seat at a back table with Sergeant Tufts. Just like the last time, the country and Western music was loud enough to cover their discussions. Spaced out over the next twenty minutes, the other three arrived and made their way to the table.

Chief Eaton was the final one to take a seat. He said, "Glad you all arrived at the time I scheduled for you. Begging your pardon, Beta, I didn't give you a time like I did for the rest. I've been keeping an eye on the front of this place from a second story window in a cheap hotel across the street." He grinned. "It's a warm-sheet place, so the desk guy didn't look twice when I said I only needed the room for a few hours."

"Master Chief," Sergeant Pickens said. "If you was usin' that room with a warm-sheet pro, d'ya really has the stayin' power for that long?"

Now everyone at the table was laughing.

It took all the control Alex could muster to wipe the smile from his face. "Okay, back to business, folks."

Alex briefed the group on the details of his meeting with President-elect Ahern. He gave them the names and as much of a bio as he could on each of the players at the president-elect's Compound. "I don't want to hear names, but give me a run down on your recruiting efforts," he said to the group.

Each man at the table reported, and it appeared the teams were at about eighty percent of the planned numbers. He asked each to forecast a date when their team would be at full strength. The replies made him smile. "Looks like we'll be there in plenty of time. Within the next week, I want each of you to run a weapons drill with your teams. Assess their capabilities to the point you're comfortable with each one. If you have any doubts, the team member is out. No questions asked—Out. Be sure each one knows the difference between 'doing it right' and 'doing the right thing.' I want to make it clear that I'd prefer to have someone who is a bit slow to fire and hits the correct target than someone who needs less time to hit the wrong one. Damn, I wish we could all hit the FBI's tactical course."

"Me too, Beta. I know with your contacts you could probably get us on the course, but wouldn't that attract a lotta' attention to us?" said Sergeant Pickens.

"You've got that right, Delta. We'll just have to use an out-of-the-way spot for this effort. Can't even use a regular qualification range. The wide range of weapons alone would draw too much attention." Alex turned to Sergeant Tufts.

"Sigma, it's up you. Find us a safe location where we can fire weapons and not attract attention. Get the word to everyone in the next two days."

Sergeant Tufts nodded.

Alex continued. "Sigma, I want one full extra set of team weapons. I'm going to pre-position them inside the Pentagon. Will that leave us short on the outside?"

There were several faces at the table that reflected surprise. Sergeant Tufts shook his head. "No sweat, sir. I'll get with my people and lay on the spares. Do you need any help getting' 'em into the building?"

"No thanks, I think I can get the job done…and in case of a problem I'd rather have just one of us involved." Almost as an afterthought, Alex asked the group if General Watkins' suicide seemed out of place. They agreed it did, but could not point to anything specific. Alex closed the meeting. "Like the old Sarge on *Hill Street Blues* used to say, 'Let's be careful out there.'"

* * *

Chief Eaton took charge and said, "I'll take point. Give me ten minutes to get back to my room across the street." Everyone chuckled again and Eaton's face turned red. "Okay, okay…" the Chief said, "I'll track each of you as you leave." Then looking at Sergeant Tucker he added, "Theta, you give us back-trail cover and leave last. Be sure no one in here has an interest is us. Beta, I'll brief you in the morning, when we're on watch."

* * *

Thirty minutes later Chief Eaton left the hotel room. He was satisfied nobody in the immediate vicinity was watching or following any of the group. He left the hotel by a back door and used an alley to approach the street running between the hotel and Roscoe's. He spent another ten minutes lounging against the building and fending off propositions from several ladies in short-shorts and fishnet hose. He forced himself to use a slow walk in the opposite direction from where he parked. After five minutes, he reversed his course and picked up his pace as he headed toward his car. He drove off, feeling comfortable no one showed undue interest in any of the group. He reminded himself to check with Sergeant Tucker as soon as possible. *It might be a good idea to have all of our vehicles checked for bugs and homing devices. I'll clear it with the Colonel in the morning.*

9:00 P.M., NOVEMBER 13th, ALEXANDRIA, VIRGINIA ⬠

As soon as Alex arrived home, Sam briefed him on his findings. There were no bugs or listening devices in the townhouse. There was a tap on the phone, but it could not monitor conversations inside the house. The break-in artist defeated the entry point sensor on the ground floor French doors. "This type of door is tough to defend, Alex. Here's an item that'll help." He handed some keys to Alex and pointed to the handcuff like device he had attached to the side-by-side doorknobs of the wooden doors. "This doesn't stop them from bypassing the sensor again, but when they do, it's tough to enter via the doors. I think I located the spot where the person ran into Caesar and what looks like blood—he gestured toward the hallway. My guess—Caesar was blocking the hall, and the guy wanted to check upstairs. He probably kicked Caesar and the cat launched an attack. There were quite a few stains on the hall carpet and the wall that supports the stairway. I have samples of the blood tucked away in the ice chest for comparison along with that other sample. From the spatter pattern, I'd say he was leaking like a stuck pig. I wouldn't be surprised if he had to put a good size bandage on the wound."

"Son-of-a-bitch. I know who broke in." Alex related the story of the man who tailed him to Georgetown earlier in the day and the nickname he gave the man.. "Sam, this guy was good—credentials allowing him into the Pentagon. Any chance he's one of your guys?"

"I doubt that he's currently with the Company. But there are any number of 'ex' operatives who aren't completely out of the business. Give me a detailed description of Mister One and anyone else you think he might be associated with."

Alex described Mister One. He also provided what details he could about the other man he and Sarah saw in the black Ford. They designated this one as Mister Two. The description was far more vague since Alex only saw the second man sitting in a car.

"One more thing, Alex, there are a lot of rumors about Mike floating around the Agency."

"What sort of rumors?"

"Well, it looks like someone is out to make Mike the bad guy. That he might have been off on some personal or non-Company business when he died. If that happens, his wife would lose a bunch of benefits under his pension."

"That's a crock of crap. What can we do about it, Sam?"

"Not much for now. We need to keep our ears open and be sure we can put Mike in a good light by the time this thing's over."

Sam and Alex relaxed over a beer and enjoyed an hour together. They covered a sweeping range of topics from recent movies to past assignments and better days. Sam glanced at his watch and rose. "I'd better get going. I've got an early get-up tomorrow. Thanks for the beer, Alex."

"You're welcome, Sam. I'd like to do this again, especially when this crap calms down and there's less pressure."

"I'll look forward to it."

They shook hands and Alex showed Sam out. As he closed the front door he was thinking, *Mike, sure hope I can trust this guy as much as I trusted you.*

NOVEMBER 14th, THE PENTAGON

Alex and Chief Eaton arrived at the River Entrance guard post within a minute of each other. They completed the security check and passed the General Officer/Flag Officer's lounge on E Ring. They turned down the corridor that would lead them to D Ring, the second internal corridor, and the one which led to the Joint Operations Center. "Colonel, just how do you plan to get those items we spoke about through that security check?"

"Wait till we're inside and I'll give you a run down." Alex punched the security code into the door lock and glanced up at the TV camera lens that stared down at him.

They went through the changeover process and settled into their positions at the watch console. Being a weekend, it promised to be a quiet day. This would be a good time to further explore and prepare the hiding place for the weapons.

Alex made a sweep of all the spaces in the J.O.C. to verify they were alone. He returned to his seat in front of the panel of phone buttons and began explaining his plan for the weapons. "First, I need to be sure that Earl is the guard on duty. He's generally thorough, but I've found I can distract him. I've already made some test runs. I'm using the briefcase Mike Reilly left for me—the one with the false bottom. I've already run some metal tools in it with no problems. Most of the weapons will fit that hidden compartment. Some will have to be field stripped to fit."

"That sniper rifle sure won't fit, Colonel. You got any plans for that one?"

"I'll have to admit, I'm stumped about the rifle. I'm not sure we need that particular weapon in here, but I'd like to have it just in case. How about it, Duke? Got any ideas how I waltz that one past the guard?"

Chief Eaton snapped his fingers, whipped his head around and said, "You don't waltz it in, you hobble it by the guard."

"What do you mean hobble?"

"You put on a fake cast and use metal crutches. It may take a couple of trips, but you can strap the barrel to your leg. Even if the metal detector goes off, you can blame the crutches. You can con the guard that far, can't you?"

"I think you've got it. I really think I could make that work."

"Colonel, once you get the weapons inside this place, where are you gonna stash 'em?"

"A while back, a friend and I stumbled onto what has to be a construction error. It's not only a secret cache, but it also affords access to the NMCC without passing their internal security post."

"Who else knows about that NMCC access?" Duke said.

"As far as I know, at this point I'm the only one. The friend I mentioned was Mike Reilly." Alex gave Chief Eaton directions to the storage room. "Check the layout but don't go through the second access door you come to. I'll cover the phones till you get back."

* * *

Duke was only gone for fifteen minutes. During that time, Alex sketched a floor plan to help him describe the details to Chief Eaton.

"Wow, you didn't mention how low the overhead is in that passageway," Duke said as he returned.

"That's why I called it a crawl space and not a passageway." Alex winked and continued, "When will you Navy guys learn some shore lingo and realize you're not aboard ship?"

Alex removed a hand drawn diagram from a shirt pocket, placed it on the console so Duke could see it, and described how the NMCC access could be accomplished.

Apparently, the restroom used to be larger. That crawlway was built with an access door or panel at both ends. Far as I can tell, it's a pretty typical area for getting to the plumbing in a restroom. When they pushed the wall in the NMCC back to make room for the expanded Cab, they left the hallway that runs between the Cab and the restroom."

"Does that put the doorway from that hall, inside or outside the security entrance to the NMCC?" the Chief said. "It's inside the NMCC security door, so it didn't cause any security problems. That hall leads to a back door in the Cab. I've seen a couple of Senior Watch Officers use it. I asked their deputies, and they described it. They weren't allowed to use the hall entrance themselves—only General and Flag officers. One of those unwritten rules I suppose."

Alex shifted in his high-backed chair. "Back to the remodeling. The end of the restroom area, past that second access panel where I asked you to stop, was dedicated to storage. For whatever reason, the storage area that runs from the D Ring corridor toward the NMCC stops about six feet short of that hallway running between the Cab and the restroom. I think that six feet was supposed to become part of the storeroom, but the wall wasn't removed and now it's just dead space."

"Sure seems like someone missed the boat, Colonel."

"You're right, Master Chief. My guess is some construction boss was in a hurry, or he was behind schedule and took short-cuts. I doubt even the building engineers are aware of the screw up. There are really two ways to get into that dead space. If you'd gone through the second access panel, you'd have been there. The other way in is from the hall behind the NMCC Cab. Inside that dead space, there's a piece of plywood held to the wall by four screws. The plywood covers a three by four foot wire mesh grill. It's probably a forgotten air return to the air-conditioning system from years ago. The grill's secured by six bolts. Get past the plywood and the grill and you're in the hallway. To your left, is the door that leads to the primary NMCC entrance hall inside the guard post. If you go right, down the hall there's a left hand turn before you reach the back door to the Cab."

"Sir, a couple more questions come to mind. Do you really think we'll need to access the NMCC? And if we need to, can we be sure all those fasteners you described aren't permanently frozen? Sounds like they've been there for a long time."

"To answer the first one—yes I think we'll need to get in there. Remember the presidential briefings we talked about? The ones giving our opponents opportunity? They include briefings in the NMCC. I plan to get with Luke Cutter and set a schedule which leaves the NMCC as the only opportunity. That way, we have a lot less ground to cover. I was thinking about your second question too. I've brought a can of rust solvent in my briefcase. I'd planned to start soaking them with it tonight. In a few days, we'll test 'em and I'll leave any tools we need to remove them in the dead space along with the weapons. Oh, that reminds me—do we have penlights on our Table of Distribution and Allowances? We'll need 'em—the dead space doesn't have lighting."

Chief Eaton pulled several small pieces of plastic film from his wallet. "Here's the T-D and A," he said dropping one of them on their overhead projector and flipping the lamp on. Alex saw "Flashlight, Penlight, Halogen - 1 per team member

+ Beta" on the list of equipment on the screen. "It's there boss. Do you want a rundown on the rest of the equipment?"

"No thanks, but leave it up there for a couple of minutes and let me make sure I'm familiar with it. This is the first time I've seen the completed list. Looks like you and Tufts did a great job. How'd you come up with the film idea?"

"Got the whole Op Plan reduced to these film strips. In a pinch, I can use a flashlight and a blank wall to read 'em. Just figured it was a good way to carry the list too."

Alex read each item on the list. He stopped after each entry to commit as much as possible to memory.

WEAPONS AND EQUIPMENT

Operations Plan - Page D – 3   Annex D - Logistics

Table of Distribution and Allowances (T D & A)

Description	Quantity (Assigned to... Team Member #)	Ammunition per Weapon
Auto Pistol, Glock 19, 9mm, 15 round magazine, 2 spare magazines	1 per team member + Beta	45 rounds
Auto Pistol, Walther TPH, .22 caliber Long Rifle, 6 round magazine, 2 spare magazines, with AWC sound suppresser	1 per team + Beta (Team Lead)	18 rounds
Auto Pistol, Calico M950, 9mm, 50 round magazine, with spare magazine and Shurfire 2581 laser aiming device	1 per team (Number 2)	100 rounds
Shotgun, Mossburg Persuader 500, 12-gauge, pistol grip, 6 round magazine	1 per team (Number 3)	18 rounds
Holster, Shoulder, Galco "Miami Classic" for 9mm Glock or 9mm Beretta	1 per weapon	
Holster, Waist, Guardian "Belly Band" for .22 caliber Walther	1 per weapon	
Rifle, Sniper, McMillian M89, .308 caliber, 5 shot magazine with scope, Leupold Vari III, 3.5-10, STD Police	1 per team (Number 4)	15 rounds
Flashlight, Penlight, Halogen	1 per team member + Beta	
Rope, Nylon, 1/4", 50 feet	1 per team	
Name Badge, Bright Yellow (Team ID)	1 per team member + Beta	
Widgets	1 per Beta, Gamma, Delta	
Voice Modifier	1 per team Leader	
Radio Communication, headset/mike for hands-free communications	1 per team member + Beta	
Radio, Miniature, 4 frequency	1 per team + Beta	
Cell phone	1 per team + Beta	
Tape, Duct, 3" by 100'	1 per team	
Lantern, Battery Powered	1 per team	
Kit, First Aid, Combat	1 per team	
Grenade, Smoke - Precision Ordinance M359	2 per team	
Distraction Device - Def-Tec AA1, "Big Bang"	2 per team	

* * *

When he finished reading, he nodded to Chief Eaton. The Chief retrieved the plastic film and replaced it in his wallet.

"Duke, get with Tucker and have him prepare fake stand-down messages," Alex said. "Better have transmission tapes set up ahead of time. May need to get 'em out to the TW units in a hurry."

"Aye, sir."

"Duke, also check the schedule for the next few days. We need a night shift when one of our team leaders is on watch. Also needs to be a night when you and I are free. We'll make a trial run through the restroom into the hallway behind the NMCC."

🏛 NOVEMBER 28th, THE WHITE HOUSE

General Osborn put out the word he wanted to speak to Corbett Chapman. An hour later, the red phone on his desk rang. He answered to find Chapman at the other end. "How the hell do you have access to this secure line?" he said.

"I still got some connections, General. What did you want to talk about?"

"My sources tell me we still have a problem with that J.O.C. Watch Officer, Hilliard. He's been sticking his nose in where it doesn't belong. The old man wants the problem resolved for good. And he wants it to happen—now."

"I'm up to my ass in alligators, General. I'll put Dickie Brocklin on it. He's been coverin' the phone taps, but he can check the tapes later I 'spose. 'Course, we'll miss any real time intercepts if somethin' important comes over the wire. Wait a minute...no sweat, General. I got a third-party I can get to do Hilliard."

"I won't tell you how to do your business, but *the man* wants something to happen A.S.A.P."

NOVEMBER 16th THROUGH NOVEMBER 30th, THE PENTAGON ⬠

On the last day of the month the schedule put Alex, Chief Eaton and Sergeant Pickens together at shift change. They brought one another up to speed.

The last two weeks of November was a busy time. The team leaders were briefed about the crawl space and Alex directed each to check out the area on their own. During their visits, they continued liberal applications of solvent on the fasteners. Chief Eaton and Alex made a dry run through the crawlway and into the dead space. They removed the plywood and the wire grill—poked their heads into the hallway—then jerked back and replaced both the access coverings. The rust solvent did its job, but the number of fasteners they needed to remove took an excessive amount of time. Alex gave the project to Pickens. "Get with Tufts and come up with some quick release devices to replace the screws and bolts. No one will see the screws in the dead space, but the replacements on the grill will have to be camouflaged on the hallway side."

Sarah, with the assistance of Mildred Harper, obtained photos of nearly all the opposition players. They both cashed favors-due with people they knew in the personnel offices of the military services. Mildred just winked when Sarah asked her about pictures of the CIA participants. They were unable to find a photograph of Mister One or Mister Two. Alex turned over what they accumulated to Duke who made sure the teams received copies of the pictures.

Alex briefed Sergeant Pickens and Chief Eaton on his contacts with Luke Cutter. It was a tough sell to President-elect Ahern, but Luke convinced the president-elect not to attend all the briefings on four different days. Ahern's schedule would include only one visit to the NMCC, and would be on the fourth night. Luke also cautioned Alex, "We've been picking up some digitized phone signals emanating from the Compound. They're not landlines, so there's a special phone in the area that transmits an encrypted signal—and it doesn't belong to any of my people. I think we have a leak inside the Compound."

* * *

During this period, Alex took the opportunity to fire all the team weapons with Sergeant Pickens. Sergeant Tufts and Pickens arranged to use a remote part of a nearby military base. "This place is costing big bucks in favors-due," he said to Alex as they arrived at a secluded glen with a natural backstop.

Alex fired the three handguns. He selected the 9mm Glock, the Beretta Mike left for him, and finally the .22 caliber pistol with the sound suppressor. "That silencer does a pretty good job," he said

As Alex put the .22 down, Hillbilly said, "Did ya notice, most of the noise came from the slide slammin' back and then loading the next round into the chamber? To make it more quiet—put your thumb on the back of the slide to stop the rearward motion. It's real quiet that way—only thing you got to remember is there's no fresh round in the chamber if you need a second shot."

Alex followed the instructions as he fired the weapon once more. *Phfft*. "Damn—real quiet," he said as he turned his attention to the remaining guns.

Next he fired the Mossburg 12-gauge. The two rounds he put through this pump shotgun cut one of the fifteen-yard silhouette targets in half. He pressed three rounds into the magazine of the sniper rifle and methodically put all three shots into a five-inch group on a target seventy-five yards away. As he reached for the Calico, Hillbilly said,

"Damn fine shooting, Colonel. You ever gone full auto with a weapon?" When Alex shook his head, Sergeant Pickens continued. "We'll build up to it. See the switch on the side of the receiver? Full back is single fire, the center position gives you a three-round burst and the forward position is for full rock and roll. Let's start with single fire."

Alex checked the selector switch and fired five times. He put all five rounds into the "vital" area of the twenty-five yard target. He moved the selector switch to the center position and switched to a fifteen-yard target. The five, three-round bursts he fired were again within the "vital" area. "That's twenty rounds. How many left?"

"No sweat, Colonel, there's plenty. That funny looking magazine on top holds fifty rounds. If I counted right, you got thirty of 'em left 'cause I put a full load in her. Go to full auto on the switch. She don't rise much as she fires, so you don't need to start low. Don't grip too tight with your left hand—just let her rest there. She'll bounce a little but if you don't hold her tight, she won't climb on you. Don't worry about your aim. Press that small button above the selector switch and just put the red dot from the laser sight on what you want to hit. Thirty rounds only leaves you about three seconds of fire on full automatic. Try to get four bursts out of what's left."

Alex managed to stretch the remaining load to four bursts, however the final one was only two rounds. He was also pleased with the grouping of the shots. They were not as tight as his previous efforts, but they would have taken down the opposition without endangering nearby friendlies.

Pickens and Alex returned to the van they were using, and Alex reached for the cleaning supplies.

"I can take care of that cleanin' later on, Colonel," Hillbilly said.

"I want to be sure I can field strip each one of these. Besides, as I recall, it's damn poor shooter's etiquette to let someone else clean guns you've fired, isn't it?"

Hillbilly nodded and they both picked up a ramrod, solvent and cleaning patches.

* * *

Also during these two weeks, Alex began the trips that would place a full set of weapons inside the Pentagon. He coordinated his trips to match the schedule of one particular guard. Earl was thorough enough, but he trusted those with authority and a security badge a bit too much. Long before this need arose, Alex developed a genuine fondness for Earl. Since he generally reported early for his work schedule, Alex often used some of that extra time talking to Earl and the other guards. It was during those times that Alex noted Earl's attention to detail sometimes drifted.

Several gunrunning trips went smoothly. Then one night Alex's heart leaped into his throat. He dropped his briefcase on the counter as usual and started to move through the airport style metal detector. Earl's general routine was to wait for the party to clear the metal detector before checking carried items. Tonight he reached for the briefcase nearly as soon as Alex placed it on the counter.

Alex cleared the metal detector in record time and reached back for his briefcase. He didn't think Earl would discover the weapons in the lower compartment, but the extra weight of two weapons might alert him. Alex opened the latches and flipped the lid up saying, "Want to check my egg salad sandwich, Earl?" He slid the case down the counter toward the guard.

"Nah, I don't much like egg salad." Earl smiled as he looked down into the briefcase and stepped back without even touching it.

The only weapon remaining was the sniper rifle and now it was time to test the crutch ploy. Alex planned two trips for the rifle after a dry run. The first trip went well and Alex felt secure enough to press on. For the first real trip, he taped part of the rifle to his leg and padded it to simulate a cast. He discussed his "clutzy accident" with Earl and told him the doctors said the severe sprain meant he would only be on the crutches for about a week. He feigned surprise when the metal detector squawked at his passage. Earl volunteered an answer. "Must be them metal crutches, Colonel. Just step on through and I'll run the hand detector over you."

Anticipating this problem, Alex brought the rifle stock in on the trip. It was constructed with minimal metal parts and shouldn't set off any of the scanners. His second trip would have to be a bluff, since there was no way the hand scanner would miss a rifle barrel strapped to his leg. For that excursion, he would make sure it was a slack time with virtually no one around. He planned to play on Earl's sympathetic nature and didn't want any witnesses to Earl's relaxed measures.

On his final trip, carrying the rifle barrel, Alex deliberately limped and grimaced as he approached the guard post. "Man, oh man. This damn ankle is killin' me tonight." Alex wasn't carrying his briefcase, so he headed directly for the metal detector. He again appeared surprised as the machine balked at his passage. Now it was bluff time.

As Earl reached for the hand scanner, Alex screwed up his face feigning pain and held his breath. If Earl came around the counter with the hand device, he would hobble back through the large detector and mutter about forgetting his briefcase—and leave the building. It might give the security guard suspicions, but it would be the best of a bad situation. The good news was that he could get away undetected. The bad news would be—the important part of the weapon would not be inside the Pentagon. For this reason, Alex left the rifle for these last two trips. If need be, they could probably get by without the sniper rifle.

Alex was still holding his breath. Earl looked left and right at empty halls. He turned back toward Alex and almost in a whisper said, "Aw, hell. Go ahead, Colonel. You look like you can't stand up much longer." Instead of running the hand scanner over Alex, Earl used it like a baton and waved Alex past the guard post.

Alex took a breath at last. *That puts a full set of weapons, ammunition, and gear in the dead space...and tomorrow's a brand new month and I've got a couple of days off.*

NOON, DECEMBER 1st, THE PRESIDENT-ELECT'S COMPOUND ⬠

Luke Cutter placed a call to Alex. There was an exchange of pleasantries about the "wrong number" Luke reached and both hung up. Less than twenty minutes later, Luke answered his phone and heard the telltale hum of the encryption device Alex was using. "Alex, I think we need a face-to-face. I've got so many questions—I guess I'm getting jumpy. For my peace of mind let's meet. How's your schedule for the next couple of days?"

"I'm reasonably free for today and tomorrow. How long would it take you to get up here to the District?"

"I can helo in to meet you. The flying time is about forty minutes. There are several places I can have the chopper put down in the District or even in Alexandria near you."

They confirmed the time and location. Luke asked one final question. "Alex, I know the weapons you're gathering. Have you got them yet?"

"Yeah, they're all in place. Why?"

"Have you considered carrying a handgun?"

"No, not really. I wasn't planning to carry anything till the final push."

"Buddy, my suggestion is to keep either the Glock or the Walther within reach. On you, if possible. I'll have a carry permit for you by the time we meet. That'll give you some protection if you're stopped by the local gendarmes."

"Okay, I'll think about it. See you tonight, Luke."

1:30 A.M., DECEMBER 2nd, ALEXANDRIA, VIRGINIA ⬟

The helicopter landed near Springfield, Virginia. Luke jumped to the ground and slipped into the right front seat of the government-issue sedan. The outward appearance of the car was nondescript. The interior was another story. It was equipped with extra weapons including the rocket launcher Alex imagined in the trailer at the Presidential Compound. It also seemed packed with passive and active electronic gear. Many of the black boxes, set to automatic mode, were continuously feeding their updates to the monitor panel between the two front seats.

Luke spoke to the driver, confirmed the destination, and added, "Bruce, better make it an indirect route. I don't want any strangers tagging along."

* * *

At the same time, Alex was cruising southbound along I-395. Even though the meeting place was barely ten minutes south of his home, he spent the better part of an hour driving. He began his trek heading south. He passed his destination, and continued south till he hit the I-495 loop. The ka-thunk, ka-thunk of the wiper blades acted as a metronome in sync with the music on the radio as they cleared the rain from his windshield. He crossed the Woodrow Wilson Bridge into

Maryland—cut north on I-295 and then took I-395 into the District. He completed a large circle and was now retracing his original route. He listened to the tires hissing on the concrete as he used all his tricks to identify anyone following him. One time he thought he spotted a tail, but the car took an exit ramp before it was close enough to identify a driver. He still felt uneasy, but chalked it up to Luke's warning earlier in the day. He cut the windshield wipers back to the Intermittent setting as the rain slackened to a light mist.

* * *

Luke and his driver were about eight minutes from their destination when a light on the computer monitor panel blinked. The men looked at the read-out and then at each other as the driver said, "I think your friend is in deep serious shit."

"If Alex is closing in on the destination, we can't get there in time." Luke grabbed the mike and broke the agreed upon radio silence.

* * *

Alex stopped three or four minutes ago. He parked near the appointed building in a deserted parking lot. He followed Luke's directions and his headlights and engine were off. Alex saw the car come around the corner of the building behind him with no headlights. *Did I get things confused? Thought Luke said he would come from the front.*

His eyes were riveted on the rearview mirror and he didn't notice the figure moving in the shadow of the building next to him.

The car stopped about twenty yards behind him and a large man got out and started toward his car. *This guy's too big to be Luke. Must be another one of his people.*

Alex pushed his door open, slid out of the car and moved toward the big guy. Big-guy was only ten yards away when he jerked his arm up, pointing toward Alex. Alex wasn't sure what was in Big-guy's hand, but his best guess was a gun.

The Shadow-man stepped away from the building and into the dim light of the scene. He shouted, "Federal Agent. Drop the gun."

Big-guy twisted his body toward the sound and pointed his arm at the newcomer. Shadow-man dropped to a crouched firing position and again demanded Big-guy drop his weapon.

Alex dove for the cover his car provided as Big-guy made his final turn. Big-guy whirled back toward Alex and two quick shots exploded in Alex's ears. He wasn't sure whether the pain he felt came from contact with the pavement or whether he'd been hit. Shadow-man was approaching Big-guy with his weapon trained on the prone figure. Without taking his eyes from the Big-guy, he shouted, "Alex, you all right?"

That isn't Luke either. Who the hell is this? Alex took stock of his condition and replied, "I'm okay, who—"

Tires screeching on the still damp concrete drowned out the rest of his words as another car hurtled into the middle of their drama. Luke and Bruce Compton were out of their car, weapons ready, and using the open car doors as shields. This second car's headlights illuminated the area long enough for Shadow-man to thoroughly check the Big-guy and to signal an all clear to Luke. They holstered their weapons and approached. Luke stopped near Alex while Compton continued toward the other two men.

"Luke, for crying out loud, will someone tell me what the hell's goin' on?"

* * *

"Come with me, Alex. I'll brief you, and then we can talk about the rest of our problems." Luke signaled with his headlights and an RV-type vehicle appeared. Luke, Shadow-man, and Luke's driver joined Alex in the RV. They began cruising the local streets. Luke and his other two agents huddled for several minutes. When they moved to the table where Alex sat, Luke began the conversation. "First, let me introduce Bruce Compton. He was with me when we arrived late."

Alex shook his hand, pulled back and said, "Hawkeye Two, right?"

"Damn good memory, Alex," Luke said. "You're right on, he was on the Comm console in the trailer the day you visited the Compound. Your benefactor here is Robert Greenburg. His radio tag is Hawkeye Six. Bruce and I couldn't make the scene in time, so I told Bob to intercede. By the way, he's been keeping an eye on you for the better part of a week. Gave him the job 'cause he's the best there is for a one-car rolling tail. Did you spot him?"

"Not really." Alex wiped his hand across the back of his neck. "Got a funny feeling, but I was never sure."

"What tipped us off was a homing signal we picked up from your car. The signal has a fairly short range. It was moving, so it meant it was on a vehicle. Figured the only one that could possibly fit that profile this time of night around here was you, Alex. And, we figured the odds were high that someone was on your tail. By then I knew I couldn't get to you in time, so I sent Bob in. He was left with no choice but to take the guy out. If he missed, the big son-of-a-bitch would have shot you."

"Damn it to hell. Chief Eaton put a team to work checking our houses and cars for bugs. They were planning to check my car tomorrow. Who was he?""Don't know yet.

My clean-up crew will sanitize the area and run down his identity. If we're lucky, we should have an ID before we finish here tonight."

"What made you think he was a threat to me?"

"I have a number of feelers out on the street. Also, your friend at CIA let me know about a couple of ex-agents who resurfaced a short time ago. He was doing a check based on the information you gave him. He also gave us an idea these two were looking for a third person. Apparently a rush job and they weren't very careful about covering their tracks. By the way, did you have a gun with you tonight?"

Alex lowered his eyes to the floor and said, "I have one with me, but I left it in the car when I first got out. I thought I screwed up the instructions and it was you pulling in behind me."

"Here's the carry permit I promised. I've just hired you and you're now an employee of the Secret Service. As long as you don't try to collect a salary from us, we shouldn't be accused of fraud. If no one looks at our arrangement too closely, this Federal permit should keep you reasonably clean in the District, Maryland, and Virginia. My friend, I suggest that you seriously consider keeping a pistol on you from now on."

For the next hour, as the RV traversed backstreets, Alex and Luke discussed possible future actions. Alex did his best to persuade Luke the most likely place for an attempt on the president-elect's life would be during the briefings in January. And the most likely location would be the NMCC.

"Why there?" Luke said.

"At the other venues, you have unlimited access for your presidential security team. I know from past history—for visits to the NMCC you'll be limited due to the cramped spaces. I've seen the current president in there without any

Secret Service people around. It's just assumed the place is safe. What if it isn't safe? What if that is the exact place an assassin plans to make the attempt? You're outside the NMCC with no way to intercede."

"I can't argue with your logic. I've been frustrated with Pentagon visits before. How can I provide protection without tipping our hand? We damn near need to catch the killer red-handed to make a case."

"Your team will be with President-elect Ahern up to the point he enters the NMCC. You'll have to trust me to cover the inside. If nothing else, we've limited his exposure to just one appearance at the NMCC, on the fourth day. Don't worry, I'll be armed for this one and I won't hesitate to use it. Besides, I've got some damn good people backing me."

"I know the president-elect trusts you, Alex. He said the general who introduced you told him that 'you've been there before.' That's good enough for me. Is there any way I could be on the inside with your team?"

"Sure, we could get you in. Wouldn't it raise red flags with the opposition?"

"Yeah, I guess it would. Let's get on to the calls my people have intercepted going out of the Compound. The first call they picked up was immediately after you left following your briefing to President-elect Ahern. Then Ahern's inner circle had three meetings where the briefing schedules were discussed. At the final meeting, when the president-elect pressed me, I told the group that you requested this particular schedule. It was the only time I mentioned your name and we captured another intercept immediately after the meeting."

"Who attended the meetings? Was it the same people every time?"

"No." Luke mentally recalled each meeting and jotted notes. "Take a look at the list of attendees at each of the meetings."

There were three names that appeared on all three lists.

"Now let's compare those three names to the people who were on hand when I was at the Compound," Alex said. "Seems like whoever it is, they may have alerted someone I'd been there briefing the president-elect." Only one of the three names appeared on that final list.

"Son-of-a-bitch, that might explain an unusual death. Did you hear about General Watkins' suicide?"

Luke nodded. "Yes, but how does that tie in?"

"Okay—let's think about the sequence of the events—this guy was there when President-elect Ahern started to refer to the general. He was about to say General Watson's name and I interrupted him, because I didn't want his name known. President-elect Ahern didn't even get the first whole syllable of the general's name out before I broke in, remember—like 'Wa.'"

Luke nodded.

"If this guy passed that along, the opposition may have gone after the wrong general. What if they assumed a 'General Wa' was someone on the Tower Watch distribution list? Was one of their own?"

"I see what you mean," Luke said. "The forensic guys weren't altogether satisfied with the suicide theory, but they couldn't put their finger on anything definite. With no other choice they let it go. Now it looks like we have a handle on the leak. I'll put someone on him and keep you up to speed."

A phone rang in the RV and Luke answered. He identified himself and said little. He asked a couple of questions, listened further and hung up. "That was a report from my clean-up crew. They have a tentative ID on the guy who was after you. They seem to think your CIA friend was right. Mister One and Mister Two hired him to put your lights out,

Alex. By the way, Mister One's real name is Dickie Brocklin and the other guy is Corbett Chapman."

Luke dropped Alex back at his car in the still dark parking lot. "I'll have Bob continue to keep an eye on you Alex, but I'm concerned about the rest of your people. I don't have the staff to cover them all. By the way, our intelligence says the opposition mentioned a 'she.' Anybody fit the female category other than Sarah?"

"Nope. Luke, I'd rather you have Bob keep an eye on Sarah instead of me."

"I wish I could Alex, but you're the key player in this operation. If the opposition takes you out, it could leave me up the proverbial creek. Brief her on what we've picked up and how potentially dangerous it could be. Have her get outta town 'til this thing is over. I'm sorry, I wish I could do more."

* * *

Alex nodded with a look of resignation on his face, knowing Sarah would never agree to those terms. They shook hands and each went back to their own vehicle. The light mist had stopped, leaving raindrops still beaded up on the top of the car. Alex looked for the spot where Big-guy had fallen. The pavement was pristine—Luke's clean-up crew did their work well. In a matter of minutes, the parking lot was as dark and deserted as it was just an hour before.

DECEMBER 3rd, SPRINGFIELD, VIRGINIA ⬠

The going-away party for Commander Jim Lawrence at the home of Ray Sanchez was rolling along. Sarah and Alex were enjoying the time away from the planning pressures. Jim's departure left Alex as the Watch Officer with the most seniority. Watch Team scheduling fell to the officer holding that dubious distinction.

Alex planned to give himself a heavy-duty workload during the coming holidays. It wouldn't be out of character. As the only single Watch Officer, he volunteered for most holidays. He didn't have any immediate family nearby and he could always push the scheduler for extra days off during the balance of the year.

He discussed the plan with Sarah and said, "I'll miss spending Christmas and New Year's Eve with you."

"Me, too." She lowered her chin to her chest and fluttered her eyelashes at Alex. "What am I going to do with your Christmas present? You know, the one where you have to be around to enjoy."

Alex grinned a schoolboy grin. As usual, he enjoyed being at a loss for words when he was near her. Changing the subject was his only defense. "By taking the extra work days, I'll be off duty the following week. That's the week the NMCC briefings for President-elect Ahern are scheduled. I've pushed for the fourth day as the only one he'll attend, but even if he goes all four days, I'll have one of my team leaders to cover every briefing day. Tufts is available on the first two days. Pickens will be off duty for the third one and Tucker is open for the final day. That may work out the best. From what I know of the teams, they're all good, but Tucker may have fielded the strongest group."

"Hey. Alex are you gonna' monopolize this pretty girl all night or can I get a good-bye dance and kiss?" The shout came from the party's honoree. Jim Lawrence was enjoying his party and advanced toward them with the gait of a sailor home from sea duty—one who had not yet attained his land legs. "Beautiful lady, may I have this dance?"

As the music faded, Jim escorted Sarah back to where Alex stood. Bowing deeply, Jim said, "Alex, I'm not near as hammered as I appear. Before things get maudlin and I forget to say it, I think Sarah and you are the greatest." He reached out to both of them and put a gentle hand on their shoulders. "I hope you two are happy forever. Sarah, you're the hardest working person in the J.O.C. Hell, in the whole damn Pentagon. How about that good-bye kiss now?"

Sarah stepped toward Jim, raised up on her toes and kissed him on the cheek saying, "Jim, I'm going to miss you."

Jim swallowed hard and took a deep breath. His eyes were moist as he said, "If this knucklehead ever comes to his senses and asks you to marry him, I hope you say yes and send me an invitation."

Thoughts raced through Alex's mind—*dangerous times, may not make it, nearly got my ass shot off last night, where would we be if...Then the answer came. That's bullshit. All we have is today.* Alex looked at Jim and then at Sarah. It was Alex's turn to swallow and take a deep breath. "Sarah, I'm goin' to let it all hang out 'cause this is a ridiculous time and place for me to ask this." Another swallow. "I wouldn't even do it if I didn't know you've got the guts to say 'no' if you need to." Deep breath. "But, if you say yes to my proposal, we can invite Jim right now." He reached out and took her hand. "Sarah, will you marry me?"

* * *

Sarah was surprised, but as usual she was not taken off guard. She was an excellent planner and long ago decided on the answer. "Yes, Alex. I accept." She kissed Alex and turned to Jim, "You're invited to the wedding. We'll just have to decide when and where it will be."

Jim looked at Alex and Sarah, his mouth hanging open, and said, "Is this a secret?" They both shook their heads.

Jim wheeled around toward the crowd and shouted, "Folks, can I have your attention?" He grabbed the karaoke microphone. "I've been looking for a way to avoid the teary-eyed platitudes and good-byes and I just found it. Sarah and Alex just got engaged. Ray, you're in luck. You just got two parties for the price of one."

Now the group used this second event to toast, and the party roared on. The added impetus kept it going long after its planned time. Ray apologized that as host he needed to leave, because he was scheduled for Watch duty tonight.

* * *

The hum of tires on the pavement was soothing. "I thought Jim was beyond calling women, 'girls,'" Sarah said. "I also saw you cringe when he called me that."

"I haven't forgotten the lecture I got for using the term," Alex said.

Sarah leaned back and relaxed as Alex drove her home. "How did you know I would say yes to your proposal?"

"I didn't. I've wanted to ask you for months now. I was just afraid of making this commitment again. Tonight, when Jim dropped that line on us, I knew it was time. I was holding my breath when I asked."

"I'm glad you did. I've known for longer than you the answer would be 'yes' whenever you asked."

"Why didn't you let me know, Sarah?"

"You said you were struggling with the commitment. Hey. Remember me, this is Sarah you're talking to. The one you confided in...the one you shared your personal dragons with. I didn't want to add to those pressures. I wanted you to have the time and the space to reach your own decision... and I was willing to invest my time by waiting."

All the tension melted and Alex reached over and took Sarah's hand. After several minutes of silence Alex said, "I hate to spoil a beautiful evening, but there are some things you need to know." Alex related the events of the previous night.

"Is there anything I can do to help take the heat off you, Alex?"

"No, I don't think so. The copies of the message traffic you've been feeding us have been invaluable, but I'm afraid they suspect you're the source of the information. I really want you to keep a low profile for the rest of the month. If you have the opportunity, read the TW traffic, but don't risk making copies. Any chance you would take Luke's suggestion about leaving town?"

"Not in this lifetime. I signed on for the duration."

"I was afraid of that. Then we'll need to be together from tonight until this thing is over. If we are, at least we'll have one of the good guys nearby."

"We can do our best," she said. "For starters, how about spending the rest of the night at my place?"

"Sounds good to me. Oh, did I leave enough food out for Caesar? Yeah, I'm sure I did. Next stop, a quiet and restful night."

"Don't count on it being too quiet, or too restful," she said resting a hand on his thigh.

Alex looked at her. He loved her smile and the sparkle in her eyes. He wondered now why he had waited so long to ask her to marry him.

▚▟▙ DECEMBER 5th, THE WHITE HOUSE

Again, General Osborn was surprised when he found Chapman on his secure phone. "What is it this time? I hope you have better news than the last time you called."

"Well as a matter of fact, it ain't all good news, General. Don't shoot the messenger, but that matter you wanted taken care of didn't get taken care of. As a matter of fact, the guy I contracted with to do Hilliard ain't been seen since day before yesterday. And Hilliard is still around."

"Damn it to hell. Why didn't you take care of the matter yourself?"

"I told you, General, I got other business to take care of. Do you still want me to take care of him?"

"No, since you've already missed him, put him on hold for now. I think we may have a better way of putting Hilliard out of action. Maybe you can handle a woman next time. Stay available."

BOOK 5

THE TURNING POINT

DECEMBER 23rd, VIRGINIA ⬠

The early days of December were a dichotomy for Alex. As he prepared for the task at hand, hours flew by—too few to accomplish what he needed to do. When he looked forward to January and the encounter in the NMCC, it seemed the time for action would never arrive.

Alex was in contact with Luke and Sam Cooke every few days. Their personal networks were bearing fruit, albeit not at the hoped for level of detail. Their sources were picking up more of the direction of movement, but the other side was cautious. The opposition still spoke in euphemisms, and pronouns, and nicknames like Batman and Robin. They seldom used actual names. Both Sam and Luke were concerned about the feminine pronouns they were picking up from the opposition.

* * *

Luke voiced his concerns, "Alex, they know Sarah's involved. They're sure she is your source to TW. Can't you convince her to get away for a while?"

"I tried, Luke. She's a tough lady with a mind of her own. I'm working on some alternatives—besides we only have a couple of weeks to go."

"So that's what it's all about. Bob Greenburg's been reporting every time he sees you, you're with Sarah. Also says he's seen your Navy Chief on a number of occasions. You pullin' shifts with her?"

"Guess you could call it that, Luke. When I'm with her, I know Bob's nearby. When I've been on duty, Master Chief Eaton's picking up the slack."

* * *

Between Chief Eaton and Alex, Sarah had precious little time she could call her own. They managed their schedules to the point one or the other was with her most of the day. One day as they, in her words, "changed shifts" she shouted at them. "Stand back you two. Give me room to breathe."

The exclamation caught Alex and the Chief in mid-stride. Trying to recover, they both stammered apologies, muttered understanding, and went back into their protective, hovering mode.

"Oh, what's the use," she said exhaling in exasperation and shaking her head. "You aren't listening. Just don't trample me in the stampede." She got into her car with Chief Eaton in tow and headed for work.

JANUARY 3rd,
ALEXANDRIA, VIRGINIA ⬠

Alex awoke from a twelve-hour sleep to the aroma of coffee brewing and bacon frying in a skillet. He smiled, picturing Sarah bustling around his kitchen. His holiday schedule was a rugged one, and he was recovering some of the lost sleep. *If I only had this much time off available for a vacation instead of what's ahead.*

Later in the day, Alex met with Sergeant Tucker to discuss the action plan and Tucker's team members. "Tuck, looks like you'll be getting the dirty end of the stick. The way things stack up, your team will back me the night President-elect Ahern visits the NMCC. Are you ready?"

Tucker beamed and his pride shone as he spoke of each member, their background, and their abilities.

"Stay close to the phone for the next four days, Tuck. As soon as I hear something, I'll alert you."

"Boss, I can get 'em anywhere quick. I'm tossing a picnic at my place on the 7th. The whole group will be there so that one call from you will alert my entire team."

JANUARY 5th, THE WHITE HOUSE

With only two days to go, General Osborn brought the colonel deeper into the conspiracy. Several calls went out from Colonel Richards as well as from General Osborn.

"What do you mean by the sixth, General? I thought this thing was supposed to happen on the seventh?"

"Ah, the beauty of it, Richards. If Hilliard has any plans—by now they're set in concrete and anchored around the seventh. By moving it up twenty-four hours we should catch them flat-footed. Besides that, just in case Hilliard does try to interfere, I've got an unpleasant surprise planned for him and the bitch helping him. Not even the president-elect will be told until a few hours before the seven p.m. briefing. Our story is that the Comm exercise is winding up a day early. This will be his last and only chance to get in on such an important briefing."

"What if Ahern decides not to come?"

"He'll come. We're doing a videotape of part of the exercise, which is scheduled to air on prime-time television. With his nose for publicity, he won't miss such an opportunity. Here are assignments for Brocklin and Chapman. Make sure you understand what you're to do and get these notes to them." He handed two sealed envelopes to Richards. "You are not to open these envelopes—"

"But, General, shouldn't I know—"

"You don't need to know the how, just the where. Here's the transmit tape for the alert message to the TW units. I want you to personally load and send it. Then destroy the tape. And...I want you in the Pentagon no later than three-thirty p.m. tomorrow. Here, this pass will get you into the VIP Lounge. Stay there till I call."

JANUARY 5th, SUITLAND, MARYLAND ⬟

The phone rang at Sergeant Tucker's home. He recognized the voice of a friend—one who worked at the White House communications center. The two shared a prepared list of phrases with prearranged meanings. They talked about the upcoming picnic for several minutes and hung up. Tucker made a short call, and then left his house.

From a pay phone, Sergeant Tucker dialed two other phones one after the other. When the second number answered he said, "Colonel H, I just got some word. Here's where you can reach me." He checked the number on the phone box and increased each number by two as he gave the last four digits to Alex.

Alex was at a pay phone near his home in eight minutes. He dialed the other pay phone and said, "Go ahead, Tuck."

"Word is, the TW alert message was transmitted a few minutes ago."

"Good work, Tuck," Alex said. "Your friend at the White House?"

"Yep, I just got off the phone with him. This is the first time any of those TW messages were left with them to send. Usually General Osborn does it himself and takes the tape back with him. Matter of fact, my friend says it was Colonel Richards who sent this one. This Richards left the tape with my buddy and came back for it later. When he dropped the tape off, Colonel Richards was bragging he was setting up transport for himself to get to the Pentagon tomorrow. Even showed off a pass to the General Officer/Flag Officer Lounge there on E Ring. My friend kept a copy of the message and called me. I guess the gist of it is that all the units are on a 'one hour standby' and the next message will deploy them. I'll have it shortly and I'll get a copy to you as soon as possible."

"Good old Quentin. All show and no go—spent too much time figurin' his next career move and didn't pay any attention to the details around him. He always did take the easy road. I wonder who set him up in the VIP Lounge. Thanks Tuck, I'll see you soon."

10:00 A.M., JANUARY 6th, THE DISTRICT OF COLUMBIA

Congress convenes. The votes of the Electoral College are delivered, counted, confirmed, and certified. Acting on suggestions from President Bancroft, his cronies in the House of Representatives and the Senate persuade the houses to vote to adjourn and to reconvene no earlier than February 15th. Both Houses of Congress adjourn by eleven a.m.

2 P.M., JANUARY 6th, ALEXANDRIA, VIRGINIA

Alex answered the phone at his home and heard, "Go secure, now." He was reasonably sure the voice belonged to Luke and there was urgency in his voice. The fact he demanded to talk on this line, one they both knew was tapped, raised the hair on the back of Alex's neck. Alex attached the encryption device to the mouthpiece and said, "What the hell is going on, Luke?"

"I just got the word. President-elect Ahern agreed to change his schedule. He's attending the NMCC briefing at 7 p.m. tonight. Alex, can you put it together in time?"

"Let me think for a minute..." Alex ticked off a dozen checklist items in his mind and snapped the answer back. "Luke, here's how we can play it. This puts the Delta Team on call. I'm going after Richards for exact details. I know where he'll be today, and now I know why he'll be there. You've got the frequency the team will use—monitor it. We play it down to the wire. If I have any doubt about The Man's safety, I'll give you a signal. I'll use the same code words you have for a contact with Gamma. If I give you the word, stop him before he enters the building. I've gotta get moving. You got anything else?"

"No, but I'm sure outta my comfort zone. I'll be there, Alex...don't wait too long to signal if you can't handle it."

Alex was afraid to risk another call on this phone. He grabbed his cell phone, dialed Sergeant Pickens and dropped the bombshell on Hillbilly. "It's a go for tonight. Best I can tell, we have under five hours to get our act together. Can your people make it?"

"Hot damn. Er...excuse me, sir. Yes, sir, we can. Home plate rendezvous?"

"You got it. There's no time to set up the military transport we've talked about. Just get your people there...fast."

Hillbilly's twang came over the line. "My folks'll be comin' in mostly from the north and the west, so they'll be able to avoid it."

"Whatta you mean, Hillbilly? Avoid what?"

"Damn, Colonel, haven't you heard about the big traffic tie-up? You're not at home are you?"

"Yes, I'm at home—no, I haven't heard any news for a while."

"There was a dee-railment on the northbound subway line somewhere near Crystal City. Then a couple of emergency vehicles responding to the Metro mess got T-boned by red light runners. Took out some traffic light controllers, and everything from the 14th Street Bridges south to past your place is at a dead stop. I heard the Shirley Highway and damn near all the surface streets are blocked. Worse mess they've had here in years. Gonna take hours to clear everything. Gonna take you a couple of hours to go 'round the affected area—if you can get around it."

"Damn. How the hell am I going to make it to the Pentagon in a half hour or less?"

Hillbilly shot back, "Hang in there, Colonel. Expect a call from Scrounger in a couple of minutes."

"Okay, but have 'em use my cell phone number."

"Roger that."

There was a click and Alex found himself listening to dead air.

As advertised, Scrounger was on the other end of the line when the phone rang seven minutes later.

"Colonel, I've gotta make this quick 'cause you need to be out the door in a hurry. Based on my talk with my buddy at the Washington Navy Yard, you got 'bout ten minutes to get to the pickup point. Oh, yeah, his name's Jason Murdock."

"How's he going to get through the traffic jam in ten minutes?"

"No jam up on the Potomac, Colonel. You need to be at the Torpedo Factory, so he can pick you up."

"Torpedo Factory?"

"Yes sir, you know that Art Center down at the foot of Duke Street?"

"Oh, right."

"He says 'be on the quay, just north of that finger wharf juttin' out—about two hundred yards north of the Torpedo Factory Art Center.' It'll be a fast looking boat. She's a forty-footer, white with green trim and the name Bon Homme Richard in gold."

"Great work, Bill. I'll be there."

"I wish I could be there too, sir. Kick ass and take names, Colonel."

Again Alex was listening to dead air. He made one more call and was out the door four minutes later. The jacket over his uniform displayed a bright yellow badge and covered two empty holsters.

* * *

He was standing at the designated rendezvous point five minutes later—three minutes to drive to the location and two minutes spent looking for a place to park. *Oh, what the hell, the grass looks good to me.* He parked on the lawn.

Seconds later the big white boat approached the quay. It carried maximum speed until the last moment. Alex watched the flurry of activity in the boat's cockpit, and was in awe of this man's ship handling abilities. The man juggled throttles and the wheel as he stopped the craft dead in the water—a foot from the quay and directly in front of Alex.

"Colonel Hilliard, Chief Murdock at your service. Welcome aboard, sir."

Alex stepped down onto the cushion of the seat behind the Chief and then sat down.

"Hang on, Colonel. I've been told you're priority cargo on a priority mission, so we're gonna' secure butts and *haul ass.*" The Chief didn't wait for a response, he rammed both throttles half open and steered slightly away from the quay. When he gained the clearance he wanted, he ripped the port throttle to idle and shoved the starboard one full open as he spun the wheel hard over to port. The result was an extremely tight turning arc. As he neared one hundred and eighty degrees of turn, he let the wheel spin back to a neutral position and brought the port throttle up to match the other one.

Without looking at Alex, the Chief shouted over the roar of the twin engines. "Each of them big MerCruisers are drivin' a three-bladed prop 'bout two feet in diameter. How's that for gettin' up to speed?" In less than fifteen seconds they were moving at top speed, the hull barely touching the water.

Alex glanced over the Chief's shoulder at the needle on the instrument that purported to report their speed. It bounced around the number 90. "Are we really going that fast, Chief?" Alex shouted to his chauffeur.

"Ninety? Aye, sir...but that's klicks. Translated from kilometers, it's only about seventy-five mile an hour," said the Chief.

ONLY seventy-five miles per hour. Alex's grip on the rail next to him tightened.

Again, the Chief shouted, "She's a beauty ain't she, Colonel? She ain't mine. These babies go for about a hundred and ten thou—no way I could afford one. This baby belongs to the Coast Guard. Confiscated under those RICO laws. They keep her up at the Yard and we do their maintenance for 'em. I borrowed her for the day. 'Course, I'm not sure if they know I borrowed her."

Alex saw the 14th Street Bridges coming into view. They passed under the railway bridge and then under the two bridges, each one providing one-way auto traffic, in and out of the area near the Pentagon to the Southwest corner of the District.

They cleared the third one, the George Mason Memorial Bridge and Chief Murdock swung the wheel hard over to port. They raced through the narrow passage on the southern end of Columbia Island and under the George Washington Parkway. For a fleeting moment, Alex thought of Mike and his last drive down that Parkway. They were aimed directly at the shore on the western side of the Boundary Channel.

When the Chief arrived at the Torpedo Factory, his approach to the quay was at about a thirty-degree angle. They were now approaching a dock that paralleled the shoreline, but they were on a perpendicular course. The dock loomed and as before, the Chief was not reducing power.

All my years of flying and not a scratch. Now I'm going to die in a boat accident.

Alex felt the ache in his forearms. He realized the pain was from the death grip he had on the armrests. He relaxed the grip and flexed his fingers.

At the last minute, Chief Murdock swung into action. Throttles were jerked to idle and the engines were backed full down to kill headway. Alex tried to follow the motions, but from then on, the wheel and throttle movements were a blur and more than he could absorb.

Chief Murdock was better than good. The boat was now parallel to the dock. The last bit of headway energy, which was sideways, carried the boat over the final foot of water that separated them from their berth. They barely touched the old tire bumper hanging over the side of the wharf. Chief Murdock reached out and grabbed a timber to steady his boat in the moderate chop.

Alex scrambled up onto the wooden timbers. Chief Murdock released his grip on the dock, saluted, and said, "Give 'em hell, Colonel." The boat's throttles were again jammed to the full open setting.

Alex returned the salute and jogged off the dock. He had three hundred yards to cover, so he paced himself using a long, loping stride. He didn't want to arrive at the big, gray building spent and out of breath.

Alex was amazed at what happened in the past few minutes between the calls from Hillbilly and Scrounger—and the ensuing trip up the Potomac River. *Never underestimate good NCOs.*

2:45 P.M., JANUARY 6th, THE PENTAGON ⬠

The boat trip bypassed the Northern Virginia traffic problems, and Alex was inside the Pentagon in record time. His phone call to Chief Eaton provided enough time for the Chief to arrive, and they met inside the River Entrance. Alex brought him up to speed as they headed for the restroom. Chief Eaton stood guard while Alex retrieved three weapons. He put two into the holsters he was wearing. Rather than the Glock, he decided to use the Beretta Mike Reilly left for him. Alex handed the Glock and two spare magazines to Duke as he emerged from the access panel.

"Duke, make sure Sarah's okay. She should be in the J.O.C. Then meet me outside the VIP Lounge. I'm looking for Colonel Richards. Do you remember what he looks like?"

"Yes sir. I'll be able to pick him out based on that picture you showed us all. I should be up there with you in ten minutes or less."

Alex ran down the hall. He swung left along the corridor to E Ring and took up a station outside the General Officer/Flag Officer Lounge. From here he could keep an eye out for Colonel Richards and use his cell phone to make coordination calls. His first call was to the J.O.C. He needed Sergeant Tucker's expertise and Tuck was on duty. By the time he reached Tucker, Duke arrived in the lounge area. "Tuck, I know they've sent out the TW deploy message by now. You've got to get to the Comm Center and transmit our TW stand-down message. Make sure it doesn't get back to the White House or to the J.O.C. Take whatever time you need. Let me talk to Colonel Sanchez. I'll square your absence with Ray."

* * *

Earlier, Sergeant Tucker prepared fourteen individual tapes—one to transmit to each TW unit commander in the field. Even though in most cases, there was more than one TW unit at a given base, this was the safest approach. It would take longer to send additional tapes, but it also reduced risks. One message with multiple addressees might accidentally find its way to the White House, the NMCC, or the J.O.C. Each of the tapes would stop at the specified unit and would not be reproduced. Except for the individualized "To:" line, they all read:

* * *

06 JAN — 1900Z TOWER WATCH TRAFFIC - SPECAT EYES ONLY

LIMITED DISTRIBUTION

FROM: TOWER WATCH ONE

TO: xxxxxxx

THIS IS A FORTY-EIGHT (48) HOUR STAND-DOWN. DO NOT, REPEAT DO NOT, DEPLOY. EXPECT FURTHER ORDERS WITHIN THIRTY-SIX (36) HOURS.

WARM REGARDS

END

Tucker made his way to the communications center and fifteen minutes later all the messages were on their way.

3:15 P.M., JANUARY 6th, THE PENTAGON ⬠

Sergeant Pickens joined Alex and Duke. Alex turned to Pickens and said, "Hillbilly, give me a rundown on your team. Who'll I be working with?"

To eliminate confusion created by last minute substitutions, they kept the plan simple. Team members took their leader's Greek letter designation and were assigned an additional number. The numbered team positions were identical for each team. Number Two always carried the Calico automatic weapon. Even if Alex forgot a name, he could call on Delta Two if he needed the automatic firepower from Hillbilly's group.

"Beta," Hillbilly said. "Delta Two is Rebecca Nathan. Staff Sergeant, Army." Hillbilly noticed Alex's expression and asked, "You're not goin' sexist on me, are you, Colonel?"

"Nope. Just intrigued. Go ahead, Delta."

"Good thing, 'cause she's got a couple of covert Ops under her belt and she's better with that Calico than I am. 'Sides that, she is a very special lady."

Alex detected more than respect when Hillbilly spoke about Sergeant Nathan. It looked and sounded like affection, perhaps more.

"My shotgunner," Hillbilly said, "is Marion Newcomb, Marine Master Sergeant. If you don't call him Delta Three, better use 'Bull' rather than Marion. He's damn good with that scattergun. He's one of the grunts I pulled outta that fire base back in the Nam, I told you about. Delta Four is Lewis

Roundtree. He's an Army Master Sergeant and he's ahead of both of us, Beta. He brought a small golf bag with him. With the head cover, that sniper rifle will look like a four wood stickin' outta the bag. He could lug it anywhere in here and get away with it."

"I admire the initiative. Has he got a nickname?"

"Guys real close call him Dozens," Sergeant Pickens said. He must have seen the quizzical expression on Alex's face and said, "You may not want to know the details, Colonel. When you said we'd have a long gun on the team, I looked for the best there was. 'Dozens' refers to the fact he's got way more'n twelve confirmed long-range hits, but he don't talk on it much. He's good—back in the Nam he even trained with Gunny Hathcock up on Hill 55. Hathcock had more confirmed kills than any other sniper over there. Finally, Delta Five is P. J. Lexington. Answers to 'PJ' or 'Lex.' He's a sergeant first-class, Army. Good people, Beta. They all pack the gear—I'd follow any of 'em walkin' point."

"That's good enough for me. Let's get busy. Get your people in and armed. Hang loose at the alcove inside the River Entrance."

Pickens left to gather his team. Duke and Alex were talking when the Chief bumped Alex's arm. "I think your man is coming, Beta."

4:15 P.M., JANUARY 6th, THE PENTAGON ⬟

Alex looked up and saw Colonel Richards approaching. Alex stepped in front of him putting a hand to the colonel's chest. "Quentin, we need to talk." Richards attempted to move around him. Alex sidestepped in front of him blocking his path again. Alex pulled his jacket open far enough so Richards could see the butt of the Beretta protruding from its holster. "Quentin, don't overestimate the security here inside the Pentagon. We are going to talk. Come with me now or I'll put a bullet in you right here, right now. Your choice."

Duke moved close behind Colonel Richards and whispered, "I wouldn't press my luck with him if I were you, Colonel. Cuz he's havin' a reeeeel bad hair day."

Alex stepped around Richards and led the way to the D Ring restroom. He preceded the other two men through the crawlway and into the dead space.

The battery lantern cast an eerie glow over the three occupants. Alex directed Richards to sit with his back against the wall. Alex knelt beside him, facing him. "Quentin, I need to know everything you know. So let's get started."

"I don't know what you're referring to, Hilliard."

"How about calling me *Lieutenant Colonel*, Quentin. I'm going to say just two words, and then you'd better begin the story." Alex slid the .22 caliber Walther from the Belly Band holster, cocked the hammer back and said, "Tower Watch."

Richards stammered, but began the story. He started with his first exposure to Tower Watch and with slow halting words brought them up to date. As the long-winded explanation continued, Alex eased the pistol's hammer forward to the safe position. The click startled Richards. Alex already knew the background information he was hearing, and felt Richards was creating a deliberate stall. He began to lose patience.

Alex felt his cell phone vibrate, answered and heard Luke Cutter's voice. "Schedule is being compressed. TopHat and White Tie are departing the Compound now. Briefing has been moved up one hour. Alex, flying time is about forty minutes. Transit time from the pad to the destination is no more than ten. You've got about an hour to go. Are you in position?"

"All my chicks are in the nest." Alex winked at Richards adding, "I'm getting a last minute rundown from a friend right now. We should know the exact details in a couple of minutes. That'll be plenty of time. I'll get back to you." Alex replaced the phone and glanced at his watch. It read four-forty.

He placed the tip of the noise suppressor against Richards' knee and said, "Knock off the bullshit this second, Quentin. I just lost the luxury of time. If I don't get the details about tonight *now*, I'll put a bullet in you before you can say, *huh*. Believe me, it'll hurt you a hell of a lot more than it hurts me. Matter of fact, I think I'd enjoy shooting you, Quentin."

"Hilliard, I don't think you have the nerve to shoot anyone."

Phffft...

The sound from the silenced pistol produced a faint echo in the enclosed space. A split second before he fired, Alex moved the muzzle from the colonel's knee to the inside of the upper thigh to avoid severing the femoral arteries. The .22 caliber projectile passed through about five inches of flesh and flattened itself against the concrete floor. Richards' eyes were wide with surprise as he stared at the hole in his thigh, and saw the blood oozing up from the wound, soaking his trouser leg. His mouth flew open in an involuntary movement as the searing pain welled up in his throat.

Alex clamped his hand over the colonel's mouth and stifled the scream. He placed the weapon against Richards' other leg and said, "Quit whining, Quentin. I'll get you medical attention as soon as you've finished your story. Now, Quentin, the details. All of them."

The words poured from his mouth with the speed of white water rushing over boulders in a narrow riverbed. Richards covered the remaining events leading up to today, and began relating the plans for this evening, as he knew them. "All I know is that President Bancroft said that after tonight, he'll be able to stay in office. I've only seen two others, a tall white guy and a shorter Black man who came to the White House for meetings. There is supposed to be another one, but I've never seen him. I know they have the military units moving toward the District and several other locations. Not much you can do now."

"You'd be surprised, Quentin. You'd be surprised. Who is going to kill President-elect Ahern? Where will it happen and how does he plan to get away?"

"What do you mean kill the president-elect?" His eyes grew wide and round and the words gushed faster. "They haven't told me all that much. If their plan includes killing someone, it'd probably one of the two guys I told you about. They're the only ones involved I know of. The third one's been missing for some time. I'm sure President Bancroft doesn't have the guts to do it himself. Whatever is supposed to happen, I think they planned to do it inside the NMCC, but I don't have any idea how someone could get away after killing the president-elect."

"By the way, what are you doing here in the Pentagon to-day?"

"I'm not sure," Colonel Richards said. "General Osborn told me to be here, and I could be a part of history."

"Not in your wildest wet dream, Quentin. The most apt scenario is to make you the scapegoat in case something goes wrong. What have you heard them say about me?"

"I overheard them say 'If…if they got hold of her, it would pull you out of the picture.' I…I don't know who they were talking about."

4:45 P.M., JANUARY 6th, THE PENTAGON ⬠

"Must be talking about Sarah," Alex said looking at Duke. Alex dialed the J.O.C. When the Watch Officer answered, he kept his voice as calm as possible. "Hi, this is Alex. Let me talk to Sarah."

Ray Sanchez said, "Alex, she got a call a couple of minutes ago. I thought she said it was from you…or about you. Anyway, she just left to meet someone. What the hell is going on, Alex? First Tucker—now you're calling for Sarah. What's up?"

"Ray, trust me…Another half hour or so and you'll know the whole story."

Alex punched the end button on his cell phone. "Duke, get out there and see if you can catch Sarah leaving the J.O.C. I've gotta bad feeling. She got a call, so there may be someone waiting for her to come out. I'll take care of Richards."

Duke moved through the access panel and disappeared into the darkness.

Alex grabbed a roll of duct tape and began working on Colonel Richards. He bound his wrists behind him and taped the colonel's ankles together. He also put a strip of the tape over Richards' mouth. Using a pair of scissors from the first aid kit, he cut the pant leg away from Richards' thigh. "I'll bandage that leg before I leave, Quentin. Don't worry, a bit of pressure should stop the bleeding. I'm sure I missed all the vital parts of your leg, so you'll be all right in a few days."

Alex dragged the colonel back into the crawlway. He taped Richards' legs to a pipe. "If you try kicking to get free or to alert someone, you'll probably pop that bandage. Might be a long time before someone finds you in here and is able to stop the bleeding. I'd lie real still if I were you."

Alex stabbed a button on his cell phone and it quit vibrating. He heard, "Beta, this is Gamma. Do you hear me okay?"

Alex responded to Duke. "You're loud and clear. Go ahead."

"Some guy grabbed Ms. Crawford. I tried to stop him, but he clubbed me with something. By the time I got up they were out the door. I'm outside the River Entrance movin' toward North parking. They're about seventy-five yards in front of me."

"Damn." Alex switched to the radio headset. "Delta, this is Beta. Are you on frequency?"

"Roger that, Beta."

"Delta, I want Delta Four on the roof of E Ring, north side. Give him the four-frequency radio. He has about five minutes to make it. You take the twelve-gauge and have Delta Three run interference for Delta Four. Delta, I want you and the rest of your team here with me. Head for the dead space."

"Beta, this is Delta, Roger that. Three and Four are movin' and they're on headset. Give 'em the brief."

Communication would be awkward. Alex would have to act as the liaison between Duke on the cell phone and the Delta Team using their radio headsets. Alex passed the details of Sarah's abduction to the Delta Team.

Alex told Duke he would call back shortly. He hung up and dialed another number, and spoke only a few minutes. He disconnected and reconnected the links to Gamma and the Delta Team.

Alex updated his team. "Gamma's description of this guy tallies with someone I've spotted before. I've confirmed from friendlies that he is not one of their people. I'm designating him 'Mister One and I'm declaring him hostile. Green light, we take him out at the first opportunity."

Alex pondered the decision he would have to deliver to his Delta Team. *What's this "we" crap? I only have to give the go ahead...Delta Four has to squeeze the trigger. I hope he's as good as Hillbilly says he is. What if it comes down to a choice of saving one or the other? What if I have to decide between Sarah and the president-elect?*

Sergeant Pickens and the rest of his team joined Alex in the dead space outside the NMCC hallway. Alex briefed them and said, "Delta Five, I want you over on the west side of E Ring. Keep an eye on the helo pad. Let us know when the presidential helicopter lands. We need to wrap up the problem in North parking before he gets here."

"Gamma, how's the situation now?" Alex was back on the cell phone speaking to Duke.

Duke came back on the phone panting. "I just moved up even with 'em. He sees me and I think I'm between him and his car. He keeps looking around like he hopes to spot another way out."

* * *

Two men jogged through the halls of the Pentagon. They wore Army Class B uniform sweaters with a bright yellow patch. One of them carried a golf bag slung over his shoulder. The two men received a number of raised eyebrows from the people who crowded the halls—most just shook a head, and no one bothered Delta Four and Delta Five on their way to the roof.

Alex relayed the latest news to Delta Four and asked, "Do you have a clear shot?"

"Delta Four. That's a negative. The woman gives him a lot of cover. It would be a real dicey shot right now. I see Gamma—he's about fifteen meters south of the two. See if he can get Mister One to turn a bit and face east."

General Osborn placed a call to the Pentagon's VIP Lounge. When the steward answered, he asked to speak to Colonel Richards. There was a short pause and the steward came back on the line. "There are no colonels here in the lounge, General."

"Are you sure?" Osborn said with an edge to his voice.

"Yes sir. I'm certain. There is no one here wearing eagles on his uniform. I even know the number of stripes a Navy O-6 wears." The sarcasm was not wasted on Osborn.

The general slammed the phone down, checked for another number, and dialed again. It took several minutes on hold for the duty NCO to locate the commander of this particular D.C. Military Police unit. "General this is Major Davis speaking, sir. I suppose you're checking to see that we got those stand-down orders. Yes sir, we certainly did and we're waiting for the next alert."

"What friggin' orders?" General Osborn stammered.

"The TW forty-eight-hour stand-down, sir. Is there something wrong?"

Covering his confusion, Osborn said, "Ah, of course, that's what I was checking. Good work, Major. We'll be in touch." Again he slammed the receiver down leaving Major Davis with a dead phone in his hand.

Osborn evaluated the slim evidence he now had. Someone sent a message to at least one of our Tower Watch units. *I've got to assume that they all received a similar message. There's not going to be any help from the military for the president's scheme. We could get another alert message out...or I can cut my losses and get the hell out of here.* The general considered his options for less than a minute. His choice to cut and run was obvious, at least to him. Muttering under his breath, he shoved a half dozen items from his desk into a briefcase and beat a hasty retreat from his office in the White House.

* * *

Luke Cutter and Alex earlier anticipated General Osborn's possible departure. As the general reached the street in his car, he found his way blocked by a government-issue sedan. Hawkeye Two, Bruce Compton, and his partner took Osborn into custody and escorted him to the Pentagon.

5:30 P.M., JANUARY 6th, THE PENTAGON ⬠

Luke's pacing was restricted to the only open area of the trailer—every two and a half steps he reversed course. His helicopter, as usual, left before and traveled faster than the one President-elect Ahern was aboard. The early departure and a higher airspeed gave him the opportunity to land first and establish the forward command center. Luke would coordinate the security team while Hawkeye Three and Four provided direct assistance for the presidential party. For nearly ten minutes, he listened to Alex coordinating his people. He glanced at his watch and said aloud to no one in particular, "Alex, it's going on six. We need to wrap this up or abort the old man's arrival."

* * *

Both Duke and the sniper provided a running commentary. Since neither one could hear the other, Alex kept each of them apprised of the others' remarks. He also knew that Luke was monitoring only the radio side of the conversations.

Duke engaged Mister one in conversation. Every time he shifted his position, Mister One maneuvered to keep Sarah between them. Duke reported that the man was armed with a handgun. "He must have had it hidden in the bushes just outside the building." Duke took his eyes off Mister One and nervously glanced around. "Beta, not many people out on this side of the building. Those I've seen either didn't notice the guy holdin' Ms. Crawford...or they decided not to get involved."

Delta Five cut into the dialogue. "The people from the first helo are in a trailer and that bird is gone. There's a second chopper inbound to the pad. It'll be on the ground in a minute or two."

Alex knew Luke would be sweating bullets by now. He used the headset radio, knowing Luke could not respond. "Luke, this is Alex. I know it looks grim from your end. Give me five more minutes."

Fearing that someone else could be overhearing their radio communications, Alex directed Delta Four to an alternate frequency. "Delta Four, how is your view from the fourth floor?"

Delta Four said, "Great view." He switched to frequency number four on the radio Sergeant Pickens gave him. He acknowledged the instructions from Alex and they both switched back to their primary headset radio frequency.

* * *

Sergeant Roundtree brought the sniper rifle back into firing position using the low wall on the rooftop as a bench rest. He peered through the optics of the variable power Leupold scope mounted atop his rifle. *Damn, wish I had a clean shot—this would be easy pickings...barely over a hundred meters. Okay, no wind to speak of, makes it all the easier...I'll leave the windage neutral.*

The current scope settings gave him a field of view of over thirty feet. Without taking his eye from the optics, his fingers located the knurled ring on the scope's tube and he began rotating it. The image in the scope grew larger and he could see less and less as the field of view narrowed. His thoughts were so intensive they were almost audible. *Oops, ten power on this baby is a bit too much. I'll just back her down a bit.* Now he could see little more than the man in the parking lot holding the woman in front of him. *Okay asshole, it's just you and me—up close and personal.* He continued squinting into the telescopic sight as he settled himself down and controlled his breathing.

* * *

Delta Five reported the president-elect's party entering the Pentagon. Alex issued a terse order to Duke.

Duke was using his pistol to focus Mister One's attention on him. He returned the Glock to its holster and said, "You win. I just got the word from Colonel Hilliard that he's coming out. He says, 'please don't hurt the girl.' Those were his *EXACT* words. If you promise not to hurt the *GIRL*, he'll give it up."

"As soon as I see Hilliard and his people outside the building, I'll let her go."

"Okay, I'll go get him..." Then Duke shouted a command. "Sarah...DROP NOW."

Hearing Sarah's name, Alex relayed the order even before Duke finished the shouted command to her and said into the radio, "Delta Four, NOW."

* * *

Delta Four held the crosshairs steady on Brocklin—the man he knew as Mister One. He had long since taken up the slack in the trigger pull. Now it was only a matter of another pound of pressure and the firing pin would be released. It would slam forward into the primer cap of the cartridge and send a projectile spiraling out of the barrel. The shot rang out as Sarah dropped through Mister One's slightly relaxed grip and she collapsed to the asphalt, limp as a rag doll. The bullet hit Brocklin in the upper-right side of his chest, drove downward and penetrated his heart. Delta Four saw the surprised expression on Brocklin's face, but it was doubtful he knew what hit him. He was dead as he landed in a crumpled heap on the ground beside Sarah.

"Beta, this is Delta Four. Clean dink. Hostile is down." He jerked the bolt back and slammed it forward—cranking another round into the chamber of the rifle.

* * *

Duke rushed to Sarah's side. He scooped up the pistol Brocklin dropped and checked the man's neck for a pulse. He reported, "Beta, Ms. Crawford's okay. Tell Delta Four he can relax, this guy is out of action...on a permanent basis."

On their way back to the Pentagon, Sarah responded to Duke's questions. "Alex never refers to a woman as a 'girl.' He knows damn well that if he called me girl, I'd brain him. When you told the bad guy those were Alex's exact words I knew something was up—it was part of a rescue plan. Chief, in the entire time I've known you, you've never called me Sarah. When you did, I knew following instructions would save my life."

* * *

Alex moved his team of three past Richards and into the dead space. As they passed the colonel, Alex said, "I really apologize for this, Quentin. I can't afford any noise for the next few minutes." Alex used the butt of his pistol to put Colonel Richards to sleep.

They removed the plywood cover, and Alex whispered into his headset mike. "Delta Team, this is Beta. External is resolved. Luke, we need a North parking clean-up."

* * *

Luke took his first breath in what seemed like an eternity. He directed two men and a small van to take charge of the situation in the North parking lot.

* * *

One major hurtle out of the way. *Now for the really big one,* Alex thought.

"Delta Three, Four and Five—take up positions outside the NMCC," Alex said in a whisper over the headset mike. "Delta and Delta Two will handle the internal with me. Delta and Delta Two—lock and load. Any questions—from anyone?" After a few seconds of silence, Alex said, "Safeties off. Radio silence now."

6:00 P.M., JANUARY 6th, NMCC, THE PENTAGON

President Bancroft and his party cleared the guard post just outside the NMCC. As Alex expected, the guard reminded the Secret Service detail that Standard Operating Procedures indicated they would need to remain outside. The security door to the NMCC closed. Bancroft opened the door that led to the hallway behind the NMCC Cab. "You take this shortcut to the briefing area. I'll take the long way around and meet you inside," Bancroft said to President-elect Ahern and Vice President-elect Ryder.

* * *

The grill fasteners were removed. Alex used the handle they installed to hold the grill in place. The hallway door to his left closed with Ahern and Ryder inside the hallway. Alex heard a rustling down the hall to his right. He set the grill aside and stepped through the opening. Sergeant Pickens and Sergeant Nathan followed.

When Chapman came around the bend into the main part of the hallway, his mouth dropped open and his eyes widened. Instead of two unarmed men in suits, he was confronted by three figures in uniform standing between him and his intended targets. All three of these meddlers had a weapon leveled at him.

"Drop it. Don't let the testosterone override the ability, asshole," Alex said. It wasn't a shout—it was barely louder than a conversational tone. At the same time, the authority in Alex's voice was intended to leave no doubt in Chapman's mind he would die if he didn't obey the command.

Alex watched as Chapman began lowering the pistol from the two-handed shooter's grip. Then Chapman jerked the weapon back up toward an aiming stance. The bullet from Alex's Beretta and a three-round burst from the Calico struck him in the chest. Like his partner before him, Mister One was dead before he hit the floor.

Along with the revulsion of seeing a man die, Alex felt a sense of purpose—some resolution. *That one's for you, Mike.*

"Mr. President-elect it's all clear. I think it's time we move into the NMCC," Alex said as he escorted President-elect Ahern and Vice President-elect Ryder through the back door of the Cab.

Alex turned his thoughts to Luke who must have heard the gunshots over his radio. He transmitted the current situation. "Luke, breathe easy. TopHat and White Tie are safe—out of the hallway and we're moving to the NMCC."

* * *

Bancroft's expression revealed his guilt. Expecting to see Chapman emerge from the hallway into the Cab, he saw both of his intended victims following Alex into the room.

* * *

"General Jordan," Alex said to the senior watch officer, "there was an attempt to kill the president-elect and the vice president-elect. The assassin is lying dead back there in the hallway. I don't think we'll have use for these any longer." He surrendered his Beretta to the Deputy Watch Officer, Colonel Jake Townsend. Alex waved his arm toward the people in the main area of the NMCC and said, "General, would you please let the folks out there know the worst is over."

The general made the announcement and turned to Alex. "When will the rest of these people be handing over their weapons?"

"We'll be turning them over to building Security as soon as possible, sir." Alex left the presidential party in the Cab and walked into the main area of the NMCC with Sergeant Nathan and Sergeant Pickens.

Alex, Sergeant Pickens, and Sergeant Nathan stood in the area just outside the Cab. Alex surveyed the large, open room, noting the people staffing the duty desks. As his eyes passed the CIA position, a blinding realization struck him. He looked back toward President Bancroft in the Cab. *You son-of-a-bitch. That's why you didn't have worries about Mister Two. You never intended him to leave the NMCC alive.*

"GUN."

* * *

Luke was exiting the trailer as he heard a female voice shout the single word. "Sweet Jesus, what now?" He cursed and wheeled back into the trailer.

* * *

Alex also heard Sergeant Nathan's shouted warning. He turned back toward the CIA desk in time to see both Agent McKee and his boss Quincannon standing.

* * *

Realizing his entire career was about to come crashing down, Quincannon made one last desperate attempt to take someone with him. Quincannon's arm was arcing up from his waistband—a pistol in his hand.

* * *

Alex heard the gunfire, but didn't see it. All he saw was Pickens's broad back. First he heard a single gunshot he assumed was from Quincannon. Next there was the distinctive staccato of the Calico. Sergeant Nathan moved toward the CIA desk to be sure Quincannon was dead from the three rounds she fired, and to disarm McKee. Only then did she allow her attention to be diverted to Sergeant Pickens who was lying on the floor.

Hillbilly took Quincannon's bullet, meant for Alex, high in the chest. Delta Four and Delta Five entered the NMCC from the back as Alex had. Seeing them, he knew he could relinquish his vigilance and go to Sergeant Pickens. PJ carried the first aid kit from the dead space and attended to Hillbilly. Alex knelt next to his fallen comrade.

"Did we get 'em all, Colonel?" Pickens said.

"Yeah, you bet your ass we got 'em all. Thanks to you and your team, we got 'em all." Alex looked at PJ, his eyes pleading for an opinion on Hillbilly's condition.

"I'm no medic, Colonel. He's losing a lot of blood and he needs help fast."

* * *

Luke monitored the events over Alex's open radio mike. "Damn it, Alex. What's going on?" he said to no one. Minutes before, when he heard the first shots, Luke alerted the medical and trauma teams which were always on standby when the president or the president-elect were on the move. "Alex, I wish I there was some way of letting you know help is on the way."

Alerted by the call from the Secret Service, the Pentagon medical team brought the gurney into the NMCC. Before Sergeant Pickens was wheeled out, Alex issued two more orders to him. "Hillbilly, don't you dare give up. That's an order. I'll tell you when you can die. You're going to be fine." Sergeant Pickens smiled and nodded at Alex. "Sergeant Nathan, Rebecca, I want you to stay with him and keep me posted," Alex said.

Only then did Alex finally remember that Luke was still in the dark about the last shots fired. He keyed his radio and said, "Luke, TopHat and White Tie are okay. Come on into the NMCC."

6:16 P.M., JANUARY 6th, NMCC CAB, THE PENTAGON

President Bancroft was directed to wait outside the Cab door under the watchful eyes of the remaining members of Hillbilly's team. Alex and President-elect Ahern discussed their next move. The president-elect was in favor of keeping the entire episode quiet and simply holding the culprits under close surveillance. "I'm concerned how the public would react to an attempted coup."

"Damn it, Mr. President-elect. If you can't trust the people who put you in office, where does that leave us? Besides that, when was the last time a secret of this magnitude was kept here inside the Beltway?"

"You've got me there, my boy. What would you suggest?"

Alex spent several minutes outlining his plan. Ahern shook his head—unbelieving, but agreed in the end.

As they were ready to leave the NMCC, Alex's radio headset crackled. "Beta, this is Delta Two, do you read?"

"You must be at the limit of the radio's range—you're about two by two—but I can hear you. Go ahead, Sergeant Nathan."

Rebecca's voice was choked with emotion and Alex feared the worst…until he heard the words, "He's hurt pretty bad, but the doctors say Hillbilly will make it. He's going to be all right."

"Rebecca, you take as much time as you need and stay with him. I'll cover for you." Alex smiled as he saw Sarah and Chief Eaton entering the NMCC. He went to her and engulfed her in his arms. He leaned forward to kiss her.

Her eyes widened and her eyebrows rose as she said, "You're going to kiss me in front of all these people?"

"Damn right I am. And I may have more surprises for you."

He turned to Master Chief Eaton and said, "Round up all the rest of the Delta Team. We'll meet in the alcove just inside the River Entrance."

When the team was gathered, Alex said, "I'll keep this short folks. In case you didn't hear the news, Sergeant Pickens was shot, but he's going to recover. Sergeant Nathan says it may take a while, but he'll be okay. Each of you performed...each of you—"

The adrenaline was no longer pumping. His muscles began a quivering, shaking dance of their own as the rage and fear he'd suppressed for so long did their best to dominate him.

He struggled to regain his composure and continued, "Each and every one of you did an outstanding job. President-elect Ahern will know your names and faces by the time I file my After-action report. You not only saved two lives tonight...you preserved a democracy. I'll make sure no one ever forgets the job you did here. I'll be in touch."

Alex brought himself to attention and saluted the team. Without any command, but in unison, they all returned the salute.

EPILOGUE

ONE MORE VISIT

11:00 A.M., JANUARY 8th, WASHINGTON D.C. ⬠

The nation was glued to their television sets this morning. Alex watched a twenty-one inch monitor in his White House office. "Pay attention, America. This is going to be a day to remember." He wouldn't need to watch too closely since it was his idea to be played out on television this day. He busied himself scratching notes on a legal pad. His own chore to accomplish as soon as the television drama was complete.

The self-assured talking head of one of the major networks was waiting to report to the country. He wore the typical uniform: dark pinstriped suit, starched shirt, blue with a white collar, red power tie and the coiled cord leading to his earpiece. The camera was on him—he smiled an easy smile and shuffled papers as he waited for his cue—

* * *

This is Ned Worthington coming to you from the pressroom near the House of Representatives. In all my years covering the political beat, I've never in my life seen such a security blanket as this one. This town usually leaks like a sieve, but our sources are unable to uncover any information on this extraordinary event.

Here we are, monitoring a joint session of the Congress. Congress was not expected to reconvene until sometime after the inauguration. I don't know how they were able to pull a quorum of both houses together on such short notice. I've been selected to provide pool coverage for all the news organizations since the orders were that only one representative of the media would be allowed to cover this event.

At this point, all we know is...President Bancroft called both Houses of Congress to meet here in the House of Representatives. We know he told them that he has an announcement to make which will be of great importance to the nation.

* * *

Worthington exuded a cool, self-satisfied demeanor, but those familiar with his style noticed more. As he spoke, he fidgeted with his pen, twirling it around and around between his fingers.

* * *

We are not able to bring you direct audio, but we do have a picture from inside the House of Representatives. You can see that picture as the small inset on your television screen. We have a staff person, Bob Winston inside the chamber, who is allowed to give us an audio update on what is being said.

Vice President Clifton, President-elect Ahern and Vice President-elect Ryder are also in the chamber. As you can see, President Bancroft has just taken the rostrum and Bob Winston tells me through my earpiece that he is introducing Vice President Clifton. Yes, would you...would you repeat that Bob?

* * *

Worthington's head swiveled slightly and listed a bit to the side. Alex glanced around as the newsman poked an index finger down the side of his starched collar and gave it a tug. Alex smiled.

* * *

Ladies and gentlemen, I know I heard Bob Winston correctly, but I'm not sure I understand what is happening. Vice President Clifton has tendered his resignation. President Bancroft is back at the microphone and has accepted the resignation… Bob Winston reports President Bancroft…citing the Twenty-fifth Amendment…has nominated President-elect Ahern to fill the vice presidential vacancy.

* * *

"Hang in there, Ned baby. You ain't seen nothin' yet," Alex said to the TV screen. Worthington appeared to need some powder to cover the beads of perspiration breaking out on his forehead.

* * *

Ladies and gentlemen, I thought the first announcement was a blockbuster, but try this one on for size. A vote has just been conducted and both Houses of Congress have confirmed the appointment of President-elect Ahern as the new sitting vice president. I doubt anything could top this.

Bob, please confirm what you just said. Ah… ah…er. I'm sorry folks…

* * *

The pen twirled faster in Worthington's hand. Now he was in imminent danger of drowning in the sweat pouring down from under the false hairline.

* * *

My last statement couldn't have been further from the reality of what has happened. Bob Winston, inside the House of Representatives, has confirmed President Bancroft has formally resigned the presidency. He has handed the resignation letter to Speaker of the House Burnside and indicated President-elect Ahern is now the sitting president. President-elect Ahern has taken the microphone and confirmed that under the Twenty-fifth Amendment to the Constitution he accepts the office of president of the United States. He indicated the transition is effective immediately, and the Chief Justice of the Supreme Court is administering the oath of office. President-elect Ahern just announced that he is nominating Vice President-elect Ryder to fill the vacant office of vice president.

The appointment of the Vice President-elect Ryder to the office of vice president has been confirmed by Congress. This is a most extraordinary turn of events.

Well, I guess this change of leadership has to be the news of the century. After this, I can't think of anything that could possibly—

My God. Excuse me again ladies and gentlemen. Bob Winston just informed me that President Bancroft, Vice President Clifton and several members of the president's—ah, the former president's—staff have been taken into custody. President-elect Ahern—ah, President Ahern—made the announcement. He also said he would hold a news conference from the White House at 6 o'clock this evening.

* * *

The once starched shirt looked more like a limp rag on Worthington. His perfectly knotted tie had been jerked down and off center. He sliced a forefinger across his throat asking for the camera to cut away. His head jerked back and forth and one hand covered his earpiece as his producer apparently issued one last instruction.

* * *

Ah...It looks like this session of Congress is over. I...we're dumbfounded. I don't know what to tell you except, stay tuned for the six o'clock news conference. This is Ned Worthington returning you to our studios.

11:55 A.M., JANUARY 8th, THE WHITE HOUSE ⬠

Alex switched off the television set on the credenza behind him. He was sitting in General Osborn's former office where he had access to more communications than he was used to. So far, the ideas he presented to President Ahern were working. The president would be returning soon to his new office in the White House—the Oval Office.

Alex turned to the next item on his agenda. He checked the notes he'd prepared during the past hour—twelve phone calls to make. The number was three fewer than the individual addressee list of those originally involved in Tower Watch. Admiral Eastland was removed from his post earlier, General Watkins was dead, and their investigations revealed that a Lieutenant Colonel Martinez of the Special Forces refused to participate when he received the Tower Watch activation order. He was the only one of the unit commanders who would not be censured or arrested.

The White House communications center set up the calls on secure lines and buzzed him as each contact was made. As each officer answered, Alex identified himself and explained that he was calling on behalf of the president. He made certain that each man understood he was referring to President Ahern and not former President Bancroft. He directed each to pay close attention, since he did not intend to repeat himself.

"Tower Watch" were the words he used to begin each conversation. Reactions ranged from indignant to fearful, but he cut them off short. "Don't insult my intelligence by trying to deny anything. You will tender your resignation as soon as I hang up. You will stipulate that you do not intend to request any benefits resulting from your military service. You will leave the military at once without any public comment.

"You will not make any statements to any person regarding this matter or your resignation. If you do, you will be arrested and placed on trial along with President Bancroft and the other members of his staff. The evidence is overwhelming and you will be found guilty, at the very least, of conspiracy to overthrow the constituted government.

"I expect an original, letter of resignation signed by you to be on President Ahern's desk by noon tomorrow. If you have any questions, or think you are being treated in an unfair manner, you may present yourself to the president along with your resignation here in the Oval Office at noon tomorrow. Lest you think we have short memories, arrangements have been established to monitor your activities from now until hell freezes over. Do you have any comment?"

None of the officers he called was able to respond to that final question. Alex anticipated that all the resignations would arrive on time. His assumption proved correct.

A few days later there was a small item on one of the back pages of *The Washington Post*. It mentioned "reliable sources" reported a number of military officers submitted resignations directly to the White House. The article further stated that while the procedure was "out-of-channels," it was assumed these officers were apparently making some type of protest. The article did not name the officers, nor did it contain any further speculation.

10:00 A.M., JANUARY 20th, THE WHITE HOUSE ⬠

Inaugural Day was finally upon them and Alex planned to watch the day's events from his office in the White House. He was amazed and surprised at the power commanded by the office of the president. He only needed to announce his name and indicate that he was "calling on behalf of the president." Doors opened, people listened.

* * *

Almost three months to the day since this whole mess started. All the time, the planning, the effort. A lot like flying. How did that guy describe it? "Hours of boredom interspersed by moments of stark terror." He laughed aloud as he remembered only the bad guys were fooled by the figment of his imagination—Alpha.

Alex reviewed the events of the last dozen days with relief and satisfaction. President Bancroft, Ray Howland, General

Osborn, Admiral Eastland and Colonel Richards were all under indictment. They were also being held in jail without bail, pending trial. Their house of cards crumbled when the note found in Chapman's pocket was revealed to Richards. The note outlined the final chore to be accomplished by Brocklin—make Colonel Richards the final "suicide" that would provide a scapegoat for the entire plot. Once he saw the note, Richards began to talk. Richards remained mute when asked about his gunshot wound. A muttered "accidental," was all he would say.

Faced with carrying most of the burden of guilt, General Osborn also began making statements. Between the two of them, it took world-class stenographers to keep up.

President Ahern's press secretary, Ted Montgomery—his role as the mole on Ahern's staff uncovered—was cited as an unindicted co-conspirator. His chances of ever holding a position of responsibility anytime in the future were less than nil.

In the days preceding the inauguration, the weapons and equipment used by the teams were returned to their rightful owners. The one exception was the Beretta. Alex decided to keep the gun Mike provided. With urging from President Ahern, the CIA concurred and cleared ownership. A few supply officers questioned the actions, but few answers were required. The president's note stating, "to be returned to military inventory without delay" cleared all the hurdles.

Based on input from President Ahern, all four shootings, the three deaths and Colonel Richards' wound, were considered. The Judge Advocate General raised an eyebrow over the hole in Richards' leg, however all possible charges against Alex and his team members were discharged. Their deeds were deemed justified, in the line of duty and actions taken under competent military authority and orders.

Two days before the inauguration, all team members assembled in the Pentagon amphitheater near the VIP Lounge.

The auditorium was packed with dignitaries. After opening introductions, President Ahern kept his comments short. "Ladies and gentlemen—there is no way we can express our thanks and gratitude to this band of intrepid warriors. They embody everything which is right, which is ethical, which is courageous in our country. You will hear each and every name as I present the medals, but you should also know some of the terms applied to this group. At first they were called a 'rag-tag band.' Later they were referred to by a term from Sir Arthur Conan Doyle's books. When faced with insurmountable odds, when the police and Dr. Watson could not provide the required assistance—Sherlock Holmes called upon his own band of young street rogues to get the job done." President Ahern paused for a moment as he looked at the people on the stage with him...and then continued.

"Most awards certificates use flowery wording like acquitted themselves in a highly professional manner, et cetera, et cetera. These magnificent folks saw a problem, recognized their duty and went out and did a job that needed to be done. Therefore, from this day forward, let this group be forever known as, and respected for being the 'Baker Street Irregulars.' It is now my pleasure to personally present each with the highest civilian medal I have the authority to bestow."

He presented the Presidential Medal of Freedom to every member of the team in Alex's group—including Sarah Crawford. When he completed the presentation, President Ahern added, "There are two people who are not able to attend this ceremony. One is Master Sergeant Rayford T. Pickens. He was wounded in the NMCC during the final stages of the attempted assassination. I will present this medal to him in the hospital. The other presentation must unfortunately be made posthumously. And I know this goes contrary to tradition and protocol...but I must recognize Michael J. Reilly, a CIA employee, who died during the early stages of the plot while assisting Colonel Hilliard. His wife,

Cindy Reilly, and their two children are here to accept this medal on his behalf."

As the ceremony ended, Luke Cutter gave Alex a thumbs-up, a big grin, and a wink. General Watson introduced his three-star boss to Alex saying, "I know he'll do a great job for the president, but we're damn sure going to miss this young man in the Air Force..."

On the day following the awards ceremony, Alex accompanied President Ahern to Bethesda Naval Hospital to visit Hillbilly. They found Sergeant Rebecca Nathan there with him. The president draped the ribbon over Hillbilly's head and wished him well.

"I'm honored, Mr. President." Hillbilly managed an extremely military salute considering he was flat on his back in a hospital bed.

When the president left, Alex stayed to talk with Rebecca and Hillbilly. He found Hillbilly would be out of the hospital in about a week, which would be followed by a two-week convalescent leave. "I'll be happy to see you back at work, Sergeant, but take your time and don't push it. I hope I'll be seeing you again, Sergeant Nathan."

"I can almost guarantee that, Colonel. Rebecca and I are considering tying the knot. We've talked it over and I'd like you to be our best man."

"Hillbilly, I'm flattered, and I'd be honored."

"Rock and roll, Colonel, rock and roll," Hillbilly said.

* * *

Alex looked up as the small clock on his desk chimed the hour. *President Ahern will occupy the office of president in his own right. He'll be leaving the White House in a few minutes to be sworn into the office he already occupies. I guess there's some irony in that. Bancroft didn't even get to stay here til the end of his term, let alone another four years.*

APRIL 6th, ARLINGTON NATIONAL CEMETERY, VIRGINIA ⬠

Alex awoke to a balmy and beautiful spring day. There was a near overcast of fluffy white clouds. He knew this would be a tough monologue, but he owed it to his friend. On the way to the cemetery, he picked up Sarah and drove through the District and around the Tidal Basin. "Mike loved to come down here this time of the year," he said. "He always said it reminded him of a fresh new beginning." Alex drove past the Lincoln Memorial and swung left over the Arlington Memorial Bridge which would lead him to the cemetery. He parked the car and walked toward a relatively fresh grave. Sarah stopped several feet short to give Alex the opportunity to talk to Mike Reilly.

Alex looked out over row upon row of white markers. They reminded him of an editorial cartoon he saw years before—a reprint of a Bill Mauldin drawing commemorating the death of President Eisenhower—the same row upon row of grave markers Alex could see and bore a simple caption: "It's Ike himself. Pass the word."

Alex knelt on one knee by the grave. "Mike, this is probably the last time you'll see me in uniform, so enjoy it, old buddy. On the way here, Sarah and I saw the cherry blossoms around the Tidal Basin. They're beautiful today."

He swiped tears with the back of his hand.

"Mike, your name and reputation are clean. No more stories, no more rumors. President Ahern awarded you the highest civilian award possible. You should have seen how proud Bobby and Liz were when they presented your Presidential Medal of Freedom to Cindy."

Alex stood to ease the stiffness in his legs.

"Mike, I came to the formal ceremony when we brought you here to Arlington National, but it just wasn't the right time to say good-bye. Don't worry about Cindy or the kids—the fund President Ahern established in your name will guarantee your family's future including Bobby's and Liz's education. Also, there are plenty of us around just to lend a hand any time they need it.

"I took a job with President Ahern with an office in the West Wing of the White House. It's actually pretty damn close to the Oval Office. How's that for an old hometown boy? I don't have a formal title yet. Guess you might call me an ombudsman. I told him the first time I said 'no' and he looked like he preferred a 'yes' man, I'd be out the door. Guess he's okay with that."

* * *

Alex was still looking down at Mike's grave when his cell phone interrupted the silence. Only one person used this phone number, so Alex answered. He listened for several minutes, then said, "Yes, Mr. President, I agree it sounds serious. I can be there in about ten minutes, I'm just across the river."

Alex raised his eyes from the grave. In the distance he could see the Tomb of the Unknowns and the member of the Old Guard who stood sentinel duty. He looked back toward the grave and said, "Mike, I'm leaving you in good hands here. I hope to see you again in a better place and a better time..."

Alex put the phone back in his pocket and looked at the pristine white marker once more. He brought himself to attention and offered Mike a Hand Salute that Hillbilly would have been proud of, and said, "Good-bye old friend. I'll never forget you or the sacrifice you made for all of us."

Tears flooded his eyes and coursed down both cheeks as Alex brought his hand down slowly and executed an about-face.

He approached Sarah and she saw clearly the pain he felt. She shared the pain and did nothing to hold back her own tears. She took his hand. As they walked toward the car, arms around each other, Alex said, "You can guess who called?" Sarah nodded and Alex said, "As soon as this meeting with the president is over, you and I are going to sit down and decide on a date for the wedding."

Sarah stopped, put her arms around Alex, and smiled. Her smile was infectious. The corners of Alex's mouth curled upward as well. The sun shone through the puffy white clouds in brilliant shafts of light, and he said, "Looks like someone is smiling from up there, too."

THE END

ABOUT THE AUTHOR

John Achor's writing assignments have appeared in a variety of regional and national publications, and he has sold over two dozen articles to an international magazine. He has also published three mystery novels featuring his female amateur sleuth, Casey Fremont. John says he enjoys writing about, "The subjects I know best: the military, flying and people I've known." After that, according to John, he lets a vivid imagination take over.

The first of his three careers spanned twenty years as a U.S. Air Force pilot. He accumulated over 4,000 hours flying planes from Piper Cubs to the military equivalent of the Boeing 707.

After the military, he entered the real estate industry. He joined a national real estate franchise as a management consultant working at the regional and national levels. Those positions led him to Phoenix, Arizona, and an affiliation with a major Savings & Loan institution.

In John's words, "When the Savings and Loan industry melted away like a lump of sugar in hot coffee, I knew it was time to develop a third career." He became a freelance computer instructor, user-developer, consultant, writer and community college instructor.

In mid-1999, John moved to Hot Springs Village, Arkansas, where he resided in the piney woods with his wife Pat and their two cats, Lexus and Betsy Ross. As you may know from his web site; these two cats are no longer with them and left a big hole in their lives and they relocated to the Omaha, Nebraska, area in 2016 where John continues to devote his time to writing mysteries and thrillers, as well as presenting seminars at state wide conferences.

www.ingramcontent.com/pod-product-compliance
Lightning Source LLC
Chambersburg PA
CBHW052033240626
47153CB00006B/2064